J
18/1/19.

MAID
(REFURB)

1 6 MAY 2022
0 6 DEC 2022

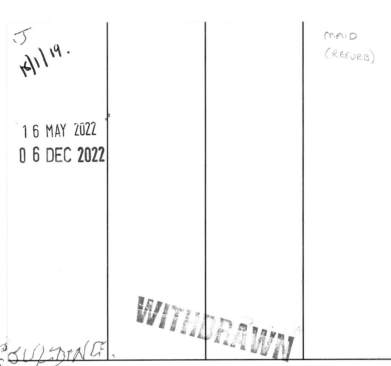

GOULDING.

Please return on or before the latest date above.
You can renew online at *www.kent.gov.uk/libs*
or by telephone 08458 247 200

CUSTOMER SERVICE EXCELLENCE

Libraries & Archives

00884\DTP\RN\07.07   LIB 7

THE PRICE OF LOVE

Lucy Collins and her brother Sam have lived next door to the Tanner family all their lives. Lucy and Robert Tanner long for the day when they can marry. Until tragedy strikes when Lucy's parents are killed in a car crash, leaving Sam gravely injured. Sam's girlfriend Patsy refuses to help, and Lucy has little choice but to postpone her wedding. Heartbroken at her loss, Lucy is devastated to discover Robert has betrayed her. With little money and unable to earn a regular wage, Lucy and Sam are forced to move into the slums of Cardiff. Lucy wonders if she'll ever find happiness again...

THE PRICE OF LOVE

THE PRICE OF LOVE

by

Rosie Harris

Magna Large Print Books
Long Preston, North Yorkshire,
BD23 4ND, England.

British Library Cataloguing in Publication Data.

Harris, Rosie
    The price of love.

    A catalogue record of this book is
    available from the British Library

    ISBN   978-0-7505-3520-5

First published in Great Britain in 2011 by Arrow Books

Cover illustration © Gordon Crabb by arrangement with
Alison Eldred

Rosie Harris has asserted her right under the Copyright, Designs and
Patents Act 1988 to be identified as the author of this work

Published in Large Print 2012 by arrangement with
Arrow, one of the publishers in the Random House Group Ltd.

Magna Large Print is an imprint of Library Magna Books Ltd.

Printed and bound in Great Britain by
T.J. (International) Ltd., Cornwall, PL28 8RW

For my daughter Pamela Sak

Acknowledgements

With sincere thanks to my editor Georgina Hawtrey-Woore and my agent Caroline Sheldon for their continued help and support.

Chapter One

The horrendous scream that rent the misty November air in Priory Terrace sent a shudder through the group of young people gathered around the huge blazing bonfire.

It also alerted their parents; men and women who were standing on their doorsteps enjoying the spectacle and at the same time keeping an eye on what was going on, ready to help, if necessary, should things get out of hand.

The younger ones had been determined to make bonfire night the most exciting event of 1920 and they wanted to do it on their own. They'd spent well over a week collecting wood and anything else that would burn and building the biggest bonfire that anyone in the terrace had ever seen.

Perched on the very top was a guy that Lucy Collins and Patsy Warren had made out of an old broom handle swathed in straw and dressed in a variety of old clothes they'd cadged from their families over the past weeks. He wore old brown trousers, a striped grey and white flannel shirt, a moth-eaten green waistcoat and a grey and black check jacket. Round his neck they'd tied a bright red muffler and even put an old bowler hat on his straw head.

The ear-splitting scream was followed by pandemonium as most of the group pulled back from the huge bonfire in fright.

13

'It's Percy Carter ... he's fallen into the fire,' sixteen-year-old Lucy Collins exclaimed in horror.

Seconds earlier Lucy's brother Sam and Robert Tanner, who were both eighteen and, along with several of the older boys, were in charge of the bonfire, had been letting off the fireworks which had been collected together before the bonfire had been lit.

The big crowd that had gathered there had been cheering as Catherine wheels spun, thunder flashes exploded and silver fountains and golden rain rose into the night sky, filling the air with shafts of coloured light and brilliant sparks. These had been interspersed with small bangers and jumping jacks which were exploding all around them.

'Out of the way, so that I can get to him,' a boy's voice rang out over the tumult.

'Sam, stop, you'll get hurt,' Patsy Warren's high-pitched voice cut through the noise.

Sam Collins paid no attention to her or to the many others who shouted warnings and gasped in horror as flames from the bonfire rippled up Percy's back.

Fortunately, Percy was wearing a heavy leather jacket and matching gloves and he appeared to have clamped his hands over his eyes and face as he fell. He was now lying face down on the burning pyre and seemed unable to move.

Ignoring the tongues of flame, Sam grabbed hold of the collar of Percy's jacket and pulled him upright and started to drag him backwards into safety. The crowd of youngsters scattered, yelling excitedly as the guy toppled from his high perch

14

and crashed down almost on top of the two boys, causing sparks from the bonfire to float high into the air and land everywhere.

Grown-ups left their doorways and came hurrying forwards, seeking out their own children and shepherding them to safety.

Brushing a lump of burning wood from her coat, Lucy Collins rushed forward to help Sam and Robert who were supporting an unconscious Percy. Very gently the two boys lowered Percy down on to the ground at a safe distance from the bonfire.

'Someone's already gone for an ambulance,' a voice called out.

'Better not touch him until it gets here,' somebody else cautioned.

Between them, Robert and Lucy tried to make Percy as comfortable as they could. When they gently moved his gloved hands away from his face they were relieved to see that it didn't look as though the main part of his face had suffered any serious burns, although his forehead and around the edges of his cheeks appeared to be bright red and looked very sore.

When Lucy turned round to see where her brother was she saw that Sam was bent over as if in pain, his hands clutched together between his knees.

'Sam, what's wrong? Are you hurt?' she asked anxiously as she went to his side.

'I'm all right, don't worry about me. Go and see what you can do for Percy. My hands are stinging, that's all. I think they're burned a bit. Probably be all right in a minute.'

Before Lucy could decide whether to stay and help Robert attend to Percy or see what she could do to help her brother, there was the sound of the ambulance approaching and of the crowd being moved back so that it could stop as close as possible to the spot where Percy was lying.

It took several minutes to lift Percy on to a stretcher and load it inside the ambulance. As the driver was about to slam shut the rear doors, Lucy told him that the boy who had pulled Percy off the bonfire had burned his hands and she asked him if he would check to see if he was all right.

The ambulance man took one look at Sam's hands and the massive blisters that were already forming and said that Sam must go along to the hospital as well.

Sam was reluctant to make such a fuss but both Robert and Lucy insisted that it was necessary and agreed that they would go with him, so all three of them were driven away in the ambulance along with Percy Carter.

'I hope someone has let Mr and Mrs Carter know what has happened to Percy and that he is being taken to hospital,' Robert said worriedly.

'Don't worry, someone will have told them and they will go straight there,' Lucy assured him.

Mr and Mrs Carter were already waiting outside the hospital as the ambulance pulled up; Mr Carter was wearing a long dark grey coat and black trilby and Mrs Carter was dressed in an expensive, well-tailored blue wool coat with a black astrakhan collar and a matching black astrakhan hat. They both looked anxious and rushed forward as the ambulance came to a stop and the men opened the rear doors and brought out the stretcher.

Mrs Carter became hysterical when she caught her first sight of Percy and saw his badly singed clothes and the huge red wheals down each side of his face where he'd not been able to shield it with his gloved hands.

His eyes were closed but he had regained consciousness and was moaning slightly. His mother bent over him to try and comfort him but one of the ambulance men laid a restraining hand on her arm.

'Better not touch him,' he warned. 'Let the doctor have a look and put a dressing on his burns first; we don't want him getting any germs in them now, do we?'

Mr Carter put a protective arm around his wife's shoulders and drew her away so that the men could carry the stretcher inside the hospital.

It was then that Clarence Carter noticed Lucy, Sam and Robert.

'Robert Tanner,' he exclaimed sharply, 'what happened? Were you and Sam Collins fooling around or something? Did one of you push Percy into the fire?'

'No, Mr Carter, we most certainly didn't,' Robert hastened to assure him. He felt angry that Percy's father should think that they would contemplate doing such a stupid thing but he was careful not to let his feelings show.

Mr Carter owned the garage where both he and Sam were apprentices and Robert knew how important it was that Mr Carter didn't get the

17

wrong idea about what had happened. 'In fact, Mr Carter, Sam–'

'Sam was the one who pulled Percy off the bonfire, Mr Carter, and his hands have been badly burned. He needs to have them looked at right away,' Lucy interrupted indignantly.

Mr Carter stared at her, frowning, almost as if he didn't believe what she was saying.

'Well, you'd better get someone to see to him then,' he said briskly.

'Yes, Mr Carter,' Robert said obediently. 'Perhaps we could come and find out how Percy is after we've done that?'

'Don't worry about Percy; we'll be staying at his bedside until we know how he is.'

'Should we come back a bit later on?'

'I've already said that there's no need. I'll tell you tomorrow if there is anything that I feel you should know,' Mr Carter told Robert dismissively.

'And make sure you're not late in the morning after all the shenanigans that have gone on tonight. Even if it is Saturday and you finish at twelve, I still expect you to do a full morning's work, remember. And that goes for you too,' he added, looking at Sam.

'It all depends on how badly his hands are burned, whether or not he will be fit to come to work,' Lucy muttered, putting her arm around Sam's shoulders and propelling him towards the desk where she could see a uniformed nurse.

Robert hesitated for a moment, wondering if he should apologise for Lucy's manner. Mr Carter was their boss so it was important that they stayed in his good books.

He was still trying to decide what to do when Mr Carter said sharply, 'Well, run along, then, Robert Tanner, there's nothing more you can do now. Make sure that Sam Collins gets home safely after he's had his hands attended to and, as I've already said, I expect you both to be at work on time tomorrow morning. I'll be speaking to you then about this matter.'

Before Robert could answer Mr Carter had turned on his heel and hurried away.

For several minutes after the ambulance had pulled away there was an uneasy atmosphere in Priory Terrace. Normally it was a very quiet, respectable street in the middle-class district of Anfield. The women didn't congregate, apart from an exchange of greeting if they met as they went in and out of their houses, or when they were cleaning their front doorsteps or windows. There was no gathering in groups on the doorstep to exchange gossip as there was in other parts of Liverpool.

The younger children were allowed to play out in the evenings but they were always called in for bed long before it got dark and they never played rowdy games or swung from ropes tied around the lamp posts.

Mostly the girls enjoyed skipping while the boys played marbles or played with their whipping tops. Hopscotch was forbidden because marking the pavement was unsightly, and if they played rounders or cricket, they had to do so without any screaming or shouting and to take great care that no windows were broken.

The men kept their front gardens neat and grew vegetables in their back gardens but if they wanted to chat to each other it was usually over a quiet bevvy in the local pub.

Then the arrival of a fire engine on the scene brought them all to their senses. As if awakening from a trance, everybody began to insist that the children, who were still outside and were mesmerised by the roaring fire as it flared up into the night sky, lighting up the entire street and casting weird shadows as well as throwing out an incredible heat, went indoors for greater safety.

'Come on, if you get this smoke on your chest, you'll be coughing your lungs up all night,' one mother scolded.

'You can watch from the window,' another consoled her youngster who seemed to be reluctant to leave the bonfire.

One or two of the older men moved over to the bonfire and kicked at it with their feet as if to dismantle it but the pyre had a life of its own and flared up at them, sending out spurts of flame that licked at their boots or caught at their flapping trouser legs, filling the air with the smell of singed cloth.

As they retreated backwards there was a gigantic explosion. A rainbow of colours hit the night sky as the fire reached the large box of fireworks which Robert Tanner had been in charge of and caused the entire contents to ignite.

The noise of exploding bangers was like a series of guns going off and it struck fear into the hearts of many of the men who were there and who not long before had been in the army and under fire while serving in France.

By now the firemen were in action and were ordering people to take shelter as they unwound their hoses and connected up to the nearest hydrant.

A couple of the men had gone into their garden sheds and were now armed with shovels and spades. They began attacking the burning mass, beating down the flames, hacking at the structure. The bonfire was so sturdily built that their onslaught proved to be completely ineffective and, rather officiously, the firemen ordered them to get out of the way before anyone else was hurt.

As the firemen turned their massive hoses on to the bonfire in no time at all they had doused the flames and the centre of the massive pile of flaming wood disintegrated until it was no longer a danger. Only the glowing heart remained, still hissing and spitting as the water reached it.

One man, more resourceful than the others, brought out a bucket of garden soil and tipped it over the remains of the glowing heart.

'That should keep it doused down; it should be safe enough now,' he commented with such satisfaction in his voice that the firemen and other bystanders laughed.

'No point in blaming the bonnie for what happened, whacker,' one of the firemen observed. 'The lads were probably doing a bit of pushing and shoving, you know what they're like.'

'I don't think so. We were all watching to make sure there was no rough stuff.'

'Then the stupid young bugger must have tripped, or else he was trying to warm his hands

21

and got too damn close.'

'Bad luck that it was young Percy Carter; you know what his old man is like and a lot of us depend on him for our living,' someone muttered.

'Don't know what the young idiot was doing here, anyway, since he doesn't live in this street, for a start.'

'Got his eye on young Lucy Collins, hasn't he? That's why he was lurking around.'

'Wasting his time, then; she's given her heart to Robert Tanner; they've been sweet on each other since their schooldays.'

'Young Sam Collins is the one I'm worried about,' another remarked. 'Did you get a chance to see how bad his hands were before he went off in the ambulance, Bill?' he asked looking over at Sam's father.

'Brave young devil, and no mistake,' someone commented admiringly. 'He didn't hesitate for a second. No, he went straight in there, regardless of all the heat or the danger to himself.'

'It was in his interest to do so, wasn't it? Don't forget Carter is his boss.'

'Get some good Brownie points for rescuing his son,' another commented with a cynical guffaw.

'He'd probably have been made foreman next week if he'd finished his apprenticeship,' someone else laughed.

'Doubt it. More likely to get blamed for what's happened. It's to be hoped that Percy isn't too badly hurt or there will be hell to pay. Mark my words, if he is, then his dad will most certainly blame it all on those two young lads.'

'Talk sense, whacker. Why should Carter do

that when they were the ones who helped him?'

'They'll have a job to convince him of that. Sure as eggs he'll hold them responsible.'

'Well, that's a load of nonsense and I'll be one of the first to stand up and tell him so if I hear him say anything like that,' a mild-looking man defended.

'You and whose army, John Edwards? You can't even say boo to that nagging wife of yours so I don't see you facing Mr Carter and telling him he's a lying bastard.'

'No, I wouldn't put it to him quite like that,' John Edwards admitted, ignoring the comment about his wife. 'There are other ways of telling a man he's wrong.'

'Instead of standing around here in the cold arguing the toss about it all, why don't we all go for a jar down at the boozer?' someone suggested.

There was a universal murmur of agreement and, putting up their coat collars and turning their backs on the sodden remains of the bonfire, they began to wend their way down the road to the nearest pub.

A few looked guiltily towards their homes, knowing that they were leaving their wives to console the children who were both dismayed by what had happened to the bonfire and fireworks they had been looking forward to and also excited by all the things that had gone on there that night. For most of them the most thrilling moment had been the arrival of the fire engine and when the box of fireworks had exploded with such an almighty bang.

Chapter Two

The minute Lucy Collins arrived at Carter's Cars on Saturday morning she went straight to her seat at the switchboard at the far end of the general office.

A tall, slim girl with neatly styled dark brown hair, she had an air of efficiency about her and she wanted to ask Mr Carter how Percy was the moment he arrived. She also wanted to tell him that Sam would not be coming in to work that morning.

There had been a heated discussion at breakfast about whether he should do so or not.

'There's no point in you coming in to work, not with your hands all bound up like that,' she'd told him firmly as she finished her bowl of porridge and reached for her hat and coat. 'Don't worry, Mr Carter knows what happened last night and all about your hands, so I'll let him know how bad they are.'

'No, he might think I was pulling a fast one,' Sam argued. 'You heard what he said to me and Robert about making sure we were at work on time this morning.'

'Yes, but he didn't know how badly burned your hands were, now did he?'

'Well, he won't know now, not unless I go in to work and he can see for himself.' Sam scowled.

'Yes he will, I've already said that I'll tell him

the minute he arrives.'

'After the way you spoke to him last night you might find you haven't even got a job when you get there,' Sam pointed out gloomily.

'Don't talk daft. Of course I'll have a job. There are only two of us on the telephone switchboard and if one of us is off, then the other is unable to handle all the calls and he knows that perfectly well.'

'Well, I'm coming to work whatever you say, so help me put my coat on,' Sam stated firmly.

'I'll help you, luv,' his mother said. She had let them argue it out but she had a worried frown on her face as she tried to slide one of his bandaged hands into the armhole of his coat and found it was impossible to do so.

'You know, I think our Lucy's right, Sam; it would be better if you stayed at home. You don't want to get the cold into those sore hands or you'll be in real trouble.'

'Get the cold in them?' Sam laughed. 'I'd have a job to do that the way they're bandaged up. Look, if you can't get my hands into the sleeves, then help me put the coat around my shoulders and just fasten a button or something to keep it on.'

'And let you go out of the house looking like a scarecrow?' Margaret Collins scolded.

'Either that or I'll go to work without putting on a coat at all,' Sam mumbled.

'You'll do no such thing. Heavens above, you'd catch pneumonia. It's cold and damp out there. Look at the way our Lucy is wrapped up. Underneath her coat she's got on a cardigan as well as a jumper and she's even put on a thick scarf.'

'I'm going into work whether you two like it or not. When I've seen Mr Carter, if he says it's all right for me to have some time off, then I'll come home again.'

'You know he won't say that,' Lucy protested. 'He always says that no matter what's wrong with you, if you concentrate on what you should be doing, then you'll soon forget about it. He even says that when it means you'll end up passing a heavy cold or the influenza to everyone else you're working alongside.'

'Well, if you're going, then you'd better get a move on or else both of you will be late,' their mother told them. 'Your dad left well over half an hour ago.'

Lucy and Sam exchanged smiles. They both knew that their father, Bill Collins, who was in charge of the Stores at Carter's Cars, was a stickler for punctuality.

As they reached the front door Sam turned round to say goodbye to his mother and as he did so he accidentally caught one of his hands against the door frame and let out a sharp yelp of pain. The colour drained from his face and for a moment he leaned against the wall as if he was feeling faint.

'That settles it,' his mother said firmly, her mouth set in a tight line. 'Our Lucy is right; you're not fit to go in to work. Come on, Sam, come back inside and settle down in front of the fire. Take the morning off and by Monday you'll have had a good rest and your hands will be feeling much better.'

Lucy could see that Mr Carter was not in a good mood when he arrived half an hour after she did. A short, squarely built man, he strode through the general office to his own private office without acknowledging anyone.

Normally he raised his trilby and nodded left and right to the row of clerks busily entering details into ledgers or making out invoices, but this morning he even ignored their chorus of 'Good morning, Mr Carter' that greeted him as usual.

His face was like a grim mask, his hard, dark eyes staring straight ahead. The clerks whispered amongst themselves after he'd gone into his office and shut the door.

'The boss looks as though he's been up half the night.'

'Yes, young Percy must be in a bad way.'

'Do you think someone should ask him how his lad is this morning?'

'Mr Carter would probably prefer it if you kept your heads down and got on with your work,' Miss Yorke, who was Mr Carter's secretary and also in charge of the general office, ordered. 'If Mr Carter has anything at all to tell us about his son, then he will do it in his own good time,' she added officiously.

A thin angular woman in her mid-forties, her thin mousy hair always in a tight roll in the nape of her neck, she had worked at Carter's Cars since the day she left school and took a proprietary interest in guarding her boss's privacy and well-being.

Lucy said nothing but the moment there was a

lull on the switchboard she walked quickly down the room to Mr Carter's office and tapped on the door.

'Lucy Collins, whatever do you think you are doing?' Miss Yorke demanded, staring over the top of her gold-rimmed glasses in stark disapproval.

Lucy ignored her. Her heart was thumping because she knew she had a nerve to approach Mr Carter without asking Miss Yorke for permission, so the moment she heard him say 'Enter', Lucy nipped inside and quickly closed the door behind her.

Mr Carter was seated at his massive mahogany desk concentrating on a ledger that was open in front of him. Lucy stood in front of his desk for such a long time waiting for him to look up that she wondered if he knew she was in the room.

When he did glance up, Mr Carter frowned heavily when he saw who it was standing there.

'Well, Lucy Collins, what is it you want? I am extremely busy.'

'I wanted to ask you how Percy was,' Lucy stuttered, the colour rushing to her face.

'Very badly burned and if I find out who it was who pushed him on to that bonfire, I will make sure that they are severely punished. You are quite sure that your brother wasn't one of them?'

'No, Sam most certainly wasn't,' Lucy said heatedly. 'Sam was the one who pulled him off the bonfire, and his hands are now so badly burned that he isn't able to come to work today.'

For several minutes Mr Carter said nothing as he studied her angry face.

'Did Robert Tanner have anything to do with

what happened?' he asked.

'Only in so far as he helped Sam to lay Percy down on the ground and then went with them in the ambulance to the hospital.'

'You were there as well,' Mr Carter said tetchily. 'I suppose it could have been you who pushed Percy.' His sharp dark eyes studied her face as he waited for her to reply.

'You know quite well that I wouldn't do anything like that,' Lucy said flatly. 'None of us know how Percy fell on to the bonfire. He wasn't even supposed to be that close to it. Robert was in charge of the fireworks and Sam was making sure that all the younger kids kept well back so that no one would be hurt.'

'Well, he didn't do a very good job, did he, or Percy wouldn't have ended up getting half burned to death,' Mr Carter snapped. 'He's quite badly blistered, especially his forehead and the sides of his face, that it's a mercy he hasn't been disfigured for life.'

'I'm very sorry to hear that, Mr Carter. I can well imagine how much discomfort Percy must be in because Sam is in terrible pain with his hands.'

'A mere detail compared to what my son is suffering,' Mr Carter stated bitterly.

Lucy bit her lip and remained silent. She could see that Mr Carter was very upset and she was aware that anything she did say he would manage to turn round so that she was the one in the wrong.

'You'd better get back to the switchboard,' he said dismissively. 'Even if your brother isn't fit to work I trust you are.'

'Yes, Mr Carter.'

Lucy felt angry and humiliated as she made her way back to her seat. She could feel all eyes were on her as she walked through the general office and she knew Miss Yorke was waiting for an explanation but she was too choked to speak.

Once she was sitting down with her headphones on she tried to shut out the rest of the world as she dealt almost mechanically with the incoming and outgoing calls.

Half an hour later, when she put through a call from Mr Carter to Mr Fitzpatrick, who was in charge of the apprentice mechanics, she deliberately listened in and her heart sank as she heard Mr Carter tell him to send Robert Tanner to his office right away.

Robert was in Mr Carter's office for well over twenty minutes and to Lucy it seemed to be an interminable time. When he emerged he was white faced and looked extremely upset. Lucy longed to know what had been said but it was impossible to ask him at that moment.

As she watched Robert stride out of the office, his head held high, she knew she would have to contain her curiosity until they finished work at midday.

He was still looking very perturbed when she arrived at their usual meeting place about a hundred yards away from the showroom. As he fell into step alongside her he said nothing but as she slipped her hand into his he gave it a companionable squeeze, and when she looked up at him he returned her smile.

Even so she knew something was wrong and was impatient for him to tell her all that had gone on. She understood that he didn't want to do so until they were away from all the other apprentices and clerks who had left Carter's Cars at the same time and who were still within earshot.

'How was Sam this morning?' he asked.

'He wanted to come in to work but Mam persuaded him he'd be better off at home. He agreed with her after he banged one of his hands as he was coming through the door.'

'You told Mr Carter about it?'

'Yes, but he said it was nothing to what Percy was suffering. He said Percy was in considerable pain because he was so badly blistered.'

'He'd probably have been burned to a cinder if Sam hadn't acted so quickly,' Robert pointed out. 'What gets me so mad is that instead of being grateful for what we did, Mr Carter more or less accused Sam of pushing Percy on to the fire.'

'Or you! He asked me if you'd done it and when I said no, he had the nerve to ask if it was me,' Lucy added with a mirthless laugh.

'When he started accusing me I nearly told him that if his son wasn't such a stupid bugger then he wouldn't have been so close to the fire in the first place,' Robert muttered.

'I don't suppose we'll ever know why he was that close, not unless he tells us and, by the sound of things, he's not well enough to do that at the moment.'

'Even when he is feeling better he's hardly likely to admit that he was in the wrong because

31

he knows how mad that would make his old man,' Robert said gloomily.

In this Robert was wrong.

Percy had always been something of a loner. When he'd first started school the other children had teased him and called him 'four-eyes' because he wore glasses and was afraid to join in any of the rougher games for fear of breaking them. Sam and Robert had befriended him. When he was about twelve and his father paid for him to attend a private school they still considered him a friend and let him go around with them at the weekends.

Although she had been Sam's girlfriend since their schooldays, Patsy, with her long blonde hair, hour-glass figure and wide smile that made heads turn, was giggly and a born flirt and often led Percy on when they all went out together, even though she confided in Lucy that he was pretty dumb.

Nevertheless, it was Lucy whom Percy appeared to be attracted to, not Patsy. The two girls were the exact opposite of each other. Lucy was quiet and sensible, very slim with dark hair and eyes and a shy smile. Even though she made it quite clear that she wasn't interested in him other than as a friend, it had been because he wanted to be in Lucy's company that Percy had come to the bonfire night in Priory Terrace.

Patsy and Lucy had been working at Carter's Cars more or less the same length of time. Patsy's father, though, had paid for her to have short-hand and typing lessons so as well as occasionally helping out on the switchboard whenever they were short-staffed, Patsy also worked directly under Miss Yorke. Occasionally, when Miss Yorke was away, Patsy even acted as secretary to Mr Carter.

As soon as Percy realised that his father was blaming Sam and Robert for his accident he explained to his father that what had happened was his own fault.

'I wanted to see what fireworks Robert had in the box and when I bent down to look at them my glasses came off and as I reached out to pick them up, I tripped over something lying on the ground and I fell forward on to the fire.'

It was a couple of days, though, before he told his father this and in the meantime Robert and Sam were regarded as the young villains responsible for the terrible accident by most of the staff at Carter's Cars. Some people even went as far as to say that Sam deserved to suffer and that his badly burned hands were his punishment.

Once the true events came out into the open, then everyone was full of praise as well as sympathy for Sam and even Mr Carter said how brave he'd been.

Although Sam was fit enough to be back at work the following week, he wasn't able to carry out his duties as an apprentice mechanic in the workshop. Instead, he was filling in his time running errands for Mr Fitzpatrick the engineering foreman and doing odd jobs around the car showroom that didn't require any practical skills.

'I might just as well stay home,' he complained when his father commented about it one evening.

'You make the best of it, son,' his father advised. 'Seeing that you're not fit to do your job, Mr Carter could have stood you off with no pay, remember. As it is, he's paying your wages in full even though you've had two days off this week to go to the hospital to have your dressings changed, so think yourself lucky.'

'He's probably only doing that because he feels guilty about accusing me now that he knows it was Percy's own fault.'

'Well, keep quiet about it; you can't expect him to admit he was mistaken, now can you? As it is, he's been saying how brave you were so that's an accolade in itself.'

'He should admit he was wrong to blame me for doing such a stupid thing,' Sam argued.

'Robert was accused as well as you and he's not had Mr Carter praising him or saying how brave he is,' Lucy chipped in.

'That's enough,' Mr Collins said firmly. 'Mr Carter is a good boss and it's only natural that he was extremely upset that such an accident should happen to his son. Let's hope the lad is better soon and out of hospital and that things get back to normal. Have they told you how long it will be before your bandages are off, Sam?'

'Probably sometime next week,' Sam mumbled. 'Mind you, they also said that it might be a bit longer before the new skin is strong enough to stand up to oil and grease. I hate having to be the errand boy around the place. I only hope that I'll be able to catch up with the other apprentices after all this time.'

'Of course you will, it's only a matter of a few

34

weeks,' Lucy assured him. 'All you need to do is ask Robert and he will tell you about anything you've missed.'

'I was wondering if I ought to go and see Percy,' Sam commented thoughtfully.

'Whatever for?' Lucy asked in surprise.

'To see how he is and to thank him for owning up that the accident was his own fault. I did ask Patsy to tell him but she said she forgot to do so.'

'How could Patsy tell him? Percy hasn't been into the office since the accident.'

'She's been visiting him in hospital. I would have thought you knew.'

'No.' Lucy frowned. 'Patsy's never said a word to me about it. How strange.'

'I think she said that Mr Carter asked her to do so to try and cheer Percy up because he is so depressed about everything.'

'Well, she's kept very quiet about it and that's not like Patsy. Usually she would be boasting about it,' Lucy observed dryly.

Chapter Three

A week later when Mr Carter summoned her to his office, Lucy wondered what was wrong and whether it had anything to do with the fact that Sam was still not able to resume his full duties as an apprentice mechanic.

It can't be that, she told herself as she took off her head phones and checked in the little mirror in her handbag to make sure that her hair was tidy. He wouldn't talk to me about it, he'd see Sam himself.

'It will be at least another two weeks before Percy is allowed out of hospital,' Mr Carter told Lucy when she reported to his office a few minutes later. 'He has asked if you will go and visit him, so you can leave an hour earlier this afternoon in order to do so.'

Lucy stared at him in surprise, wondering why she was being asked to do so. Knowing how Percy felt about her she wondered if she dared refuse.

As if reading her mind, Mr Carter said, 'Percy has requested it. He seems to need to see some-one his own age to cheer him up and he said there was something he wanted to talk to you about. I can't allow both you and Patsy Warren to have time off, of course; she will have to take over the switchboard this afternoon so that you can leave early. She'll probably welcome the break; she's been in to see him every day since his accident.'

After she'd promised Mr Carter that she would go and see Percy that afternoon Lucy went back to her switchboard feeling very uneasy. She didn't really want to go and see him because she knew he had a crush on her and she didn't want to do anything that might encourage him in any way.

Since Mr Carter was telling her he wanted her to go and was giving her time off, she had no alternative but she didn't think that Robert would be too happy when he heard about it and there was no way she could keep it from him.

She was also concerned about being late home because her mother would be wondering where she was. Without asking Miss Yorke for permission she put a call through to the showroom and asked Mr Fitzpatrick if she could speak to Sam so that she could tell him where she was going and her mother wouldn't be worried when she didn't arrive home at the usual time.

Lucy was shocked at how ill Percy looked. Without his glasses he looked quite different; not nearly so studious or owlish. His face was bandaged and there was a metal cage over the bed to support the bedclothes and keep them from touching his body.

He seemed to be very anxious to know how Sam was; in fact, it was the very first question he asked.

'Well, his hands are recovering but he still can't do his normal job,' she told him. 'At the moment he's helping out in the showroom. I'm not sure how long it will be before he can go back into the workshop.'

'Is he upset about it interfering with his apprenticeship?' Percy asked worriedly. 'I feel it is my fault.'

'I don't think that he looks at it like that at all,' Lucy assured him. 'He is keen to complete his apprenticeship, of course, but a couple of weeks shouldn't make that much difference.'

'I don't know,' Percy admitted gloomily. He bit down on his lower lip as if there was something else he wanted to say and didn't quite know how to put it into words. Finally, avoiding Lucy's eyes, he gulped, 'Do you think your Sam would like a driving job?'

'You mean instead of becoming a qualified mechanic?'

'Well, in the long run it might be a better job for him. If his hands are as bad as both you and my dad say they are, then perhaps he shouldn't do manual work.'

Lucy shook her head. 'I really don't know. It's probably never entered his head. He hasn't got much longer to go before he finishes his apprenticeship.'

'Dad thinks he might get rashes or something from all the oil and grease and if that happened then he would probably have to stop working as a mechanic anyway. Can he drive a motor car?'

Lucy shook her head. 'Not as far as I know. I suppose one day he will want to learn to drive, but at the moment he is happy enough dealing with the mechanical side of motor cars.'

'Being able to drive as well as knowing what goes on under the bonnet might be to his advantage,' Percy persisted, staring shortsightedly at Lucy.

'I expect you're right, but I really don't know. Is this why you wanted me to come and see you?' Lucy asked in relief.

'Yes.' Percy nodded. 'We wondered if you would know what Sam would say if it was suggested to him that he became one of our drivers.'

'So is it your dad's idea?' Lucy asked.

'We've talked about it. I've been worrying about Sam while I've been lying here. I feel it is my fault he's been hurt and I know that if it hadn't been for him, then probably I would have burned to death. I want to do something to make it up to him and to help in some way. I thought changing to a driving job would be the perfect answer and Dad agreed that he would arrange it.'

'Perhaps you should have asked Sam to come and see you, not me,' Lucy prevaricated. 'I don't know how he would feel about it.'

'You do think it would be a good idea, though?'

'In some ways, yes,' she agreed hesitantly. 'It depends on how Sam feels about it, though, doesn't it?'

'Would you ask him, Lucy, and let me know?'

'You want *me* to ask him?' Lucy exclaimed in a startled voice. 'I don't know about that. I think it might be better if the suggestion came from you or your dad.'

'No.' Percy shook his head. 'You ask him, and then if he doesn't like the idea, we need say nothing more about it. If Dad asks him, he might think he has to agree because the boss has suggested it.'

'If I ask him, he might tell me to mind my own business and he mightn't like the idea that we've all been talking about him behind his back.'

'What about if you mention the idea to Robert first and see what he thinks? Sam and Robert are good mates so perhaps Robert could talk to him.'

Lucy was saved from answering by the bell signalling the end of visiting time.

'You will do something and let me know? Promise me,' Percy pleaded as Lucy said goodbye and made to leave.

'I'll think it over,' she promised.

'Talk to Robert about it,' Percy called after her as she moved away from his bed.

Lucy thought about Percy's suggestion all the way home but she couldn't decide what to do for the best. When she met Robert later that evening she was so preoccupied that he wanted to know what was wrong. When she tried to dismiss it with a smile, claiming that she felt tired, he wasn't satisfied.

'Has it got something to do with you going to see Percy in hospital without saying a word to me about what you were going to do?' he said.

'I didn't have much option, Robert. Mr Carter asked me to go; in fact, he more or less said I had to go and he gave me time off work so that I could do so.'

'Why was he so keen for you to visit Percy, anyway? Patsy has visited him most afternoons, hasn't she?'

'Yes, she has,' Lucy agreed, 'and I don't think that Sam is very happy about that either.'

'You know quite well that he isn't and I feel the same way. The difference is that he keeps quiet about it because he doesn't want to upset Patsy. Anyway, he knows she is always flirting and there is nothing in it and that it doesn't mean a thing. You're different. Was Patsy there as well?' he added.

'No, she had to look after the switchboard while I was away from the office.'

'In other words, Percy wanted to see you instead of her. You do know that he wants you to go out with him?'

'I know, but what can I do about it?'

'Not visit him in hospital for a start and don't talk to him any more than you have to do.'

'I don't,' Lucy protested, her face pink with embarrassment. 'I have to sometimes, though, when he comes into the office or when he's with a group of us and he says something to me.'

'That's different. I know you have to speak to him then but try and avoid being on your own with him. It's not that I'm jealous,' he went on quickly, 'but the others all laugh about it and keep ribbing me and saying that if I don't watch out then I am going to lose you to Percy Carter and I don't like it.'

'Well, you certainly don't think there's any truth in what they're saying surely,' Lucy defended.

'No, of course I don't.' He pulled her into his arms and hugged her. Then he kissed her on the mouth; a long, hard, possessive kiss that left her breathless.

'You've been my girlfriend since the first day you started school. I stopped the other kids from bullying you and I've been looking after you ever since,' he laughed as he released her.

'Except when it came to Patsy not wanting me around because I was a few months younger than her. You never took my part then.'

'Well, that was different.' He grinned. 'She was in the same class as me at school so I couldn't fall out with her, now could I?'

'No? Why was that? Did you hope people would think she was your girlfriend because she was so pretty and so popular?'

'Of course not!' He pulled a face. 'You are the only girl I've ever been interested in and you know how much I love you,' he added as he hugged her again and kissed her on the cheek.

Reassured, Lucy smiled up at him. She knew what he was saying was true but it was nice to hear him admit it, nevertheless.

'This weird mood you're in has something to do with that visit to see Percy, though, hasn't it?' he commented thoughtfully. 'Come on, what did he say that's upset you so much? He didn't try to make a pass at you, did he?'

'Percy make a pass at me in his condition!' She laughed dryly. 'You should see him, Robert. I had quite a shock because he was in such a dreadful state.'

Robert listened in silence as she related all about Percy's face and the cage to keep the bedclothes off his body.

'That's pretty bad, but I don't think that's what's made you so contemplative,' he said. 'There's something else worrying you, isn't there?'

'Yes,' Lucy admitted. 'It was something Percy suggested.'

Taking a deep breath she told Robert all about Percy's idea for Sam to take driving lessons and become a driver for Carter's Cars instead of being a mechanic.

There was a long silence when she finished as Robert contemplated what such a change would be like for Sam. Like her, he was uncertain if Sam would want to be a driver.

'He loves being a mechanic, you know,' he said at last.

'I agree and that's why I'm worried about suggesting the idea of being a driver to him,' Lucy pointed out. 'As a qualified motor mechanic he would have a job for life, so it's his future I'm worried about.'

'On the other hand,' Robert said thoughtfully, running his hand through his shock of fair hair, 'he was saying the other day that he's not enjoying working in the showroom and being a general dogsbody, so he might welcome the idea.'

'How can we be sure?' Lucy frowned.

'By doing what Percy suggests and asking him, I suppose,' Robert sighed. 'Let's ask Sam if he'd like to come out for a drink with us tonight and then we can tell him what Percy has suggested and find out how he feels about it.'

'That's a good idea as long as he doesn't invite Patsy along as well because I'm sure it is her idea that he should become a driver,' Lucy said. 'Perhaps I should suggest to her that we go to the pictures tonight, just to make sure.'

'No,' Robert shook his head firmly, 'you were the one Percy asked to talk to Sam about this, so you must be there. I agree with you that we don't want Patsy along as well, so don't say anything to Sam when you get home. Later on this evening I'll call round and then invite him to come out for a bevvy.'

'Just the two of you,' she said with relief.

'No, you must come as well.'

'Won't Sam think that is rather strange? He is bound to suggest that if I am coming we ought to take Patsy along as well.'

'I'll deal with that if he does. I'll tell him that since we are only going for a quick half it's not worth going round for her.'

'Surely it would be much better if it was just the two of you?' Lucy persisted.

'No,' Robert said firmly. 'You must be the one to tell him what Percy has suggested. I'll talk it over with him afterwards, if he wants to do so, but as we said before, it is up to him what he decides to do.'

Chapter Four

Lucy watched the changing expressions on her brother's face as she repeated what Percy had suggested. At first his dark eyes widened with astonishment. Then his thick brows drew together in contemplation of the idea and his eyes narrowed speculatively.

When she'd finished speaking he took a long drink of beer from his glass and then looked questioningly not at her but across at Robert who had remained silent the entire time Lucy had been talking.

'What do you think about it?' he asked.

Robert picked up his own glass and stared down into it as if seeking an answer. 'I don't know what to think, it's up to you, whacker, isn't it?' he said at last.

'I'm well aware of that,' Sam stated, 'but I wondered what you thought of the idea.' He looked at Lucy. 'Do you think they mean it about me packing in my apprenticeship and becoming a driver instead? Or do you think it is something that Percy has dreamed up himself while he's been lying there in his hospital bed with nothing else to do and that probably his old man knows nothing about it?'

'He told me that he and his father had talked it over,' Lucy assured him.

'So do you believe him?' Sam persisted. 'I'm wondering if Patsy's had something to do with it. She's always saying she wished I had a white-collar job; one where I didn't get all oily and my hands stained with grease from the cars. Do you think she's the one who has put the idea into Percy's head?'

'I really don't know,' Lucy said uncertainly. 'It was Mr Carter who asked me to go and visit Percy, though, and he said there was something Percy wanted to talk to me about.'

'Yes, but he didn't give you any idea what it was,' Sam muttered, picking up his glass again and staring into its contents.

Robert drained his own glass and began fastening his coat as though ready to leave. 'Why don't you mull over the suggestion, Sam, and then if Mr Carter does ask you about it, at least you will know what sort of answer to give him,' he suggested.

Sam was very quiet as they walked home and he went indoors ahead of Robert and Lucy who lingered on the doorstep to say goodnight to each other.

'I hope we've done the right thing in telling him,' Lucy said worriedly as Robert took her into his arms and held her close.

'We've done what Percy asked you to do and now it's up to Sam to decide what he wants to do. It's none of our business what the outcome is, so let's forget it and not talk about it any more,'

Robert told her firmly as his lips sought hers.

Lucy sighed and said no more but the thought that perhaps Sam was right in thinking that it had been Patsy's idea went round and round in her head and she wondered if it was the right decision for Sam to make. As a fully qualified mechanic he would be able to work anywhere; as a driver, she wasn't sure what his prospects would be.

Learning to drive was something most young men wanted to do but very few had the opportunity so she could understand what a temptation it must be for Sam. Since his hands were still tender after all this time, then perhaps it was a wise decision. If he hesitated, then he might not get another chance and if he ended up with some sort of skin problem from the oil and grease he came into contact with daily, then he would bitterly regret having turned down such an opportunity.

On the other hand, Lucy mused, if it was simply because Patsy fancied having a boyfriend who always looked clean and spruced up, then it was regrettable for Sam to sacrifice all the years he had spent as an apprentice simply to please her.

She wished Robert had been prepared to talk about it, but he didn't seem to understand why she was so concerned. He'd practically said that it wasn't up to her and that it had to be Sam's decision and that he should be left to make his own mind up.

She wondered if Sam would mention it to their parents and if so what her father would advise. He'd always seemed to be so proud of the fact that Sam was learning what he termed a proper trade.

It was two days before Sam said anything about Percy's suggestion and then it was to announce to the family over dinner that Mr Carter had arranged for him to have driving lessons.

'Driving lessons?' Bill Collins's eyebrows shot up in surprise as he laid down his knife and fork and looked across the table at his son. 'Why on earth is he doing that?'

'So that I can be a driver,' Sam said, concentrating on the food on his plate.

'A driver!' There was a mixture of curiosity and pride in Margaret Collins's voice as she stopped eating and looked questioningly from Sam to her husband and back. 'This is all rather sudden, isn't it? I thought you were helping out in the showroom until your hands were better and you could go back into the workshop.'

'As far as I know we already have all the drivers we need, so why go to the trouble of training you for the job?' Bill Collins asked. 'It will only be another couple of weeks or so before your hands are completely all right again and then you'll be fit enough to complete your apprenticeship.'

'No, Dad. The idea is that I become a driver instead of being a mechanic.'

There was an uneasy silence as Mr and Mrs Collins both mulled over this piece of news. Lucy wondered again whether it really was Mr Carter's idea or had Patsy persuaded Percy into suggesting it.

Her father didn't appear to be too happy about

47

the arrangement but her mother seemed to think that it was some kind of promotion. She kept saying that Mr Carter must think a great deal of Sam to suggest something like this.

As the discussion continued Lucy could tell that Sam seemed to be in favour of learning to drive and so, in the end, Lucy didn't think it fair to spoil things for him. If it was what he wanted, then even though it might have been due to scheming on Patsy's part, she reasoned that it might be best to leave things as they were.

At work, Patsy took all the praise for Sam's change of direction, boasting to all the girls and making out that it was a step up the ladder for Sam. She took a delight in pointing out whenever Lucy was within earshot that Robert was still a 'grease monkey' but Sam was on to better things.

Lucy waited to see if Mr Carter would ask her about her visit to see Percy but he made no reference to it.

Robert merely shrugged and said he thought she was being silly when Lucy confided in him that she was sure the idea that Sam should learn to drive was all Patsy's doing.

'What difference does it make whether you are in overalls or a driver's uniform as long as you have a job? That's all that matters these days. Sam's lucky that he didn't get stood off when he wasn't able to work.'

'Mr Carter could hardly do that when it was his son that Sam saved, now could he?' Lucy protested.

Robert didn't answer and seemed to be so reluctant to talk about it that Lucy wondered whether he was jealous and whether he would have preferred to be a driver himself rather than a mechanic. Then she decided that the best thing to do was to put it all out of her mind. It was none of her business, she told herself, and as long as Sam was pleased about what he was doing then that was all that mattered.

She and Robert had so many other things to talk about. Robert had now finished his apprenticeship which meant that he was on a man's pay, so their dream of getting married was uppermost in their minds.

They talked about it every time they met and eventually decided that as it was almost Christmas they would wait until the following year. Robert favoured a spring wedding, around Easter time, but Lucy thought they should wait until June.

'There's so much to prepare and Mam says she's worn out after all the worry over Sam,' Lucy pointed out. 'Anyway, it will give us more time to decide where we are going to live.'

'That's true,' Robert agreed. 'My mam has said that we can have a couple of rooms and live with them if we want to do so.'

'My mam has said the same.' Lucy smiled. 'I'd rather we found somewhere of our own, though, wouldn't you?'

'If we can afford it; if we live with our parents, there won't be much rent to pay each week. I know I'm on a man's pay now but it will be hard going at first unless Mr Carter lets you go on working. Carter's Cars doesn't employ married women.'

They finally agreed to aim for mid-July and decided they would both save hard until then for all the things they were going to need.

'After Easter we'll work out if we can afford to take furnished rooms,' Robert promised. 'I don't think we should tell anyone outside the family about our plans until closer to the date though,' he added.

'I agree. If Sam knows, then he's bound to tell Patsy and you know what she's like; she'll tell everybody,' Lucy warned.

'Yes, that's true. She'll be telling Sam that it was time they were married and want to make it a double wedding,' Robert laughed.

Sam certainly appeared to be extremely happy at the moment, Lucy thought. He had taken to driving like a duck to water and every evening as they sat around the table eating their meal, he regaled them with details of his progress.

The one thing which seemed to irritate Sam was that although Percy Carter was now out of hospital and recuperating at home, Patsy was still visiting him every afternoon. Sam didn't think this was necessary, and eventually Lucy decided she ought to ask Patsy why she was doing it.

It became obvious that the other girls in the office were wondering the same thing when someone brought up the subject a few days later while Miss Yorke was out at lunch.

'Mr Carter asked me to do it because he says Percy looks forward to seeing me so much that it's the highlight of his day,' Patsy retorted, giving them all a supercilious smile.

'Percy doesn't usually have much to say for himself when he's here at work so what on earth do you find to talk to him about?' one of the girls giggled.

'Well, I tell him all about what's going on here in the office and news about his friends, and after that we play board games. Percy loves to play Snakes and Ladders and Ludo.'

'Those are kid's games!' another of the girls laughed.

'Does that matter as long as he enjoys them?' Patsy defended, tossing her long blonde hair back defiantly.

'Probably more entertaining than listening to you jabbering on about nothing,' the girl agreed.

'I bet you get up to a lot more than that,' someone commented and there was general laughter all round.

Lucy kept silent because, like Sam, she didn't think that Patsy should be visiting Percy now that he was at home, but she didn't want to cause trouble and she knew that Patsy would repeat any comment she made to Sam.

'You're only taking advantage of getting off early every day, Patsy Warren. Are you really going to see him, or do you go shopping or something?'

'She daren't do that, Mr Carter would know and then she'd be in trouble,' another girl pointed out.

It worried Lucy that the others also thought it was strange and she kept wondering whether she ought to talk to Sam about it. Each time she intended to do so, however, he started regaling her with tales about his driving skills and he was so enthusiastic about how much he was enjoying driving that Lucy thought perhaps she was worrying needlessly and said nothing.

It was several weeks before Sam was considered to be a competent driver. The first time he was allowed to take a car out on his own he came home bubbling with excitement.

'Has Mr Carter told you yet which vehicle you are going to be responsible for?' his father queried. 'You'll probably have to be a co-driver at first because I haven't heard that anyone is leaving and we have enough drivers in the Stores as it is.'

'I've been told that I'm going to stay on in the showroom and that I will be delivering new cars and returning cars to their owners after they've been serviced,' Sam told him.

'Delivering new cars! You haven't had anywhere near enough experience to be doing something as responsible as that.' Bill Collins frowned. 'You take care, my lad, we don't want any more accidents, you know.'

'It's Mr Carter's decision; he says I am a very good driver,' Sam mumbled.

Bill Collins shook his head but said no more. It was left to Lucy to shower praise on Sam and wish him well.

Patsy positively glowed with pride when early in the New Year she informed everybody that Sam had been instructed to drive Percy and Mrs Carter to the hospital when Percy had to go back for his final check-up.

'It shows how much Mr Carter thinks of Sam

to choose him to do something like that,' Patsy boasted.

'He's simply making use of him, and saving himself having to drive there,' one of the clerks scoffed.

Once again Lucy took no part in the bantering that went on in the office but when she got home she did congratulate Sam and told him that he must be a good driver for Mr Carter to trust him so much.

Mr Collins, however, still continually expressed his doubts about Sam's ability as a driver, saying that he was too young to have the responsibility of driving customers' cars.

Then, as Easter approached, to prove to his father how good a driver he was, Sam summoned up the courage to ask Mr Carter if he could hire one of the cars to take his parents out on Easter Sunday.

'I'd like to take them out for a drive and then stop somewhere for afternoon tea. It would be a real treat for my mam and I thought it would be a way of saying thank you to both of them for all the worry they've had ever since the accident.'

'I suppose I could permit that,' Mr Carter agreed. 'Only your parents, though, and I don't want you to go driving too far or too fast, so no showing off, remember.'

'I'll be extremely careful, Mr Carter, I promise.'

'Right. Where were you thinking of going?'

'I'm not too sure, sir,' Sam said hesitantly. 'I thought perhaps Southport or Chester.'

'Hmm!' Mr Carter looked thoughtful. 'I think perhaps Southport might be the best choice. You are still too inexperienced to drive in a city like Chester.'

'Southport it will be, then.' Sam smiled. 'My mam will love that and we can have tea at one of the cafés on the front and then walk along the promenade.'

'Make sure you park in a suitable place and lock the car before you leave it,' Mr Carter warned.

Margaret Collins was so excited when Sam told them about the proposed outing that evening when he arrived home that she could hardly eat her meal.

'Do you know which car it is we're going in?' she asked.

'Does it matter all that much?' Bill Collins commented. 'Most of Carter's Cars are black, aren't they?'

'Some of them are bigger and shinier than others,' his wife murmured.

'I won't know which car until I finish work on Saturday,' Sam told her. 'Then I'll be given the keys and I've been told to collect the car at one o'clock on Sunday and to have it back in the garage again before five o'clock.'

'Four whole hours of driving around,' Margaret Collins exclaimed in amazement. 'Can you believe it, Bill?' she asked, smiling across the table at her husband.

'We won't be driving all of the time,' Sam told her quickly. 'There is a limit on how far I can go.'

'Oh dear.' His mother looked puzzled. 'What are we going to do, then, and exactly where are we going?'

'You will have to wait and see,' Sam told her.

'Don't worry,' he added with a smile, 'I have it all planned out and I know you are going to enjoy every minute of it.'

'Perhaps you ought to take your mother and Lucy on this outing instead of me,' Bill Collins suggested.

'No, it's got to be you and Mam, that's what I've arranged with Mr Carter. He said the two of you and no one else,' Sam emphasised.

'Well, he's not to know now, is he, whether it's me and your mam or your mam and Lucy sitting in it. Come to that, there's room for both of us and Lucy as well. I can sit in front with you and Lucy and your mother can ride in the back.'

'That's not the point,' Sam muttered. 'I gave my word, and since he's been good enough to let me have the car for the afternoon, I'm not going to go against his wishes.'

Chapter Five

Lucy didn't have to work on the Good Friday which, that year, 1921, was early and fell on the twenty-fifth of March. She spent most of the day helping her mother to prepare for the special outing on Easter Sunday.

'I can't believe that our Sam will be taking your dad and me out in a motor car,' Margaret Collins said over and over again, her plump, round face beaming. 'I do wish you were coming along with us as well, Lucy, it would be such a lovely treat for you,' she added in a wistful voice.

'Never mind, I've got plans of my own,' Lucy assured her. 'I'm going out for the afternoon with Robert.'

'I'm sure there would be room for both of you,' Margaret Collins mused as she kept her head bent over an enamel bowl while Lucy poured a jug of lukewarm water over her head to rinse out the Amami shampoo from her hair.

'We can't come with you, Mam. Sam told you that Mr Collins said it was to be you and Dad and no one else. You don't want Sam getting into trouble, now do you?' Lucy said firmly.

After she had dried her mother's shoulder-length hair with a towel and then combed it into a neat knot in the nape of her neck, Lucy offered to help her to put together everything she intended to wear on the Sunday.

'I'm not really sure what to put on,' her mother said worriedly. 'I want to look smart.'

'Then wear the cream dress and jacket that you've already bought,' Lucy suggested.

'Oh, Lucy, I can't do that. That's special for when you and Robert get married later in the year.'

'Surely you can wear it again for that,' Lucy told her. 'No one else will know.'

'I'm not so sure,' her mother said dubiously.

'You could always treat yourself to a new hat and gloves for the wedding and then it would look completely different.'

'No, it wouldn't feel right. I must keep it new for your wedding,' her mother insisted.

'You could always buy something else; it'll be

months till our wedding.'

'I'm not sure I should be so extravagant because there's so much else we have to spend money on for your bottom drawer.'

'Nonsense. I've been collecting things for ages. I've all I need to start off with and I can always borrow things I'm short of from you,' Lucy said, smiling.

'Well, yes, that's if you decide that you and Robert are going to make your home here. You haven't told us yet what you've decided to do. Your dad was only saying the other day that if you and Robert are going to move in here, then he will have to start decorating the two rooms in readiness.'

'We'll talk about it after this outing is over,' Lucy promised.

'I want to make your wedding day the talk of Priory Terrace,' she went on, her eyes shining. 'I can see you now in your wedding dress, holding your father's arm as you walk up the aisle to where Robert is waiting, and our Sam standing there beside Robert in a smart new suit.'

'And Patsy as my bridesmaid,' Lucy reminded her.

'Mmm! Well, I hope she behaves herself and doesn't start flirting with all the men like she usually does.'

'Mam! You know it's just her way because all the men think she is so pretty.'

'Rubbish! You are going to be the one looking beautiful. Anyway,' her mother said briskly, 'all this chatter's not helping me to decide what I am going to wear when Sam takes us out. I suppose

I could wear the red dress that I wore on Christmas Day, but I'm not sure which hat and coat to wear with it.'

'Your winter coat, of course,' Lucy told her. 'It's still March and the wind can be quite cutting.'

'Not if we are inside the car, surely,' her mother protested, her face creasing into a frown. 'It's not like standing around waiting for a tram, now is it?'

They discussed it at length and finally agreed that her three-quarter-length coat with a fur collar would be ideal even though it was dark blue and her dress was red.

'Oh dear, and my hat is black,' Margaret Collins sighed. 'That won't look right, will it?'

'In that case, why don't you wear my dark red one and it will go with your dress?'

'You mean that little one with the tiny brim that looks like a pudding basin?'

'It's called a cloche hat and they are the very latest fashion, Mam. It will look far better than wearing a black one and, anyway, the brim on your black one is so big that you will probably knock your hat off trying to get into the car.'

Reluctantly, her mother agreed to try it on and then seemed genuinely amazed at how well it looked. The face-framing hat flattered her and the colour suited her extremely well, making her look younger than she was.

'Don't let on to your dad or Sam what I am planning to wear, I want to give them a surprise,' Margaret Collins said smiling conspiratorially as she took off Lucy's hat and smoothed down her hair which was now slightly disturbed.

Her mother talked so much about the forth-coming outing, wondering where Sam was taking them and worrying about what the weather would be like, that Lucy began to feel that she would be glad when it was all over.

'Very well, I'll keep what you're wearing a secret,' Lucy promised as she took the hat from her. 'Now, can we go and have our meal? I'm meeting Robert at two o'clock.'

She was almost relieved that she had to go to work on Saturday and that she was extremely busy on the switchboard so that the time flew past.

Although the rest of them dressed up in their best to go to church on Easter Sunday morning, to Lucy's surprise her mother didn't wear her red dress.

'No one will see what I have on under my big coat. I want to keep that dress and your hat to wear later, because that's going to be such a special occasion, and I want to look my very best then,' she reminded Lucy as she fastened on her wide-brimmed black hat and picked up her bag and gloves ready to leave.

After church, Lucy offered to clear up after their meal and told her dad he'd better go and spruce himself up while Sam went to fetch the car.

'No need to go showing off by bringing it right here to the door, we can walk to the garage,' Bill Collins protested.

'No, Mam wants to find it waiting for her when she walks out of the front door,' Sam insisted. 'Letting the whole street see it arrive and then being driven off in it is half the treat for her.' He grinned.

'Well, I'll walk along to the garage with you, Sam,' Bill muttered, following Sam out into the hallway and picking up his flat cap and reaching for his coat that was hanging there.

'Oh no, Dad, you can't go out dressed like that,' Lucy intervened quickly. 'For a start, you are not going to wear that cap. It's a smart trilby-and-no-muffler day,' she added laughing.

Sam took advantage of the interruption to disappear and with a sigh of resignation Mr Collins went to find his trilby as Lucy had requested.

Five minutes later, Lucy felt really proud of them both as they stood in the living room, waiting for the car to arrive. She opened the front door the moment Sam pulled up outside but one or two of the neighbours were already on their doorsteps curious to see what was going on.

Before Mr and Mrs Collins could get into the car, Patsy appeared. There was a look of astonishment on her face as she spoke to Sam and asked him what was happening.

'I'm taking my mam and dad for a spin and then somewhere for afternoon tea,' he said, grinning.

'You planned all this and yet you never said a word to me about it?' Patsy pouted, tossing her hair back from her face. 'Did Mr Carter say you could use the car?'

'Of course he did; I wouldn't be outside my house with it otherwise, now would I?'

Patsy waited until Mr and Mrs Collins were settled in the back seat and then looked enquiringly at Lucy.

'I suppose you are going with them as well, are you?' she asked.

'No,' Lucy shook her head, 'Sam wants it to be a special treat for Mam and Dad.'

Patsy beamed, her pretty face suddenly lighting up. 'Then I shall come as well, Sam. I can sit in front beside you.'

'Sorry, Patsy, but that's not possible. Mr Carter said I could only take Mam and Dad.'

'That's not fair.' Patsy scowled. 'What am I supposed to do all afternoon? I was expecting you to take me out.'

'I'll be back before five and we'll go out this evening,' Sam told her as he turned on the engine.

'No, that's not good enough.' Patsy shook her head, her mouth set in a tight line. She clung on to the car door as Sam engaged gear and began to pull away.

'Come on, Patsy, don't spoil things for them. It's not Sam's fault that you can't go as well; he had to promise Mr Carter he would only take my mam and dad,' Lucy told her, taking her arm and pulling her away.

'Mr Carter probably meant that he didn't want you riding around in one of his cars pretending to be Lady Muck,' Patsy told her, shaking free of Lucy's restraining hand.

Lucy couldn't think of a suitable answer as Patsy stalked off home in high dudgeon. She felt sorry for Sam, though, because she knew that Patsy was very angry and would have quite a lot to say to him when he came home.

Knowing that there was nothing she could do about it and that Robert would be arriving almost any minute, she went back indoors to get ready to go out.

Robert had promised to take her across to New Brighton because the fun fair was open over Easter and he knew how much she loved going on the rides with him, but suddenly her heart wasn't in it. She even wondered if he would prefer to stay home since they had the house to themselves, something that rarely happened.

Robert arrived long before she was ready and he was shivering as he came indoors. 'It's chilly out; there's a keen wind and it will be bitterly cold going over on the boat,' he told her.

'The kettle's boiling, would you like a cup of tea first, to warm you up?' Lucy asked.

'That sounds like a great idea,' he agreed, as he rubbed his cold nose against her cheek after kissing her.

As they settled down on the sofa to drink their tea Lucy said, 'We don't have to go out this afternoon, you know; not if you'd rather stay here.'

He looked at her quizzically. 'What do you want to do? I planned the trip over to New Brighton because I know how much you enjoy the rides.'

'We have got the house to ourselves,' Lucy murmured. 'Sam isn't planning to be back until five o'clock and that's almost four hours away.'

'Mmm,' Robert murmured, putting his cup down on the table and pulling Lucy into his arms, his mouth covering hers. His lips travelled down her neck and back up again and he nibbled gently on the lobes of her ears. 'Perhaps we should change our plans and take advantage of that and stay here; we can always go over to New Brighton next weekend,' he whispered.

Cocooned in the warmth and quiet of the house, Lucy acquiesced and relaxed in Robert's arms. She loved him with all her heart and was always eager for his kisses and embraces but usually these were very constrained because they had so little privacy.

Now, knowing that there would be no interruptions, Lucy nestled up closer to Robert and made no protests when he slipped his hands inside her clothing and became far more intimate than he had ever dared to be before.

She was carried away by Robert's ardour. Her own feelings were in turmoil; she had never before felt such desire or need. She wanted the strange and slightly shocking sensations that sent shivers of anticipation through her entire body to go on for ever.

When he gently eased her from the sofa and lowered her on to the rug in front of the glowing fire, she made no resistance. As he undid the buttons on her blouse and, peeling it away from her shoulders, began to kiss and fondle her breasts, she stiffened for a brief moment then gave a quivering sigh followed by a little cry of delight as his mouth took possession of first one and then the other.

Eagerly she started to unbutton the front of his shirt. As her hands touched his bare chest she drew in a sharp breath and then pulled him closer to her own naked body, closing her eyes as their flesh melded together and she felt the intense heat from his body enveloping her.

Robert raised himself on one elbow and looked

down at her quizzically, almost as if asking for permission to go on. At that moment Lucy knew she could deny him nothing and smiled in anticipation of what was to follow.

After that they were so intertwined that it was as if they were one. Every throb of their pulse, every breath they took and every movement they made seemed to be in unison. They lost all sense of time or place as their passion, which had been restrained for so long, completely engulfed them.

The loud hammering on the front door followed by a pounding on the window startled both of them and brought them back to reality with an unnerving jolt.

They stared at each other in alarm, then Lucy pulled away from Robert, fighting back a feeling of shame at having been caught in such a compromising situation.

Their moment of sheer bliss had been completely shattered and, for a few seconds, neither of them seemed to know what to say or do. Lucy pushed her hair back from her flushed face and tried to think who it could be hammering on the door.

'Surely Sam hasn't brought my mam and dad back from their ride already,' she gulped, her brown eyes wide with distress as she looked at Robert.

'It's far too soon for them to be coming home,' Robert agreed. He looked at the clock on the mantelpiece. 'They've only been gone just over an hour. Anyway, the door isn't locked, so they could have opened it. It must be someone else.'

'What are we going to do? Perhaps we should stay quiet and pretend we're not here.'

'No, we'd better not do that in case it is important. You stay there; I'll go and see who it is.'

He reached for his clothes, pulling on his trousers and shirt and fastening them as quickly as he could.

There was another loud hammering on the door and Lucy hurriedly put on her own clothes and tried to smooth down her tousled hair as she heard Robert call out, 'All right, I'm coming; there's no need to bash the door in.'

With shaking hands she tried to straighten the crumpled rug and pick up the cushion that was lying on the floor and put it back on to the sofa.

She walked over to the fireplace and stared at her reflection in the over mantle as she smoothed her hair, wondering if anyone could tell from her appearance what had just happened in the last hour or so.

She looked perfectly normal, she told herself as she heard Robert returning.

Her feeling of bravado was immediately forgotten when she saw that he was accompanied by a policeman; she could only stare at them in silence, afraid to ask why he was there.

Chapter Six

'Are you Lucy Collins?' the policeman asked, removing his helmet and placing it on the table before taking out his notebook.

'Yes!' Lucy said in a trembling voice, her colour rising. What on earth was a policeman doing calling on them? she wondered. They'd never had a policeman at the door in the whole of her life. He was so big and burly that he seemed to fill the room.

She felt a frisson of fear rising inside her, making her heart thud faster. Surely she and Robert couldn't be prosecuted for what they had been doing, she thought anxiously.

The policeman consulted his notebook again and then cleared his throat hesitantly. 'I'm afraid I have some bad news for you, miss,' he said awkwardly. 'The motor vehicle that your brother was driving has been involved in a serious accident—'

'Accident?' Lucy's voice was shrill with fear. 'What sort of an accident? My mam and dad are in the car with him; he was taking them to Southport as a treat...' Her voice faded away and she looked helplessly at Robert who immediately moved across the room and put his arm around her protectively.

'Yes, Miss Collins. The accident took place at Blundell Ince, a small village about halfway between here and Southport,' he paused and consulted his notebook. 'It seems a horse strayed on to the main road and when the driver took evasive action to try and avoid it, the animal reared up and collided with the vehicle and the driver lost control of the steering. Two of the wheels skidded off the tarmacked road and into a deep ditch, causing the vehicle to overturn. The driver and passengers were all trapped inside the vehicle.'

Lucy gasped.

'Are they badly hurt?' Robert asked.

'The driver was taken to hospital with severe injuries; I'm afraid I don't yet have the details of exactly what they were.'

'What about the two passengers who were in the car?' Robert persisted, his arm tightening around Lucy, who was white faced and trembling as they listened to the policeman's report.

The officer's mouth tightened as he studied his notebook. 'I'm afraid, sir, that both the passengers in the back of the vehicle died at the scene of the accident.'

Robert frowned. 'Are you quite sure about that?'

'It was a very deep ditch and there was considerable impact when the car plunged into it–'

'It's not true,' Lucy interrupted. 'Sam was taking Mam and Dad for a day out, so he wouldn't let something like that happen to them.'

'I'm sorry to have to bring you such distressing news, miss, but I'm afraid it is true and you will need to go along to the hospital mortuary to identify the bodies,' he added, looking not at Lucy but at Robert.

'How soon do we have to do that?' Robert asked,

glancing uneasily at Lucy.

'Right away, if you can. It's best to get it over with as quickly as possible,' he advised.

'Yes, I understand,' Robert said stiffly.

'Now, is there anything else I can tell you?' the officer asked as he tucked his notebook back into his top pocket and picked his helmet up from the table ready to leave.

'No, I don't think so.' Robert looked enquiringly at Lucy but she shook her head and gave a small shiver as she clutched at his arm as if for reassurance.

After the police officer had left, Robert patted her shoulder and then gently pushed her into an armchair. 'Sit down and I'll make a cup of tea before we go,' he told her.

She offered no resistance but did as Robert asked; she was still sitting there, staring into space as if completely mesmerised, when he brought in the tea.

Neither of them spoke; Robert had no idea what to say, he still couldn't believe that such a terrible thing had happened and he wasn't too sure that Lucy had taken in everything the policeman had said.

To his surprise, when she had finished drinking her tea, Lucy put the empty cup on the table and said in a quiet, determined voice, 'I'd better be going to the hospital to identify the bodies, hadn't I? Are you coming with me?'

'Of course I am.' He stood up and picked up her cup and his own and carried them through to the kitchen.

'Leave them on the side,' Lucy called out. 'I can

see to them when we get back. The policeman did say to go along there as soon as possible.'

Without waiting for him to reply Lucy went out into the hall and took down her everyday grey coat and hat from the hallstand and put them on before Robert could help her.

Outside there was sunshine and clear skies. 'Good job we didn't go over to New Brighton, although it would have been a lovely day to walk along the shore,' Lucy commented as they walked towards the nearest tram stop.

Startled, Robert looked sideways at her. She was speaking in such a normal voice that he was slightly taken aback. The look of stunned disbelief had gone from her face. She wasn't smiling but she was holding her head high and stepping out as if enjoying their walk in the March sunshine.

He didn't know what to say. He felt he ought to warn her about what lay ahead but he couldn't find the right words. It was going to be a tremendous ordeal and he wondered if she would be able to cope with it. They would also have to visit Sam afterwards and he wasn't sure if Sam knew about what had happened to his parents when the car overturned or not; or how he would take the news if they were the ones who had to tell him.

To Robert's amazement Lucy remained icily calm when they were shown into the mortuary. He expected her to cringe away when the green sheet was pulled back from the body on the first trolley to reveal her father.

Instead, with a small sigh she bent and pressed

her lips to the waxen figure before nodding and confirming in a low, firm voice that this was her father, forty-five-year-old Bill Collins.

Without wavering, she repeated the process when they uncovered the body of her mother, 'Margaret Collins, forty years old,' she stated after implanting a light kiss on her mother's forehead.

'If you're ready, then we'll go and visit Sam,' she murmured turning to Robert.

Sam was in a small side ward with only three other beds in it. Lucy hesitated as the sister started to lead them towards the one in the corner of the room that had the curtains drawn around it and Robert quickly took hold of her hand and squeezed it.

As the sister drew one of the curtains aside they found a nurse was setting up a drip and they had to wait until she had finished.

One of Sam's arms was heavily bandaged and the wrist of his other arm was in splints and supported above his head. One of his legs was encased in a plaster cast from ankle to thigh and there was a metal cage over it to keep the bedclothes from pressing down on it. His face was badly lacerated and both his eyes were surrounded by dark bruising. Lucy could see that his mouth and lips were very swollen and she wondered if he had lost any of his teeth.

His eyes flickered open as they approached but although Lucy spoke his name he simply stared vacantly into space and moaned as though he was in pain.

'He doesn't even know me,' Lucy whispered in

a shocked voice as she stood helplessly at the bedside staring down at him.

'Your brother is heavily sedated at the moment, Miss Collins,' the sister told her.

As the tears began to trickle down Lucy's cheeks Robert put his arm around her shoulders and gently drew her away from the bed.

'I would suggest that you go home and come back tomorrow or the next day and hopefully by then you will find he not only recognises you, but is also able to speak to you,' the sister advised.

'Does he know what happened and that our parents are both dead?' Lucy whispered, her voice trembling.

'No.' The sister shook her head firmly. 'He was unconscious when he was brought in.'

'Who is going to break the news to Sam?' Lucy asked, her voice full of concern. 'He's going to be so terribly upset,' she added with a deep, shuddering sigh.

'It would be best not to tell him about what happened until he is much stronger,' the sister said firmly. 'Next time you come we will discuss the matter; perhaps it would be better to leave it until he is on the road to recovery himself.'

'He is going to be all right, isn't he?' Lucy gulped.

The sister hesitated for a second. 'Your brother is young and healthy and if he was quite fit and strong before the accident then he should make good progress given time and patience.'

'Will he make a complete recovery?' Lucy repeated, emphasising the word *complete*.

Again the sister hesitated. 'He will need a great

deal of nursing care for some considerable time after he is discharged from here,' she said evasively.

'I think we should go now,' Robert suggested, taking Lucy by the elbow and propelling her away from Sam's bed.

'Yes, that's very sensible,' the sister murmured giving Robert a grateful look.

'It is all right to come back tomorrow, though?' Lucy asked.

'Yes, but there may not be a great deal of improvement in his condition by then, so it might be better if you left it for a day or two.'

Lucy shook her head. 'Please don't ask me to do that,' she begged. 'I'd like to stay now and sit by his bedside so that I am here for him when he does waken.'

'No, no. You can do nothing for him at the moment,' the sister told her firmly. 'He needs complete rest. Come back tomorrow, if you really feel you must. Mid-afternoon would be best. By then I hope you will see some improvement in your brother's condition,' she added briskly as she ushered them out of the ward.

Once they were outside the hospital Lucy seemed to be so overcome with grief that Robert wondered if he ought to get a taxi cab to take them home. As soon as he mentioned this, though, Lucy shook her head emphatically.

'No, Robert, I would prefer to walk. I'll be all right in a minute,' she told him, taking great gulps of air and scrubbing at her tear-stained face with her handkerchief.

'Are you quite sure? You were so brave when we went to the mortuary.'

'It was because they only seemed to be asleep. It was such a shock when Sam opened his eyes and didn't recognise me, or even look at me, that was what upset me the most,' she babbled.

'The sister explained that was because they had sedated him; they had to do that, Lucy, because he was probably in terrible pain after they'd seen to his injuries.'

'If he's in so much pain tomorrow, he still may not be able to speak to us or even recognise us,' she said unhappily.

'Give it a few days and he'll be over the worst,' Robert said consolingly. 'He's being well looked after and they're doing all they can for him,' he assured her.

By the time they arrived back in Priory Terrace most of the neighbours had already heard rumours about the accident and were anxious to know more.

Lucy was still too upset to talk about it so Robert told them as much as he knew.

'You should have come and let me know right away and you should have taken me to the hospital with you when you went to see Sam,' Patsy said furiously. 'Which hospital is he in and what's the name of the ward?'

'There's no point in going there now, he is so heavily sedated that he doesn't know anyone,' Robert told her.

'He'll know me,' Patsy told him defiantly.

'No, Patsy, he won't. He's very badly injured and he's practically unconscious. His eyes aren't focussing and he can't speak,' Lucy told her. 'He has broken one of his legs as well as an arm and the wrist on his other hand has a plaster on it as well. There are also cuts all over his face and I think he may have lost some of his teeth.'

'You're exaggerating!' Patsy looked accusingly from Lucy to Robert and back again. 'You're trying to frighten me and put me off because you don't want me to visit him.'

'No, Lucy is telling you the truth, Patsy. We were told it would be better to leave visiting for a day or two until he's stronger,' Robert affirmed. 'Anyway,' he added quickly when he saw she was about to argue with him, 'they won't let you see him, even if you go along to the hospital. The sister said it was better if he didn't have any visitors until he was stronger.'

'Then why did they let you in today?' Patsy asked, tossing her head, her blue eyes accusing.

'We're family,' Robert said quietly.

'Lucy might be, but you're not.'

'Patsy, it's no good arguing about it. I don't make the rules. Go along if you want to, and don't blame me if they turn you away,' Lucy said wearily.

'At the moment Sam won't know you and he certainly won't be able to talk to you,' Robert added as he took Lucy by the hand and headed for her house.

'Bring Lucy in here, son,' Robert's mother, Barbara Tanner, called. 'I've a pot of hot scouse waiting for you both.'

As Robert took Lucy into his house, which was next door to her own, he gave her a reassuring hug. 'Mum's right, you'll be better staying in with us for the moment because people will be banging on your front door asking for news about the accident and I'm sure you don't want to deal with that sort of thing.'

Lucy shook her head. 'I'll be all right. I need to be on my own to think through all the things I'm going to have to do. There's the funeral to be arranged and I don't know where to start.'

'Come in for a minute or so and have something to eat and a cup of tea before you go home and we'll talk about it. I'll help you, you don't have to see to everything on your own, you know,' he reminded her.

Chapter Seven

It was four days before Sam was fully conscious. When they finally broke the sad news to him about his parents he was overcome with remorse and blamed himself for what had happened. Lucy found it so difficult to comfort him that she was in tears.

'Why couldn't I have been the one to die?' he raged. 'I'm always having accidents of one sort or the other and now I'm going to be completely useless. I might never walk again or be able to drive even if Mr Carter does keep my job open for me. All I'm going to be is a burden on everyone else for the rest of my life.'

Lucy reached out and gently took his hand. 'You certainly will be, if you are going to adopt that sort of attitude,' she told him as she brushed her own tears aside. 'In three months' time your broken arm and wrist will both be as good as new and you'll be walking again and be able to do just about anything you want to do as long as you follow all the advice the hospital has given you.'

'You mean like having massages and doing regular exercises,' Sam said moodily.

'That's right, and I'm going to make sure you do them,' Lucy vowed in a voice that brooked no argument.

'How will you manage to do that? You're going to be the sole bread-winner until I'm better, so you won't have time because you'll be out at work every day.'

'That's right. So because I'm going to be so extremely busy I shall expect you to be cooperative. Even if you're at home on your own for most of the time, it doesn't mean you can forget all about doing your exercises.'

It was a further six weeks before Sam was allowed to come home from hospital. He was unable to walk and because of his broken arm and wrist he wasn't able to use crutches, so it meant that he had to be pushed about in a wheelchair. By then the double funeral for Bill and Margaret Collins had taken place.

Robert and Lucy had debated for a long time about whether they should try and delay the internment until Sam came out of hospital. In the end they decided that perhaps it would be better to get it all over with before he came home because he still seemed to be reluctant to talk about what had happened.

Robert's parents helped Lucy to make all the

arrangements and most of the people in Priory Terrace followed the hearse. Robert stayed at Lucy's side throughout the entire service, holding her hand and giving her the courage to go through with the terrible ordeal she had to face.

In the weeks that followed Lucy had to put her own life on hold. It wasn't simply a matter of going to work, cleaning the house and preparing all their meals. She also had to supervise Sam's medication and take him back to the hospital for regular check-ups. Time and time again she had to tell Robert that she couldn't spare the time to go out with him, not even for a walk.

More important still it meant delaying their wedding; in view of what had happened Lucy knew it was impossible to go ahead with their plans to be married in July.

'Do we have to postpone it?' Robert argued. 'By then everything will have settled down, Sam should be fit again and well enough to go back to work.'

Although she was as disappointed as he was, Lucy was adamant.

'Sam's not the problem,' she pointed out. 'It's the fact that it's far too soon after the death of my parents.'

'Would you prefer us to leave it until next year?' he asked. 'Perhaps early in June?'

'Yes. Sam will be back on his feet again by then and all our worries will be behind us,' Lucy agreed smiling.

'In the meantime, surely Patsy could help look after Sam occasionally so that we can go out together now and again,' Robert insisted. 'After all, she's always claimed that she and Sam are going to be married one of these days so he's as much her responsibility as yours.'

'Yes, you're right,' Lucy said thoughtfully. 'She should have plenty of spare time now,' she added with a wry smile.

Robert frowned. 'What do you mean?'

'Well, lately Patsy has been too busy dancing attendance on Percy Carter to spend much time with Sam,' Lucy reminded him, her mouth tightening with annoyance. 'Sam's quite miserable about it and says he can't understand why she has to bother about Percy now that he is better.'

'Probably because he takes her out for expensive meals,' Robert pointed out.

'Yes, but that's going to have to stop. I overheard Mr Carter telling him off about doing that because Percy's been putting the meals on his expense account and Mr Carter said he wouldn't stand for it,' Lucy commented.

'Oh dear, have you been listening in on the boss's calls?' Robert grinned.

'No, I don't listen to people's calls – well, only for a second, to make sure that I've made the right connection. Believe me, that switchboard is far too busy most of the day for me to spend time eavesdropping on calls,' she told him rather tartly.

'So how do you know about what Mr Carter told Percy?' Robert asked.

'They were arguing about it in Mr Carter's office and their voices were raised so much that everyone in the general office could hear what was being said.'

'Did Mr Carter mention Patsy by name?'

'Yes he did; and what's more, he said Percy has got to stop seeing her.'

'Whew!' Robert let out a low whistle. 'That will put paid to that little flirtation.'

'Yes, and I'm pleased about it; after all, it's not been fair on Sam since she's supposed to be his girlfriend.'

'Well, there you are, then. Like I said, Patsy can help to look after Sam and take some of the strain off your shoulders. We never have the chance to go out together on a Saturday or Sunday afternoon unless we take Sam with us in his wheelchair and that rather spoils things for us, doesn't it?'

'It's not much fun for him either. He hates having to be wheeled around.'

'Perhaps he'd enjoy it more if Patsy was the one pushing his wheelchair. Why don't you ask her if she'll take him out next weekend? I'm sure she will, if you tell her that we have to go somewhere on our own.'

Although Lucy was in full agreement with Robert's idea, it didn't work out as either of them had hoped. Lucy gave Patsy time to greet Sam and have time to talk with him before she brought up the idea only to find that Patsy wasn't at all keen on taking Sam out and it was only after a great deal of persuasion that she agreed to do it.

'I suppose I could take him along to the park on Sunday afternoon as long as it is only for an hour,' she finally agreed reluctantly.

'That's great! I'll make sure he's all ready when you call round for him.'

'Don't say anything to him in case something

crops up and I can't manage it.'

'I think I should tell him because it will be something special for him to look forward to and he is rather depressed at the moment,' Lucy murmured.

Sam seemed to be quite buoyed up at the idea and for the first time since he'd come out of hospital he settled himself in the wheelchair without his usual grumbling.

It was a glorious summer day, the sun was shining and there was only the lightest of breezes. Lucy was looking forward to being with Robert so much that she felt quite excited as she put on a red and white cotton dress and red jacket.

She hoped that there would be time for them to go across to New Brighton but unless Patsy agreed to look after Sam for the whole afternoon, that wouldn't be possible. She would have to try and persuade her to take Sam back to her place for tea and then she and Robert could collect him on their way home.

'Are you going somewhere special? You look as though you are dressed up for a wedding or a garden party,' Robert teased when he arrived.

'It's new; I intended to wear it on Easter Sunday when we went out in the afternoon but so much happened that day that I never got to wear it. Do you like it?'

'I think you look absolutely terrific,' he assured her. 'Good job I put on my new flannels and sports jacket. I only wish we were going somewhere special.'

Robert agreed with her whole-heartedly when she suggested that they should take a trip to New

Brighton if Patsy looked after Sam for the whole afternoon.

'Great idea. Mr Warren might like to see Sam and have a chat with him and I'm sure Mrs Warren would be happy to invite him to have tea with them.'

Patsy was almost half an hour late and they were all becoming uneasy, wondering whether she was going to turn up at all or whether she had forgotten about their arrangement.

She gave no explanation when she did arrive but said she could only manage an hour so they wouldn't be able to spend very long at the park.

Sam looked so disappointed that Lucy felt angry. In as calm a voice as she could manage, she told Patsy that she and Robert wanted to go to New Brighton and went on to suggest that Patsy took Sam back to her house after their walk.

'I'm sorry but that's not possible,' Patsy told her. 'I've arranged to go out later on this afternoon.'

Lucy and Robert looked at each other in dismay, knowing that meant their own outing was impossible.

'Well, in that case, you'd better get going right away,' Robert said sharply. 'I'll manoeuvre the wheelchair outside on to the pavement for you.'

'Why are you dressed up to the nines, Lucy? That is a new dress and jacket, isn't it?' Patsy went on. 'I don't think I've ever seen you wearing red before. You usually go for muddier colours and, of course, lately you've always been in black or some dark colour. I'm not sure red suits you; it's far too bright for your colouring, if you know what I mean.'

'There you are, then, Patsy. He's all yours, so enjoy your walk,' Robert said as he propelled the wheelchair over the doorstep and out on to the pavement.

Gingerly, Patsy took hold of the handles. 'I've never pushed one of these things before,' she murmured, tossing her hair back. 'I feel really nervous.'

'You'll find it's not very different from pushing a pram,' Lucy said, smiling.

'I've never pushed one of those either; it's terribly heavy, isn't it?' Patsy grimaced as, cautiously, she pushed the wheelchair a couple of yards.

'It won't be once you get used to it,' Robert assured her.

'It's all right for you because you're so strong.' Patsy smiled, her big blue eyes staring at him admiringly.

'Lucy manages to push me to the hospital when I have to go there,' Sam pointed out.

'She's so much bigger than me,' Patsy countered. 'In fact, Lucy's almost twice the size I am. She doesn't wear high heels like I do,' she added, looking pointedly at Lucy's sensible flat-heeled shoes and then at her own pencil-thin high ones. 'I think high heels make your legs look more attractive, don't you, Robert?'

Lucy bit her lip. She knew Patsy was quite capable of pushing the wheelchair and, what was more, she resented her exaggerated comments as well as the way she was flirting with Robert. It also worried her that Patsy protesting so much was making Sam very uncomfortable as well.

'Come on, I'll get you going,' she offered. 'Like

Robert has said, once you start moving and get used to it, then you'll find it's not difficult at all.'

'No, I'll push it and we'll walk with Patsy to the end of the road, then she can carry on to the park and we'll go on down to the Pier Head,' Robert said briskly. 'Even if we haven't time to go over to New Brighton this afternoon we can still go and take a look at the Mersey,' he added.

There wasn't room for them all to walk abreast on the pavement so Lucy found that she was walking on her own a few paces behind the other two.

'Why don't you come to the park as well?' Patsy suggested when they turned into Priory Road and were about to go their separate ways.

Lucy sensed Robert looking at her and deliberately avoided his eyes because she didn't want to have to trail along behind Patsy and Sam for the rest of the afternoon.

'No, Sam's been looking forward to having some time on his own with you,' Robert told Patsy.

'Could you take the wheelchair across the road for me, then?' Patsy asked in a pleading voice, looking at Robert wide-eyed.

'No, you do it and we'll stand here to make sure you can manage it,' Lucy told her, taking hold of Robert's arm as he was about to do what Patsy asked.

'Very well.' Patsy gave a toss of her head and bumped the chair down the kerb, causing Sam to yelp with pain as the rough movement jarred his leg.

'Go easy,' he muttered holding on to the side of the wheelchair.

When she reached the other side of the road Patsy hesitated for a moment then tipped the wheelchair backwards so violently in order to get the wheels on to the kerb that it tilted sideways. The next minute, before Robert could reach them, Sam had been thrown out on to the roadway.

Patsy was most contrite. Her big blue eyes filled with tears as she looked helplessly at Robert and protested that it wasn't her fault and that she'd already told them that she couldn't manage on her own.

'You could be a bit more careful, Patsy.'

Lucy tried to hide her anger as Robert righted the wheelchair and she tried to help Sam up from the ground, but she knew her voice was strident.

'I didn't do it on purpose,' Patsy snuffled. 'I told you the wheelchair was too heavy for me to manage.'

'Well, come on, give me a hand to get Sam up off the ground and back into it,' Lucy urged.

'I think he's too heavy for me to help lift him and I'm shaking like a leaf, it was such a shock.'

'You move out the way, Patsy, and I'll help Lucy,' Robert told her.

To Lucy's immense relief it appeared that although Sam was rather shaken he wasn't hurt apart from some gravel cuts on his right hand which he had instinctively put out to try and save himself. He tried to make light of the matter the moment he saw how upset Patsy appeared to be.

'It looks as though we'd better go to the park with them after all,' Robert murmured apologetically in Lucy's ear.

She nodded although she felt near to tears because her carefully made plans were all going so wrong. She knew she was being childish but she had so looked forward to spending some time alone with Robert that she couldn't help feeling very frustrated. What was more, she was quite convinced in her own mind that Patsy had deliberately tipped the wheelchair over.

Once again she found herself trailing behind as Patsy pushed the chair along the paths and Robert kept a restraining hand on it.

Patsy was so busy chattering and looking up into Robert's face and laughing at what she'd said that several times she almost crashed into posts and seats. In the end Robert suggested that she should walk alongside the chair and hold Sam's hand and he and Lucy would push the chair.

His arm went round Lucy's waist and he gave her a companionable squeeze as if to indicate that he knew how she was feeling and was as fed up with the arrangement as she was.

When they reached the park Patsy looked at her watch and gave a gasp of fake horror.

'Is that the time already?' she gasped. 'I really will have to fly. You'll be safe enough with Lucy and Robert looking after you won't you?' she said airily.

'Do you really have to go so soon?' Sam protested. 'I've been looking forward to this outing so much.'

'I'm afraid so. Perhaps we can all go out again sometime soon and you can teach me how to handle Sam's wheelchair,' she added smiling coquettishly at Robert.

With a wave of her hand and an airborne kiss, Patsy hurried off.

'I've messed your afternoon up completely, haven't I?' Sam said bitterly.

'Of course you haven't, we always enjoy coming to the park, but we thought you'd like Patsy to take you for a change,' Robert told him blithely.

'Come on; let's speed things up instead of dawdling along as we've been doing ever since we left home,' Lucy said as she began pushing the wheelchair.

'Right; we'll take a brisk walk around the park and then let's see if we can find a café open and have a cup of tea and some fancy cakes,' Robert suggested.

'Or we could go back home and then you two could go over to New Brighton like I know you wanted to do,' Sam told them. 'I don't mind; I'm getting used to being on my own.'

He looked so dejected that both Robert and Lucy magnanimously declared that they didn't want to go to New Brighton.

'If that was what we wanted to do, then we could have taken you with us,' Robert pointed out. 'In fact,' he added, 'why don't we do that next Sunday? We can make a whole day of it, how about that?'

'Do you think Patsy will come as well?' Sam asked eagerly.

'We can ask her, but she may already have something planned,' Lucy sighed.

Chapter Eight

Lucy found her life was increasingly frustrating. Sam's leg was taking far longer to heal than had been expected. Also, when the wheelchair had toppled over, the impact of his hand with the pavement had torn the skin on his palm which was still thin and tender from the fire and an infection had set in. This not only caused him a great deal of pain but it also meant that he had to have fresh dressings on it every day for several weeks.

For the first few weeks after the car accident, Miss Yorke had been understanding about letting Lucy have time off to take Sam to hospital but as the weeks extended into months she started to raise objections whenever Lucy asked and told her she would have to ask Mr Carter herself for permission.

'Why don't you ask Patsy to take a turn at taking Sam to the hospital?' Robert suggested when Lucy mentioned the matter to him and said how curt Mr Carter had been.

'What's the good of asking Patsy when she always says that she can't manage the wheelchair on her own and that she isn't prepared to take the responsibility?'

'Well, I can't very well ask for time off; we're far too busy,' Robert protested.

'Exactly, which means that I am the one who

has to do it all the time,' Lucy pointed out.

Arranging to take Sam to hospital wasn't Lucy's only worry. It was now over five months since the accident and she was finding that her meagre wage was nowhere near enough to cover all their household bills.

Night after night she found herself unable to sleep because she was trying to think of ways they could economise and worrying about how she was ever going to pay all their debts if they didn't.

Mr and Mrs Collins had not had any personal insurance so there was no compensation after the accident. They had been hardworking and practical but Lucy had been forced to use most of their savings to pay for the funeral. Now she was finding that dipping into what little there was left in order to pay the rent each week meant that she and Sam were rapidly becoming penniless.

As well as that, because of all her other responsibilities, in addition to going to work each day, she was desperately tired. Often she felt either too exhausted or was too busy with household chores to take Sam out at the weekends. In desperation, she once again asked Patsy if she would be willing to do so.

At first Patsy said that she was far too busy but when Lucy pressed her she reluctantly said that she'd take Sam out if Robert went with them in case she tipped the chair over again.

'If Robert has to go with you, then he may as well be the one to take Sam out,' Lucy grumbled. 'I was hoping that if you could take Sam for a walk, it would give Robert a chance to do some of the odd jobs around our house that need attention and also give us some time together; I hardly ever see him alone these days,' she added wistfully.

'Sorry, Lucy, but the wheelchair is far too heavy for me to push,' Patsy maintained with a dismissive little shrug.

'Sam's going to be very disappointed; he's been looking forward to it,' Lucy persisted. 'He says he doesn't see very much of you at all these days.'

Patsy was adamant and, knowing how fed up Sam was with being on his own so much, Lucy finally agreed to her demands. At first Robert protested that he didn't see that it was necessary but reluctantly he gave in rather than disappoint Sam.

Once the routine was established Lucy couldn't help feeling rebellious from time to time as she watched Robert, Patsy and Sam setting off for a walk on Saturdays and Sundays while she stayed at home. As she started to clean the house or tackle the pile of washing and ironing after she'd waved them off, she felt it was so unfair and wondered when it would ever end.

It was almost the end of September when Mr Carter summoned her to his office and Lucy thought it was because he wanted to know why she hadn't yet asked to take her annual week's holiday.

She intended explaining that because she'd had so much time off she was willing to forgo a holiday this year and to ask him if he would be good enough to let her go on having the occasional half-day whenever she needed to take Sam to hospital.

Mr Carter didn't even look up from the papers in front of him when she went in to his office; he merely indicated with a brief movement of his head that she was to sit in the chair on the other side of his desk.

As she sat there waiting for him to speak she felt more and more nervous. She kept twisting her handkerchief between her hands as she mentally went over what she was going to say and wishing he would hurry up and pay her some attention.

When he finally did look up his face was very stern above the high collar of the white shirt he was wearing with his immaculate dark grey suit. Lucy's heart started to pound because she sensed that there was something wrong, and it wasn't anything to do with her annual holiday.

'I'm sorry to have to say this, Miss Collins, but I am afraid matters can't go on like this any longer,' he said curtly. 'I am going to have to replace you. We need a switchboard operator who can be relied on and so far this year you have had–' he paused and looked down at the piece of paper in front on him to check the number of occasions when she'd taken time off.

Quickly, before he could start to speak again, Lucy tried to explain what she intended doing about her holiday, hoping that he would then see that she was cooperating as much as she possibly could to overcome the problem.

Mr Carter waved her to silence before she was halfway through her explanation.

'I'm sorry, Miss Collins, but I've talked it over with Miss Yorke and I've given the matter very careful thought and my mind is made up. I am dispensing with your services,' he said firmly.

Lucy shook her head in disbelief. She tried to speak but all she managed was a feeble croak. She didn't know what to say to make him rethink the matter.

'It will also be necessary to dispense with your brother's services as well,' Mr Carter went on. 'This firm isn't large enough to carry passengers. Everyone employed here is expected to pull their weight and there are half a dozen other people waiting to fill any vacancy that comes along.'

The colour drained from Lucy's face. It was bad enough that she was going to be out of work but for Sam to lose his job as well was quite un-thinkable. Although he'd not received any wages since the accident she was hoping that once he was earning again they would be able to manage on their combined income. The unfairness of it made her angry.

'Sam's hands have given him so much trouble because they were so badly burned when he saved your son from the bonfire,' she reminded Mr Carter.

'Oh no!' Mr Carter shook his head firmly. 'The reason your brother has to go to the hospital for treatment is because of the car accident, Miss Collins.'

'Yes, that as well,' Lucy agreed, her colour rising.

'Let me remind you that your brother com-pletely ruined one of my finest vehicles and that has cost me a great deal of money,' Mr Carter stated in a voice that brooked no argument.

'Both my parents died in that accident,' Lucy reminded him in a small voice. 'Do you think I am ever likely to forget it?'

'Yes, and your brother was driving the car,' Mr Carter reiterated sternly.

'The accident wasn't Sam's fault. It was caused when a horse that was running loose on the road reared; Sam did all he possibly could to avoid it.'

'Most unfortunate, but he was in charge of the car at the time,' Mr Carter stated flatly.

'Don't you think that Sam has suffered enough without losing his job as well?' Lucy pleaded.

'Possibly.' Mr Carter nodded solemnly. 'Nevertheless, my decision remains unaltered.'

Lucy bit her lip as she stared at him across the desk. The tears which she had managed to hold in check began to roll down her cheeks and she felt too choked to say anything more. She could see from the hard look on Mr Carter's face that his mind was made up and that no amount of pleading would change things.

'A formal letter of dismissal is already in the post to both you and your brother,' Mr Carter went on in an implacable voice. 'I have enclosed a reference, but if a prospective employer requires further details, then you may refer him to me. I wish you both well.'

'You wish us both well?' Anger made Lucy's voice so high that it was almost a scream. 'You take our livelihoods from us and then wish us well? We have both worked for you ever since the day we left school and until the accident never taken a day off because of illness or for any other reason.'

'Good day, Miss Collins; I have nothing more to say on the matter. You may leave immediately.'

Lucy went on sitting there for another minute, studying Mr Carter's hard-set features as he concentrated on the papers in front of him. Then with a sigh of resignation she left his office, leaving the door open behind her.

As she went out into the general office she tried to hold her head high, knowing that all eyes were on her, determined not to let anyone know how upset she felt, particularly Miss Yorke because she was positive that it had been Miss Yorke who had complained about her frequent absence.

She walked across to the switchboard with the intention of pulling out all the plugs as a symbol of rebellion, but Patsy was already sitting in her place, headphones on, busily connecting callers to the various departments.

Without a word, Lucy opened the small drawer at the side of the desk where she kept her few personal items. Collecting them together she picked up her coat from the peg behind the door and walked out of the office without a word to anyone.

As she made her way home Lucy wondered how on earth she was going to break the news to Sam. He'd had so many things go wrong for him in the last few months that he had become depressed and this would be the final straw.

It wouldn't be easy for him to find a new job because he was no longer fit enough for any physical work, and somehow she didn't think he would take kindly to being a clerk; that was even if he could find a position of that sort.

She would have to find another job as well, and girls who were capable of operating a switchboard were two a penny. She knew she had been lucky to get taken on at Carter's Cars as soon as she left school. Her father had been working there and so she and Sam had been given preferential treatment.

One look at Sam's face as she went into the living room told her that he had already heard the news. The letter from Mr Carter was open on the table and alongside it was an unopened envelope addressed to her. She knew from what Mr Carter had told her earlier what it contained, so she ignored it.

Sam picked it up and waved it in the air at her. 'Does this say the same thing as mine does?' he demanded as he dropped it back on to the table.

She hesitated, wondering if she denied it whether that would make him feel better or worse. Before she could make up her mind his shoulders slumped and he looked so upset that she went and put her arms around him and hugged him.

'Yes,' she murmured. 'It's more or less the same as yours.'

'How long have you known?'

'Mr Carter called me into his office and told me about an hour ago. It looks as though we are both finished at Carter's Cars.'

'What are we going to do?' he asked, pushing her away.

She gave a falsely bright smile as she released him. 'It will be a fresh start for both of us, won't it? Probably all for the best.'

Sam shook his head but didn't answer. They both knew in their hearts that making a fresh start wasn't going to be easy for either of them. In fact, it was impossible for Sam even to contemplate until he was completely better.

What was worrying Lucy, though, as she went through into the kitchen to make a cup of tea, was how they were going to manage for money until she found a new job.

Lying awake that night she toyed with the idea of asking Robert if they could get married and if he would move in with them. He was now earning good money and she would probably be able to manage on his wages.

If only Patsy married Sam and she moved in with them as well, then they wouldn't have any money problems, she mused.

The more she thought about it the more Lucy felt that it was a good idea. If they all lived together then she could cook the meals and do all the housework until Sam was well enough to go to work. Then she would find herself a job and everything would be in easy street.

It was the first thing that came into her mind when she woke up the next morning. She wished she'd thought about it when they were talking it over the night before; now she would have to wait until evening before she could discuss it with Robert.

She decided to talk it over with Sam while they were having breakfast and see if he was in agreement with her idea.

Sam admitted it had possibilities but he wasn't as optimistic as she was that the other two would agree.

'If Robert wanted to do that, then wouldn't he have mentioned it?' he questioned as he pushed his cup across the breakfast table for a refill.

'He probably never thought of it; I didn't until after I was in bed and going over everything again in my head,' Lucy told him as she picked up the teapot.

'Let's think about it for a while and if we still consider it to be a good idea, then we can put it to them and see what they think,' Sam said tentatively as she passed his cup of tea to him. 'I'm not too sure if Patsy will still want to marry me now that I'm a cripple.'

Chapter Nine

Lucy stayed downstairs long after Sam had gone to bed that night, wondering if the plan she'd outlined to him earlier really was feasible. Sitting there in front of the dying embers, she thought back over all that had been happening over the past few months.

Before the bonfire accident, she and Robert had been planning to be married early in the summer. After her parents had been killed and Sam had been so badly injured, they had postponed it until the autumn.

It was now the end of September and their wedding seemed to be as far away as ever. In fact, Robert hadn't even mentioned anything about them getting married for the last couple of months and sometimes she wondered if he still wanted to marry her.

They saw so little of each other these days; there

was never the time or opportunity for them to go out together. Whenever Sam was taken out at the weekend it was Robert and Patsy who went with him, not her. In fact, Lucy thought resentfully, Patsy appeared to see more of Robert these days than she did.

She sighed and picked up the poker and began raking out the ashes from the bottom of the grate and then dampening the fire down with small pieces of coal and cinders so that it would keep alight overnight. She stopped halfway through. There was no real need to do this, she told herself, because now that she didn't have a job, she wouldn't have to rush off to work in the morning.

She shivered and dropped the poker. No job! As long as she could remember her life had revolved around the office at Carter's Cars and working on the switchboard there; to no longer be a part of it seemed impossible.

Lucy wondered if perhaps she ought to ask Patsy to have a word with Percy Carter, to see if he would speak to his father and persuade him to change his mind about Sam's dismissal. She knew she was going to find it difficult to get another job, but for Sam with all his disabilities, it would be almost impossible.

When she finally plucked up the courage to ask, Patsy looked at her rather disdainfully. 'I don't think so,' she smirked. 'Have you forgotten that Mr Carter has forbidden Percy to have anything more to do with me?'

'Sorry, Patsy, I had forgotten about that,' Lucy said quickly.

'Anyway, Percy isn't around, so I couldn't ask

him even if I wanted to do so. Mr Carter sent Percy off to London to do a business studies course. I shouldn't imagine it will do him much good, you know how thick Percy is,' she giggled.

'On the other hand, it might be the making of him,' Lucy commented. 'I imagine he had plenty of time to think about his future while he was in hospital after the bonfire accident,' she added thoughtfully. 'It was very kind of you to visit him as much as you did; in fact, I never knew you were so friendly with Percy.'

'I wasn't, really, but it got me some time out of the office, didn't it? And I thought that Mr Carter might be impressed and consider me for promotion.'

'Patsy!' Lucy couldn't keep the shock out of her voice. 'Whatever sort of promotion did you think you would get?'

'Deputy to Miss Yorke, of course.'

'She's not that old; surely she's not thinking of retiring?' Lucy said in amazement.

'I don't know.' Patsy shrugged. 'She will do one day and someone will have to take her place as Mr Carter's secretary and be in charge of the general office. And since I often deputise for her, then I would stand a better chance than anyone else, wouldn't I?'

'Well, that makes sense, but since she won't be retiring for five or perhaps ten years, surely you will be married to Sam long before then?'

Patsy shrugged again. 'Perhaps, perhaps not. Sam's still a cripple at the moment,' she pointed out.

'Nonsense! He's improving all the time. It will

only be a matter of another couple of weeks, or perhaps a month, before he is fit enough to go back to work.'

'Except that he hasn't a job to go back to now that Mr Carter has sacked him,' Patsy reminded her.

'There are plenty of other places where they would be glad of someone with Sam's skills,' Lucy pointed out.

'What skills? He has earned himself black marks as a driver, no one would trust him with their cars in a hurry and as for working as a mechanic, well, he hasn't completed his apprenticeship, so that rules that out, doesn't it?'

Lucy bit her lip to stop herself uttering aloud the sharp comments that came into her mind. There was no point in arguing with Patsy and antagonising her, Lucy decided. Obviously, she wasn't going to be able to help so really there was nothing else to be said; there was certainly no point in suggesting that as soon as Patsy and Sam got married they all lived together, because at the moment Patsy didn't seem to want to commit herself.

Lucy felt very depressed and unhappy as she thought about the future. Even so, she didn't intend to sit down and cry about it; it wasn't in her nature to admit defeat, she told herself grimly.

Tomorrow she would buy a copy of the midday edition of the *Liverpool Echo* and look through the situations vacant columns and if she could find anything at all that was remotely suitable, she would apply right away that afternoon.

Until she did manage to find some sort of work,

she would be able to spend more time with Sam. In fact, she resolved, she'd tell Patsy that there was no need for her to come round at the weekend because she and Robert would be taking Sam out.

It would give her a chance to see something of Robert; they needed to spend more time together. She'd seen so little of him lately that they were almost like strangers. Then she had a better idea; instead of asking Patsy not to come round, she'd suggest that Patsy should stay at home with Sam while she and Robert went out together.

Finding an office job proved to be impossible and as the weeks passed and their debts mounted, Lucy became quite desperate and knew she would have to find some other way of earning money. She was not only behind with the rent, but also owed money to the coal man, the butcher and the grocer, even though they lived on the cheapest of foods that she could find. Sam needed new clothes and so did she; the skirts and blouses that she had worn to the office were now shabby and Sam had grown so thin while lying in bed that none of his clothes fitted him.

Finally, in desperation, she applied for a job as a charlady at one of the large office blocks in Old Hall Street near the Pier Head. She'd still be working in an office, she told herself, even if it was emptying the waste bins and polishing the desks.

When she was told that they would give her a week's trial, Lucy was delighted even though the wage was far less than she'd been used to getting at Carter's Cars.

She had to be there by seven each morning, which meant leaving home before half past six, and she did find that was something of a struggle when she'd been used to starting at half-eight in the morning.

She didn't have time to wake Sam to give him his breakfast before she left so she prepared something for him the night before and left it on the kitchen table and told him he would have to get himself dressed and downstairs.

The first morning he tried to do so, but couldn't manage the stairs on his own, so from then on he simply stayed in bed until she arrived home again around mid-morning and then she prepared a meal which combined both breakfast and a midday meal.

The cleaning job was hard work and by the end of the trial week she felt so exhausted that if it hadn't been for the fact that they owed so much money, she would not have accepted the job even when they offered it to her.

There were four flights of stairs to clean as well as offices on each of the floors. Emptying the wastepaper baskets and dusting the desks was the least of her problems; what she really hated having to do was cleaning the lavatories and washbasins.

The payment she received was so meager that as Christmas approached she knew she had to find some other work that paid better or some kind of part-time job that she could do after she'd finished her cleaning work in the morning.

The weather was turning quite cold and although she tried to be frugal with both food and heating, their debts were still mounting and the coal man would now only deliver if she had the money ready to hand to him before he tipped the sack out in their shed.

Sam's hand was now healed and he was able to use a stick to walk so he was able to get around quite well on his own and they no longer needed the wheelchair. It had cost a few shillings a week to hire, so she was pleased to be able to return it and claim back the deposit they'd been asked to pay on it.

Lucy had also hoped that now he was able to get around he would be able to find a job. He had only been a few weeks short of completing his apprenticeship and she wondered if it was possible for him still to do so. Then, as she saw him hobbling around, she knew it was out of the question. How could he be on the floor underneath a motor car to do repairs when he was in such a state?

She wasn't sure if he would still be able to drive a motor car or whether he had lost his nerve. They'd never talked about the accident but Patsy's harsh words about no one ever trusting him again as a driver haunted her.

There was one other solution to their financial problem but it was one she'd talked to Robert about before and she didn't want to follow it up until she absolutely had to do so, because she didn't know quite how to broach the matter to him again. Until now pride had stopped her from telling him how difficult she was finding it to make ends meet. Now she wondered whether she should come straight out and tell him the truth or try to pay off all the outstanding debts after they were married and she had more money.

She was positive she'd be able to clear them in next to no time once Robert's wages as well as her own were coming in and that would make life so much easier.

The only trouble was it would make it look as if she was marrying Robert as a solution to her problems instead of because she loved him, she thought miserably.

If only she could clear off all her debts first, she'd feel so much better about suggesting they should get married, she decided. If she could find some extra work over Christmas, then it might be possible, she told herself. It would be wonderful to be able to start 1922 with a clean slate.

Her daydreams escalated as she contemplated the possibilities if this happened. She and Robert could have a spring wedding.

In mid-December when she managed to find a temporary job washing up in a hotel and knew it would last over Christmas and the New Year, it seemed as though this might be a real possibility.

Like her charring job, Lucy found it was much harder work than she had anticipated. As she tackled never-ending piles of glasses, dirty plates, dishes and greasy pots and pans, her back and feet ached. The amount of waste she scraped off the plates horrified her. How could people leave such delicious-looking food when so many others were hungry or even had to cut back as she'd had to do lately? she wondered.

As she stood up to her elbows in dirty, greasy water until well after midnight all over the Christmas holiday, Lucy tried to work out how she was going to deal with matters in the new year.

The first thing, she resolved, was to have a quiet word with Patsy and ask her if she really was serious about getting married soon and also what she thought about getting married at the same time as she and Robert, and then Sam and Patsy sharing the house with her and Robert.

The opportunity came on New Year's Day. Lucy arrived home in the early hours of the morning after a gruelling night's work. Fortunately she had no office cleaning that day and she planned to go straight to bed for a few hours before getting up and cooking a meal for herself and Sam.

Footsore after her long walk home, she was more than a little annoyed to find Sam, Patsy and Robert still there; all of them asleep. Patsy and Robert were on the sofa and Sam in an armchair.

As she went into the kitchen to make herself a hot drink Patsy woke up and padded in after her.

'You're up early,' she yawned.

'I've only just finished work,' Lucy told her, 'and once I've had a hot drink I'm off up to bed. Shouldn't you be at home?' she asked rather pointedly.

'We stayed up to see the New Year in,' Patsy said as she yawned again. 'It was fun. We went down to the Pier Head and there were crowds down there all singing and dancing as the klaxons and ships' hooters sounded. You should have come.'

'I would have liked to have done so, only I had to work,' Lucy reminded her as she spooned some tea leaves into the big brown pot and poured the boiling water from the kettle on to them. 'Do you want a cuppa?'

'Might as well.' Patsy sat down at the kitchen table and put her head down on her folded arms. 'I'm so tired I could sleep the clock round,' she moaned.

'Have you made any plans for 1922?' Lucy asked as she poured out the tea and pushed one of the cups across the table to Patsy.

'Heavens, no. The plans I make never seem to work out. Other people always manage to muck them up for me,' Patsy muttered as she took a sip of her tea.

Suddenly, without a word, she was off her chair and dashing for the sink.

'What's wrong? Is it the tea?' Lucy asked as she heard Patsy heaving and hurried to her side.

'Must be something I've eaten,' Patsy gasped. 'It happened yesterday morning and the morning before. Strange thing is, it seems to work off after an hour or so and I feel fine for the rest of the day. Do you think I should go and see a doctor?'

Lucy stared at her aghast. 'You don't really need a doctor to tell you what's wrong, do you?'

Patsy looked at her blankly. 'Well, I don't know what's causing it, do you?' she asked, flicking back her hair defiantly.

'It sounds as though you're pregnant.'

The colour drained from Patsy's face. 'Oh no, don't say that; I can't be,' she gasped.

'Oh, Patsy, I am sorry,' Lucy sympathised.

'Not half as sorry as I am. I told you other people always muck up my plans,' Patsy muttered resentfully.

Lucy bit down on her lower lip thoughtfully; she had been waiting for an opportunity to suggest that Patsy and Sam got married but this hardly seemed to be the right moment. Yet there would be no alternative once Sam heard Patsy's news, she reasoned.

Chapter Ten

Lucy sat nursing her cup of tea for a long time. She didn't even look up as Patsy scraped back her chair and went back into the living room. Her mind was racing and a phrase her mother had used so often about being careful what you wished for in case it came true kept going round and round in her head.

She had wanted Sam and Patsy to be married and had even considered them living with her and Robert. One big, happy family all pulling together and able to make ends meet because they'd all be working.

She had never given any thought to there being a baby to consider as well. It would mean that Patsy wouldn't be able to work and that would put a fresh drain on their resources. Instead of it solving their money problems, she could see them getting ever deeper into debt.

She was still sitting there brooding over this new problem and feeling too tired to even walk upstairs to bed when Patsy came into the kitchen again.

'Do you want another cup of tea?' Patsy asked and Lucy was aware that she no longer sounded full of confidence.

'Yes, all right,' Lucy agreed. 'Then perhaps we can talk over what is to be done while we're drinking it.'

'There's nothing to talk over,' Patsy stated. 'He'll have to marry me.'

'It's all very well saying that but as you pointed out earlier, Sam hasn't got a job, so how is he going to support you and find money for the baby? There are a hundred and one things you are going to need and you haven't even anywhere to live.'

'What's Sam got to do with it?' Patsy asked. 'I wouldn't dream of marrying him, not now that he's a cripple.'

'Patsy!' Lucy tried to keep the anger from her voice but it was impossible. She thought the world of her brother and to hear Patsy speak so disparagingly of him was hurtful.

With an effort to remain calm she looked across at Patsy and asked, 'Does Sam know about this?'

'You mean that I'm pregnant? I shouldn't think so; I didn't know myself until you told me just now.' Patsy shrugged. 'Fancy you thinking that it might be Sam's baby,' she giggled, tossing back her hair and staring at Lucy in amusement.

'This baby isn't Sam's,' Patsy went on defiantly before Lucy could speak. 'I don't know why you should think it could be.' She gave a shrill laugh. 'He's been laid up for the last nine months so common sense should tell you he isn't capable of anything like that.'

Lucy stared at her wide-eyed. 'If it's not Sam's, then whose baby is it? Surely not Percy Carter's?'

'Don't be daft!' Patsy said scornfully. 'Have you forgotten he was in hospital when I was visiting him?'

'You also went out with him afterwards until Mr Carter put a stop to it,' Lucy reminded her.

'This baby has nothing at all to do with Percy Carter or your Sam,' Patsy reiterated. Her blue eyes narrowed as she studied Lucy's puzzled face. 'No, the father is someone else and, as I have said, he'll have to marry me, won't he?'

'Surely it depends on whether he's free to do so,' Lucy said.

'He's single so I see no reason why he can't,' Patsy mused. 'What's more, he's crazy about me.'

'Then you've nothing to worry about, have you? Except having to break the news to Sam,' she added bitterly. 'Or aren't you going to tell him yet in case this other bloke turns you down?'

'He certainly won't do that,' Patsy boasted.

Lucy bit her lip and shook her own head in despair. Patsy seemed to be making light of the problem but she couldn't do that; there was so much at stake.

'Sam means nothing at all to me; he hasn't done for a long time,' Patsy went on. 'I can't stand sick people and I certainly don't want to be tied to a cripple for the rest of my life.'

'You don't mean that,' Lucy protested. 'You've been going out together for years. Sam said you were planning to be married after he'd finished his apprenticeship.'

'That was then, this is now,' Patsy quipped. 'Boy and girl stuff. So much has happened since then.'

'Sam still loves you; he couldn't understand why you didn't visit him more when he was in hospital,' Lucy sighed.

'Well, now you have the answer. I was fed up with him, so why should I waste my time going to the hospital to see him?'

'Yet after he came out of hospital you were willing to take him out at the weekends in the wheelchair.'

'Yes, but only because it meant Robert could come as well,' Patsy told her smugly.

'So are you going to tell me whose baby it is?' Lucy demanded.

'Of course, if you really want me to, and I suppose you will have to know sooner or later,' Patsy said with a little smile. 'It's Robert's baby.'

'Robert's baby!' The colour drained from Lucy's face. She felt faint. This couldn't be happening, she told herself. She'd been working too hard and she was so tired that she was hallucinating. How could Patsy be expecting Robert's baby, or think that Robert was going to marry her? Robert was already her lover and had asked her to marry him and the only reason that they weren't already married was because of the bonfire incident and then the terrible accident last Easter.

Lucy took a deep breath, clenching her hands into tight fists to try and quell the pain inside her. 'Is this true?'

'Oh it's Robert's baby, all right,' Patsy affirmed and there was a look of triumph on her face as she looked at Lucy.

'I could tell that Robert liked me and after the accident you became such a drudge that you were no fun at all to be with so you can't blame Robert for preferring my company.'

'Had you forgotten that we would have been married by now if it hadn't been for all that has happened lately?'

'No one has mentioned it for months and you never seem to have very much time for Robert these days,' Patsy pouted.

'So you thought it was all right to steal him from under my nose while I've been trying to look after Sam? If you had any feelings at all for Sam, then you would have done more to help nurse him,' she added accusingly.

'I kept telling you that I didn't like sick people and now that Sam's probably going to be a cripple for the rest of his life I don't want anything more to do with him.'

'Why do you keep on saying that he's a cripple?' Lucy frowned. 'He might have difficulty in walking at the moment but I would hardly call him a cripple. Apart from a slight limp he walks as well as any of us.'

'He's out of work and I don't see him ever getting a proper job again,' Patsy stated.

'So you decided to ditch him and latch on to Robert, did you?' Lucy said in a scathing voice. 'Pinched him from under my nose because I was too busy looking after Sam.'

'It started out as a bit of fun,' Patsy admitted. 'Flirting and the odd kiss.'

'And you made the most of that and encouraged him even further,' Lucy accused.

'I didn't take it seriously until the day Robert told me he loved me,' Patsy declared.

'I don't believe you!'

'He said that he was miserable because these days you had no time for him.'

'So you offered him a shoulder to cry on and a great deal more besides,' Lucy said bitterly.

'One thing led to another, you must know what he's like,' Patsy muttered giving Lucy a wide-eyed innocent stare.

'You certainly seem to know him a lot better than I ever did,' Lucy said crisply. 'I can't believe that all this between the two of you has been going on behind my back.'

She got up from the table and moved away quickly, not wanting Patsy to have the satisfaction of seeing the tears in her eyes. She loved Robert so deeply that it was like a knife turning inside her. They had been sweethearts since their schooldays; they'd walked home hand in hand, sharing all their secrets and planning what they would do when they were older.

She felt so stupid; to think that this had been going on all these months and she hadn't noticed. Her love for Robert was as strong as it had ever been and even though he had betrayed her she knew she would never stop loving him.

'I'm going to tell Sam right now,' Patsy stated, pushing back the chair and heading for the living room.

'Patsy, do you have to do this now? It's the middle of the night, why don't you think about what you're doing?' Lucy begged as she followed her.

'No, Sam may as well know; we can all start the New Year with a clean slate then,' Patsy declared

111

as she pushed open the door to the living room.

'What do I need to know?' Sam yawned. 'I'm dog tired, I was thinking about going to bed.'

'You can after I've told you my news,' Patsy told him. 'I'm expecting a baby, Sam.'

Sam's jaw dropped. 'A baby?' He looked questioningly at Lucy. 'You knew and you said nothing?'

'Patsy only told me a few minutes ago, Sam.'

'Actually, Lucy, you were the one who said that I was pregnant when I told you that I'd been sick every morning for the past couple of weeks,' Patsy corrected her.

'So does that mean it could be a mistake?' Sam said in a puzzled voice.

'No, I'm pretty sure that Lucy is right. Anyway, whether I am or not, it settles things between us, Sam.'

He looked at her, bemused. 'What do you mean?'

'Well, it's not yours, is it?' she said with a high, shrill laugh.

'Are you saying that you've been knocking around with someone else and that it's his baby, that it's all over between us, Patsy?' he asked in a stunned voice.

'It looks like it, doesn't it?' She tossed her head defiantly. 'You wouldn't want to bring up some other bloke's kid, now would you?'

'Whose child is it, then?' Sam asked, looking from her to Lucy.

Robert roused himself and sat up straight on the sofa. 'Is this true, Patsy?' he asked in a shocked voice. The colour drained from his face, leaving it taut and grey.

She nodded. 'Are you pleased?'

Robert ran a hand through his thick fair hair in a gesture of despair but didn't answer.

'Are you telling us that it's his baby?' Sam asked in disbelief.

'I'm terribly sorry, Lucy, I seem to have let you down,' Robert said awkwardly.

'Let me down!'

The anguish in her voice made Robert look even more contrite. 'I'll go on helping you with Sam and so will Patsy for as long as you need us to do so,' he added rather lamely.

'Both of you get out of my house now; right away,' Lucy said agitatedly. 'I can't bear to be in the same room as either of you.'

'And don't ever come back,' Sam added bitterly as Robert propelled Patsy towards the front door.

As the front door slammed behind them Lucy pulled the cup of freshly made tea that Patsy had put in front of her closer, staring down into it as she stirred it round and round, trying to come to terms with the situation.

How on earth could this have happened without her noticing what was going on? she asked herself. Patsy and Robert had been thrown into each other's company a great deal since the accident but Sam had always been there with them. Anyway, she had never thought that Robert even liked Patsy. He always said she was a flirt and that her mother spoilt her. He said he hated her shrill laugh and the way she tossed her hair and made eyes at all the men.

Yet Robert, staid, sensible Robert whom she'd

thought was in love with her and planning to marry her, had been carrying on with Patsy behind their backs. And now Patsy was in trouble and what was even more disastrous was that it seemed she was determined that he should marry her.

All the plans she had been making about her marriage to Robert and even about Sam and Patsy marrying and living with them were now useless. The best thing she could do was forget all about them, Lucy thought bitterly.

Wearily she dragged herself upstairs to her bedroom after Robert and Patsy left. Perhaps this was all a nightmare or else she was imagining it because she felt so desperately tired and exhausted, she told herself.

Lucy slept until midday; when she went downstairs she found Sam staring moodily into the fire.

'I bet you're starving,' Lucy said apologetically. 'Give me ten minutes and I'll rustle something up for our meal.' She reached for her pinafore, slipped the straps over her head, and tied them.

'There's no hurry,' he told her. 'I'm not really hungry.' He ran a hand through his short hair and her heart ached for him as she saw the utter misery in his eyes. 'I've lost my appetite after what Patsy told us last night. It looks as though we're both losers,' he went on bitterly. 'I've lost Patsy and you've lost Robert.' He reached out and took Lucy's hand. 'It's all my fault; if I could turn the clock back, then I would.'

'It's not your fault any more than it's mine,'

114

Lucy told him. 'I should have seen the signs and done something about it. I suppose I have been neglecting Robert for the past few months but he seemed to be so supportive that I thought he understood.'

'So you're blaming Patsy for this awful mess, are you?'

'I don't know what to think,' Lucy murmured dejectedly. 'It's the way things go in life; there's certainly no point in blaming ourselves for what's happened.'

'What are we going to do now, then?' Sam probed. 'This isn't what you had planned for 1922, is it?'

'No, you're right,' Lucy sighed. 'I was planning to marry Robert. I was even going to suggest that you and Patsy got married as well and that we all lived here together. That way we would have been able to meet the bills. As it is, we are heavily in debt and I don't know how we are going to survive.'

Although she struggled to stop them the tears began rolling down her cheeks. Unable to restrain her pent-up emotions she began to sob, heart-rending sobs that came from deep inside her. Sam held her close, smoothing her hair and whispering words of comfort until finally her sobs abated and, apart from the occasional gulping sound, she was calm once more.

They spent the rest of the day assessing their situation. There was only one thing they could do, Lucy decided, and that was to find somewhere cheaper to live.

'Or perhaps we could take in lodgers,' Sam suggested. 'That way we would be able to stay on here.'

'If we do that, then we will have to pay off the rent arrears and that will take us at least a year, or perhaps longer.'

'So what is the answer?' Sam frowned.

'Probably the best thing we can do is skedaddle one dark night and tell no one where we are going so that no one can trace us,' Lucy said dolefully.

'Are you sure about that?'

'I'm sorry to be letting down the people we owe money to like the coal man and the grocer, but I don't think there is anything else we can do,' she muttered.

'Where do we go? We've no money for train or boat fares so we won't be able to go very far.'

'I know that. It will have to be somewhere in Liverpool, but there are lots of streets and courts off Scotland Road where they'd never think of looking for us.'

'Patsy and Robert will wonder what's happened to us,' Sam pointed out.

'I imagine they will both be relieved that we have gone and that they don't have to face us,' Lucy reminded him.

'What about all the neighbours, though? They're bound to wonder what's happened to us and they might even start making enquiries to try and find us.'

'I doubt it,' Lucy said bitterly. 'After a couple of months they'll have forgotten all about us.'

'Let's leave it until tomorrow and see what we think then,' Sam argued. 'I don't like the idea of giving up our home so easily. We've lived here all our lives. If Patsy and Robert don't like having to face us, then let them be the ones to move away.'

'We're not doing it because of them,' Lucy reminded him. 'We're doing it because we owe so much rent as well as money to so many tradesmen that it is the only way we can start afresh.'

She stood up and moved towards the kitchen. 'Think about it while I make us something to eat. I really do think it would be for the best.'

Chapter Eleven

It took Lucy and Sam almost a week of debating what to do for the best before making up their minds that they had no alternative but to move to somewhere cheaper.

Their credit with the local shops had already run out and they were forced into selling what they could of their possessions; all the ornaments and trinkets that their mother had loved as well as their father's tools and anything else that would bring in a few shillings.

Their minds were finally made up for them when the rent man threatened that unless they paid their back rent in full before the end of the week he would be sending the bailiffs in and Lucy was left in no doubt what action to take; finding somewhere cheaper to live was the obvious answer.

They both agreed that it would have to be some-where in the Scotland Road area and Lucy spent a couple of days trailing around looking for some-where suitable. It had to be rooms that were al-ready furnished because if they were seen moving furniture out of Priory Terrace, that would alert the neighbours and the debt collector would be on their heels right away.

Finally, in desperation, Lucy decided to rent two furnished rooms in a three-storey house in Hans Court, even though it was not what she was looking for and she wasn't at all sure that Sam would settle there.

The area was overrun with children, dogs and vermin of every description, but as Mrs Sparks – the officious-looking grey-haired landlady – was quick to point out, she was lucky to find rooms where the rent was only four shillings a week.

'I've got someone else coming this evening to have a look,' she stated as she stood in the door-way, arms akimbo, while Lucy took another look at the two rooms. 'If you want me to let you have them then I need two weeks' rent in advance.'

'I'll take them,' Lucy told her as she counted out the money and put it into the woman's grimy hand. 'There you are, so can you give me the key, and I'll be back soon with some of our things.'

When she went home and told Sam what she'd done and warned him that it was a pretty slummy area, his face dropped.

'We've got to get away from here before the bailiffs arrive so I'm going to start sorting out the stuff we'll be taking with us and begin carrying it there. If we're careful and take it bit by bit, then none of the neighbours will notice. I can take a bagful on the way to work and you can do the same midmorning and again later in the day when you go for a walk.'

'I think we're mad to walk out and leave so much of our furniture behind,' he grumbled.

'It's the only way we can go without anyone knowing where we've gone,' Lucy reminded him.

'They won't be out of pocket if they sell off what we're leaving behind,' Sam said sourly.

'Good! That eases my conscience quite a bit,' Lucy affirmed. 'From now on I am determined never to get into debt again.'

'As soon as we've moved I'm going to try and get work of some sort, even if it is only selling newspapers on the street corner,' Sam told her.

They waited until after dark that night to leave Priory Terrace for good. It was a bitterly cold January night and as she raked out the fire and cleaned out the grate so that the house was left neat and tidy, Lucy wondered how they were going to manage to keep warm in their new place because there was only a tiny black iron grate in the larger of the rooms and nothing at all in the smaller room.

Sam was waiting impatiently for them to get going so, taking a last look round at the only home they'd ever known, she brushed away the tears that were running down her cheeks with the back of her hand and squared her shoulders.

'Time for off,' she said, struggling to give him an encouraging smile which Sam ignored.

Both of them were carrying large bundles as they left Priory Terrace and caught a tram as far as Exchange Station.

'I thought if we walked from here, if anyone happened to see us on the tram, they'd think we were going somewhere by train,' Lucy told him as they made their way along Scotland Road, Sam walking rather slowly because he was finding it difficult to manage the bundle he was carrying as well as his stick.

'This is a funny time of night to be arriving,' Mrs Sparks greeted them when she opened the door. 'I'd already locked up for the night. Not running away from the law, are you?' she asked suspiciously.

'No, of course not,' Lucy said with a forced laugh. 'We couldn't make it any earlier because we wanted to come together and so we had to wait until I finished work.'

'Oh yes? So one of you has a job, then?' Mrs Sparks commented, looking questioningly at Sam's stick.

'This is my brother, he was involved in an accident but he is almost better now,' Lucy explained.

'Brother? You never mentioned a brother. When you gave me the names Sam and Lucy Collins, I thought you were married; a husband and wife. You never mentioned that it was your brother who would be sharing the rooms with you.'

Lucy looked at Sam worriedly. Surely this woman who had taken two weeks' rent, eight shillings of their money, wasn't going to turn them out into the street because they were brother and sister?

'Does it make any difference?' Sam asked. 'As long as you're getting the rent for the rooms regularly, surely that is all that matters,' he added sharply.

'Well,' Mrs Sparks sniffed, 'I'm not at all sure about that. I keep a respectable house.'

'I'm sure you do, Mrs Sparks,' Sam told her heartily.

'So what sort of sleeping arrangements are you going to make then?' Mrs Sparks asked, her sharp eyes fixed on Lucy.

'If it makes you feel any happier, let me assure you that I will be sleeping in the living room and my sister will be using the bedroom,' Sam told her.

'Well, I suppose that makes it all right, then,' Mrs Sparks admitted reluctantly.

'Now if we can come inside out of the cold I'd be grateful. I find standing around out here on the doorstep is making my bad leg ache,' he sighed, before giving her a broad smile.

Both Lucy and Sam found living in Hans Court very constraining. Within days of moving in, Lucy knew she had made a terrible mistake and wished she had given Sam's idea about lodgers more thought.

She had always prided herself on being level-headed and thinking things through before taking any action, but this time she had certainly not done so; she would have given a great deal to go back to their clean and comfortable three-bedroom house.

She knew that everybody would be talking about the way both she and Sam had been jilted as well as the disgrace of having the bailiffs in, and pride had made her act impetuously. There had been only one thought in her head and that was for her and Sam to get as far away from Priory Terrace as possible.

Well, she'd certainly done that, she thought morosely. The only thing to be said in favour of her action was that they should be able to manage to meet all their bills.

Their living conditions were abysmal. The two rooms were small; the main room had a low cupboard with a gas ring on it in one corner which was curtained off to serve as a kitchen. The furniture was old and decrepit and it made Lucy even more dismayed that she had left all their good furniture behind at Priory Terrace.

She knew she should have listened to Sam's idea. At least they would have been able to go on living in relative comfort and both of them would have had their own bed to sleep in. That had been her pride again, she thought miserably. She couldn't bear the thought of the neighbours feeling sympathetic because she had to take in lodgers.

That wasn't the only reason, of course. There was the further shame, which she found difficult to face up to, namely Robert's betrayal.

She had no idea how Sam felt about the neighbours finding out that Patsy was expecting Robert's baby. If he felt anywhere near as hurt as she did, then it was breaking his heart so probably he was as glad as she was to get away before all the sniggers and whispers about what had happened started to circulate.

There were moments when she wondered if she

was in some ways to blame for what had happened. She loved Robert and had thought that he felt the same way about her, and she had taken it for granted that he knew all this. Looking back, she wished she'd found more time to be with him and that she had told him how much she cared about him.

Most of all, though, she blamed Patsy. Patsy was a flirt and always had been, and Lucy even wondered if Patsy had become interested in Robert on the rebound when Percy was told to stop seeing her.

She probably thought that Robert was the next best thing, Lucy thought ruefully. Now that he'd finished his apprenticeship at Carter's Cars and was earning a decent wage, he was quite a catch; she doubted, though, that Patsy would stay faithful to him.

She wondered where the two of them would set up home. She had a feeling that it might be with Patsy's family or Robert's. Most likely it would be at Patsy's place, she mused, because Patsy would be relying on her mother to help her look after the baby.

The fact that Patsy was expecting Robert's baby was the bitterest pill of all, but it was no good blaming him or Patsy for the mess she was in now, Lucy told herself. Abandoning their home and running away as if she was the guilty one was entirely her own fault and now she had to make the best of the situation.

The drawbacks to living in Hans Court were so numerous that every day seemed to be worse than the one before. It took up to half an hour to boil the heavy iron kettle on the pitifully small fire in the iron grate. Yet to boil up the tin kettle on the small gas ring cost so much that she dreaded having to do it.

Sam was quite resourceful; he suggested keeping the iron kettle full and over the fire all the time and then pouring enough from it into the tin kettle to make their tea.

'It will only take a couple of minutes to boil whenever we need it. The hot water in the iron kettle will usually be hot enough for washing up or for when we want to have a wash.'

Getting washed was also something of a problem. When they had been at Priory Terrace they'd had a proper bathroom; here in Hans Court they had to wash in a bowl in the kitchen and then tip the dirty water into a bucket and carry it downstairs and empty it down the drain outside the back door. Sam couldn't manage to do it very well because of his stick, so it was a chore that was usually left to Lucy.

The lavatory, which they had to share with the other families in the house, was out in the backyard and was a dank, evil-smelling place which Lucy hated having to visit, but there was no alternative.

The only salvation as far as she could see was that, if they were frugal, they could manage on the money she earned from charring and, as soon as they were settled in, she intended to look around and try and find some extra work or even a second job like she'd had before.

Sam was making considerable progress and he was also determined to find a job so that they could move to something better as soon as possible. There was so much unemployment in Liverpool, however, that even when Sam was lucky enough to get an interview, the moment a prospective employer noticed that he was using a walking stick, the interview was immediately over.

It seemed that no one wanted the liability of employing a man who was not one hundred per cent fit and this made Sam increasingly depressed and irritable.

'You'll have to start your own business, luv,' Lucy joked in an attempt to cheer him up.

'That's not such a bad idea.' Sam nodded. 'What sort of things do men going to work need most but probably haven't got the time to shop for?' he mused as he helped her to get their evening meal ready.

'Lots of things, I imagine; everything from ciggies and matches to sarnies for their lunch.'

'Mm, but I would need quite a bit of money to buy stock to sell those sorts of things.'

'We could try and save it,' Lucy offered. 'It might take a few months but it's not impossible.'

'We're living on bread and scrape most of the time as it is,' Sam told her bitterly as, one at a time, he put the bowls of soup she'd prepared on to the table. 'No, I must think of something I can do right away and which doesn't cost very much to set up.'

'Well, I can't think of anything except begging – that's unless you fancy becoming a shoeshine boy?' Lucy laughed as she sat down and started to eat.

'That's it!' He waved his spoon in the air jubilantly. 'That's what I'll do. I'll stand down at the Pier Head each day and as all the toffs from Wallasey come off the boat I'll offer to shine their shoes for tuppence a time.'

'You can't do that,' Lucy exclaimed aghast. 'Supposing someone we know from Priory Terrace saw you!'

'No one from Priory Terrace is likely to be coming off a ferry boat from Wallasey, now are they, especially first thing in the morning?' Sam argued.

'No, you're probably right,' Lucy agreed reluctantly. Did it really matter all that much if they did? she thought cynically. It would probably have broken her parents' hearts to know that Sam was thinking of becoming a shoeshine boy and that now she went out charring. Then, on the other hand, she thought philosophically, they would have been proud of the fact that instead of grumbling about losing their jobs they'd both found another way of earning a living.

'You haven't got the tools for the job, though, have you?' she asked.

'What sort of tools do I need? I said I'd polish their shoes, not repair them.'

'You will need tins of black and brown shoe polishes, separate brushes for putting on the polish, a duster of some kind or a soft cloth to give the shoes a final polish, and something for the men to rest their foot on while you work on their shoes.'

Sam looked so crestfallen as she listed all the things that he was going to need that Lucy quickly tried to think of how they could obtain them.

'A small wooden box or crate from the greengrocer's, or a big biscuit tin from the grocer's would be ideal,' she said quickly. 'What's more you could carry all your brushes and polishes inside it.'

Sam's face brightened. 'That sounds a good idea. Is it going to cost very much for all the cleaning materials, do you think?'

'Leave it with me for a couple of days and I'll see what I can find,' Lucy promised him.

Three days later and Sam was in business. Carrying the large tin was not too easy for him so Lucy found an old sack and attached a strong webbing strap to it which he could put on crosswise over his shoulder. It was still heavy and somewhat clumsy but Sam was so determined that he managed.

The first day was disappointing as he only had three customers. Lucy did her best to cheer him up, pointing out that no one had expected him to be there and that he was bound to do better the next day.

'I'm not so sure,' Sam grumbled. 'They're in such a rush as they come off the boat that they're probably afraid to stop in case they get pushed over and trampled on.'

'Perhaps you should change your pitch, then. Move further away from the actual Pier Head so that the crowds have had a chance to thin out before they reach you. Pick somewhere halfway up Water Street or one of the other roads leading towards the Exchange and all the offices around there.'

'Yes,' Sam nodded in agreement, 'I suppose I could find a better spot.'

'If you found somewhere under the Goree Piazza, then you'd have shelter when it rains. They don't call it the Docker's Umbrella for nothing, you know,' she added with a smile.

By the start of the summer Sam was doing a steady trade and sometimes earning as much as eight shillings in a week. Even after he had replenished his stock of polishes and occasionally replaced one or other of his brushes because the bristles were so worn down, he was still making good money.

Each week when he handed most of it over to Lucy, she set aside at least half of it because they were both determined to move away from Hans Court as soon as they could save up enough to do so.

Living there in the winter had been bad enough but now, in the heat of summer, it was almost unbearable. They found their two rooms were smelly and stuffy and when they opened the window the air was foul because of all the rubbish piled up in the court outside.

As well as mice and cockroaches to contend with there were countless bluebottles and other flies everywhere. Lucy made sure that every morsel of food was kept covered over, otherwise, within minutes, it was swarming with flies.

'It's only the end of June and it will be even hotter and smellier in July and all through August,' Lucy sighed as she mopped at her face. 'Perhaps it is time we took the plunge and moved to somewhere else.'

Things really came to a head when a family with two boys aged about ten and thirteen moved into the other two rooms on the same landing.

They were not only extremely noisy but the boys also seemed to be up to every kind of prank imaginable.

Lucy and Sam tried to ignore their carryings on but when they started taunting Sam because of the way he walked, they both decided that they'd had enough and that it had to stop – especially when the boys started following him down the street, calling out names and imitating his limping gait.

When Lucy appealed to their mother to ask them to stop mocking Sam, instead of being apologetic or even sympathetic, she was extremely abusive.

'You think yourself too good to be living in Hans Court, don't you?' she sneered. 'I've heard what the others have to say about you. They all think that you're a stuck-up bitch who walks around with her nose in the air and has no time for anybody else.'

Lucy looked bewildered. 'I don't know what you're on about. I'm out at work most of the day, I haven't got time to stand on the doorstep gossiping.'

'You've got time to bad-mouth my two lads, though.'

'I simply asked you to tell them to stop calling out names after my brother,' Lucy said stiffly. 'If you won't do it, then I'll have a word with Mrs Sparks.'

'A fat lot of good that will do you, luv,' the woman responded with a grating laugh.

'I wouldn't be too sure about that. Mrs Sparks always maintains that she keeps a very respectable house,' Lucy told her spiritedly.

'Maybe she does, but my two lads are her bloody grandsons and she thinks the sun shines out of their arses, so you certainly won't find her telling them off or listening to your griping on about what's only a bit of fun on their part.'

'It really is time we started looking for somewhere else to live,' Lucy told Sam wearily when she told him about her exchange with the woman later that night.

They counted out their savings and although they still didn't have as much as they'd planned, Lucy felt sure that, providing they budgeted very carefully, it was going to be possible.

Chapter Twelve

Lucy and Sam spent as much time as they could trying to find new accommodation which they could afford, but it wasn't easy. Some days Lucy felt so despondent that she wondered if they were ever going to manage to get away from Hans Court.

The rooms to let which were advertised in the *Liverpool Echo* were all far too expensive for them. They spent their evenings walking around those streets in the Scotland Road area which looked slightly better than where they were living to see if there were any cards in the windows or in the nearby shops advertising rooms to let.

A couple of times they thought they were in luck only to find that when they went to the house, someone had already pipped them at the post and rented the rooms.

'Never mind, we'll go on saving until we have enough to move to somewhere really nice,' Lucy told Sam each time he became downhearted about it. 'At least we can do that as long as we're both earning money. You're doing better all the time with your shoe-cleaning job and I have my charring one, and occasionally they still ask me to do a stint at the hotel at midday.'

The summer heat was overpowering and made both of them irritable. Little things which normally wouldn't have worried Lucy made her snappy. The noise from outside in the court where children were shouting and screaming every evening until long after it was dark made her head ache. The smells of cooking that wafted through the house made her feel nauseous.

A lot of the women gathered outside in small groups in the evenings, smoking and gossiping and exchanging confidences. Although Lucy longed for a breath of fresh air she didn't dare join them because she knew that she would not be made welcome.

She and Sam had not made friends with any of the other occupants of the house since they'd been living in Hans Court. Lucy remembered what Maggie, Mrs Sparks's daughter-in-law, had told her when she'd complained about her two boys and knew that they regarded her as stand-offish. Apart from Mrs Sparks, few of them ever passed the time of day with her, not even when they passed on the stairs.

Lucy tried not to think about all the friends and neighbours she'd known as she'd been growing up in Priory Terrace. Things had been so very different then. Her family had often sat out in the pleasant little back garden, especially on hot summer evenings, waiting for the sun to go down and the air to be cooler before they went to bed.

Another thing which irritated Lucy was that now that it was summer the people living in Hans Court strung their washing out on lines that stretched across from one side of the court to the other.

Often they didn't take the trouble to put their sheets and clothes through the wooden mangle that stood in one corner of the court and was available for all to use. The weather was so hot they knew that whatever they put on the line would be dry in next to no time but, several times when she'd been going out, Lucy had found herself soaked because someone had just hung washing on the line which was still dripping wet.

The other thing which Lucy found almost intolerable was the smell from the lavatories which seemed to permeate through the entire court. The one in their own backyard was bad enough and attracted hordes of flies which meant that it was impossible to have the windows open, but mingled with all the others in Hans Court the smell was quite overpowering.

During the first week of September the weather changed; it was so wet that Sam found his usual customers hurried up Water Street from the ferry to their offices and didn't stop for a shoe-shine so his takings were pitifully low and this depressed him even more. Added to this, he found that the damp weather made his leg ache and this only served to remind him what a burden he was on Lucy.

He knew how much she hated having to live in Hans Court and how disappointed she was because they couldn't seem to be able to find somewhere better. Perhaps he shouldn't be relying on her to keep looking but do something himself.

The next day, as soon as the morning rush was over, he packed up his things and took them back to Hans Court, then set off on his own to see if he could locate a place to rent.

Previously, they had looked in the myriad of streets between Hans Court and Scotland Road but today he made his way to the other side of Scotland Road. He decided to start at the top where Scotland Road and Cazneau Street met and to check out all the streets on the right-hand side as he walked down.

The houses were pretty much the same, long rows of grim terraced houses, but it was an area they hadn't looked at before.

He had no idea where to start so he went into a newsagent's shop on the corner of Lawrence Street, intending to buy a packet of cigarettes and then ask whoever served him if they knew if there was anything up for rental.

Inside the shop was a large noticeboard with all sorts of things pinned on to it, ranging from notices of local dances, to items for sale and, in one corner, rooms to let.

He was studying them hopefully when a small,

dumpy woman with grey hair and bright blue eyes in a round, pleasant face tapped him on the shoulder.

'You looking for somewhere to live, chooks?' she asked.

'Right first guess,' he said, turning and smiling at her.

'I suppose you want somewhere with no steps or stairs,' she commented, nodding her head in the direction of his walking stick.

'I carry this for protection more than anything else. I can manage stairs as long as there're not too many of them,' he said, grinning.

'What about steps, steep stone steps?'

'Yes, them as well, as long as I take my time,' he said solemnly. 'Why do you ask?'

'I do take in lodgers but there are half a dozen steps up to my front door. You won't find anything about them on that noticeboard because the couple only moved out this morning and all my other rooms are taken. Do you want to come and take a gander when you've bought your ciggies?'

'I'll come with you right away. I only came in here to see if they knew if there were any rooms to let round about. Here, let me carry that for you,' he said reaching out and taking her shopping bag.

'Sure you can manage it with your gammy leg?'

'Quite sure. My name's Sam Collins, by the way. What do I call you?'

'Most folks call me Berky on account of the fact that I come from Birkenhead. My full name is Mrs Brenda Mason but there's not many around here who use it so you'd better call me Berky or they won't know who you're talking about.'

'Right then, Berky, shall we get going?' Sam smiled. 'Is your place very far from here?'

'No, it's the next road up, Horatio Street.'

It took them only a few minutes to walk there and as they reached number twenty, Berky held out her hand for the shopping bag. 'I'd better carry that now since you're going to need all your wits about you to get up these steps.'

'I can manage.'

Sam's voice was much terser than he had intended and he bit his lip, wondering if he'd blotted his copybook, but to his immense relief Berky laughed merrily.

'That's what I like, a man with guts. Get up those steps, then, and let's see how you get on and don't go falling backwards or you might squash me as flat as a pancake.'

As Sam stood on the top step waiting for her, Berky puffed, 'Push the door open, then, lad; it's not locked.'

He did as she asked then waited for her to join him and precede him into the house.

'Got manners as well, have you?' she said, her voice laced with satisfaction. 'Come on through here to the kitchen, then, and sit yourself down. The kettle is on so we'll have a brew-up before I show you the rooms.'

The kitchen, although not very large, was spotlessly clean and welcoming. Sam sat down in the armchair by the fireside while Berky made a pot of tea and then bustled about unpacking her shopping and putting it away as she waited for

135

the tea to brew.

'Here we are, then,' she exclaimed as she poured out two cups and held one out to him. 'I've put sugar in and stirred it, so all you have to do is drink it,' she commented as she moved back to the table and pulled out one of the two wooden chairs.

'Thanks.' Sam stood up and then, putting his cup of tea on the table, pulled out the other chair. 'You come and sit in the armchair,' he told her.

'I'd sooner sit here with you,' Berky told him as she stirred her tea. 'If I make myself too comfortable, I won't want to walk up all those stairs to show you the rooms.'

They drank their tea in companionable silence for a minute or two. Then Berky drained her cup and stood up. 'Come on, then, lad, I haven't got all day to sit around swilling tea. Come up and see the rooms.'

The two rooms were such a vast improvement on the ones he and Lucy had in Hans Court, that Sam's mind was made up the moment he saw them. The bedroom was about the same size but it had a single bed which left room for a wardrobe and a chest of drawers which had a cheval mirror on it. Everything was spotlessly clean and all the furniture, although far from new, was well polished.

The larger room had a large curtained off alcove at one end with a scrubbed table with a gas ring on it and a row of three shelves up over it. There was a chintz curtain around the bottom of the table to screen the slop pail and wash bowl that was underneath it.

Apart from that it was pretty much the same as they had now, except that there was a colourful rag rug in front of the grate, two comfortable armchairs and a round table covered with a red chenille cloth.

'Well, what do you think?'

'Seems all right,' Sam said cautiously. 'Depends on how much rent per week you're asking.'

'Five shillings.'

Sam pursed his lips in a long silent whistle. It was a shilling a week more than they were paying now but the rooms were so much better that he was confident Lucy would agree they were well worth it. They wouldn't have to go on saving money each week so he was sure they would be able to afford it.

'I'll have to ask my sister because it's more than we're paying at present,' he said cautiously.

'Your sister?' Berky looked taken aback. 'You never said you were sharing with your sister.'

'I'm sure she'll approve,' Sam said quickly.

'Your sister might, but I'm not sure that I do,' Berky told him sharply. 'There's only one bedroom.'

'That's all right. She'll use the bedroom and I'll sleep in the living room on the sofa.'

'Oh you will, will you? It probably hasn't entered your thick skull yet that there isn't a sofa.'

'Oh!' Sam looked around the room. 'No, you're right,' he agreed. 'In that case, I'll have to pull the armchairs together and sleep on them, won't I?' he added cheerfully.

'What sort of night's sleep do you think you would get doing that?' Berky asked crossly.

137

'If that doesn't work, then I can always make up a bed on the floor,' Sam told her.

Berky shook her head. 'That's no good either, not with that gammy leg of yours. No, you need a proper bed. You could have the box room; it's only a slip of a room and I'd have to clear it out. It's the dumping ground for all the bits and pieces I don't use, but I could find places for them elsewhere.'

'You'd want more rent, though, and I'm not sure we can afford it.'

'Another shilling a week, that's all.'

Sam hesitated. Would they be able to afford to pay six shillings a week every week? He wasn't at all sure they could. Lucy always tried to make every penny do the work of two as it was, and they certainly couldn't cut back on what they spent on food. She did most of their shopping late on a Saturday night when the baker, the butcher and the greengrocer were literally giving things away because they knew they wouldn't keep fresh over the weekend.

He knew Berky was waiting for his answer and he didn't like the idea of losing such comfortable living accommodation but, remembering how they'd had to skedaddle in the middle of the night from Priory Terrace because they owed so much money, he didn't want to commit them to more than they could afford.

'What about we say sixpence a week more for the box room?' he suggested.

Berky fixed him with a long stare, her bright blue eyes so hard that he thought she was going to refuse, and was wondering whether to agree to the six shillings if she insisted.

'Very well, you win. Fool to myself, mind,' she added wryly. 'Five shillings and sixpence but I shall expect you to give me a hand to clear out that box room and also to pay for the bed to go in there. Is that a deal?'

'I suppose so; it sounds fair to me,' he added quickly.

'If you are worried about how much a bed is going to cost you, then don't be, because I know a second-hand dealer who will come up trumps; he'll let you have one for a few bob. I'll come along with you when you go to buy it to make sure he doesn't palm you off with anything ropey.'

As they shook hands Sam felt that for the first time in a very long time he really had achieved something worthwhile. He knew how much Lucy hated living in Hans Court and he couldn't wait to go and fetch her and see her face when she saw what he had found for them.

Lucy couldn't believe her ears when Sam arrived home and broke the news to her. When he went on to describe everything she thought it must be too good to be true.

'How much is she asking for the rooms?' Lucy asked.

'Five shillings and sixpence a week.'

'How much? We only pay four shillings here!'

'Get your coat on and we'll go round to Horatio Street right away and you can see them for yourself,' he told her. 'I know you're going to approve of the place and you'll like Berky. She's quite a character – as different from Mrs Sparks as chalk from cheese – but I'm sure you'll take to each

139

other on sight.

'She has a son called Barry but he goes to sea and is not due home for a couple of months. So she said that if we want to move in right away then I can use his room until we've got that box room sorted out.'

'It certainly sounds wonderful but she'll want two weeks' rent up front and I'm afraid I can't quite manage that until I get paid on Friday,' Lucy told him.

'No, she doesn't want any money up front. She said that she expected the rent to be paid promptly every Friday night and I told her I was sure that would suit you,' Sam told her with a beaming smile. 'In fact,' he went on, 'all we have to do is pack up our belongings and then tell Mrs Sparks that we're leaving.'

'What if I don't like the rooms?' Lucy said hesitantly. 'They're going to cost us a lot more.'

'You will like them and they're a hundred times better than what we have here. We'll both have our own bedroom and everywhere is clean and well looked after. If you still have doubts and you want to see for yourself, then we can go now and do that right away.'

'No.' Lucy took Sam's hand and squeezed it. 'I'm sure you're right and I am as pleased as you are that we are going to be able to get away from here.'

Together they packed up their few belongings, both of them eager to get away from Hans Court.

Mrs Sparks looked quite affronted when Lucy told her that they were leaving right away and that as she had paid two weeks in advance she wanted a rebate.

'You can want all you like, but you won't be getting it,' Mrs Sparks told her. 'What about all the wear and tear to my furniture?'

'We haven't caused any damage and as for wear and tear, well, that's what we paid rent for, isn't it?' Lucy said defiantly.

They haggled for almost half an hour and in the end Lucy was quietly triumphant when Mrs Sparks finally agreed to refund them one week's rent.

'That will help to pay for the bed you have to buy for the box room,' Lucy told Sam.

As they left Hans Court, Mrs Sparks came out and stood on the doorstep, her arms folded. 'Sling yer hook, you toffee-nosed uppity pair,' she called out after them.

Sam raised a hand to acknowledge they'd heard, but neither of them turned round or took the trouble to reply or say goodbye.

Chapter Thirteen

Eager though she was to move away from Hans Court, Lucy felt slightly dubious about what sort of place it might be that Sam had found for them. She knew he had also been looking for somewhere but she was a little taken aback that he had settled on somewhere without asking her to have a look at it first.

He was so enthusiastic about the woman called

141

Berky and how good the rooms were that Lucy couldn't help feeling it was all too good to be true.

As they cut through Ennerdale Street into Hawley Street and then turned left and began to walk along Scotland Road, she wondered where on earth he was taking them.

'I hope it isn't going to be much further,' she said worriedly, 'because it's going to mean a long walk to work in the morning from here to Old Hall Street.'

'Don't worry, Horatio Street is the next turning,' he told her cheerfully.

As they went up the steps to the front door she had to agree that it certainly looked a much better area and nowhere near as depressing as Hans Court.

Berky greeted her with such a warm smile that Lucy's remaining doubts about Sam's choice began to vanish. He was right about the neighbourhood and about their new landlady, who seemed to be so kind and motherly that Lucy took to her at once. If the rooms were as good as he said they were, then it really was going to be a great improvement on Hans Court.

'Take your belongings upstairs, then, and settle yourselves in and once you've done that, come back down here and have a bite to eat and a cuppa with me,' Berky insisted.

'Well, what do you think?' Sam asked eagerly after Lucy had had a chance to inspect their two rooms and unpack and put away their few belongings.

'I can hardly believe we've been so lucky,' Lucy

told him, giving him a big hug. 'Everywhere and everything is spotlessly clean and there's even enough tea, sugar and bread to last us a few days to give me time to go shopping.'

Half an hour later they were seated around the table in Berky's cosy kitchen tucking into shepherd's pie and peas and chatting away as if they were old friends. Afterwards, Berky proudly regaled them with stories about her sailor son, Barry, and showed them a photograph of him in his uniform.

'Now if there is anything you need, come and ask me, and if I've got it, you're more than welcome to it,' she told them. 'That is anything except money,' she added with a chuckle.

When Lucy took their first week's rent down the following Friday night and asked how much they owed for the two extra days they'd been living there, Berky shook her head and told her that they owed nothing.

'You're more than welcome,' she told her. 'I'm enjoying your company. All the other rooms are let out to married couples and they keep themselves to themselves so it's nice to have someone to talk to now and again.'

The following week Sam helped Berky to clear out the box room and, between them, he and Lucy distempered the walls and Berky found some bright chintz curtains to hang at the window. Then on the Saturday, the three of them went to Paddy's Market, which was not too far away, and managed to find a second-hand single bed that was almost as good as new.

Lucy found that she was enjoying living with

Berky. When they had been in Hans Court she had often felt lonely and miserable but now because she had Berky to talk to whenever she had the time to spare, she felt much more content.

In addition, their living accommodation was so much better and, now that Sam had a bedroom of his own, she often had their two rooms to herself and so she felt far more relaxed.

By the time Barry came home on shore leave in October both Sam and Lucy felt that Berky had told them so much about him it was as if they had known him all their lives.

He had Berky's sunny nature but he was much slimmer than Lucy had thought he would be and not as tall as she'd expected. Indeed, he was not very much taller than his mother but she appeared to be shorter than she really was because she was so round and cuddly. He had her bright blue eyes and Lucy imagined that her hair had once had the same auburn tinge in it as his had.

They all got on extremely well and once or twice Lucy and Sam joined Barry and Berky for their meal in the evening and afterwards spent an hour down in Berky's kitchen listening to his tales of where he'd been on his last trip.

The night before he was due to go back to his ship he asked Lucy if she would go dancing with him.

'Sam can come as well, of course, if he'd like to,' he told her when she hesitated.

'Thanks, but no thanks,' Sam told them. 'I'd soon get fed up of having to sit watching you two circle round and round to the music and I don't

144

see any girl wanting to dance with a chap with a gammy leg and a walking stick.'

Lucy was about to protest but he gave her a look that brought the colour to her cheeks and she said nothing. Later, when they were on their own, and she was getting ready to go out, he said teasingly, 'You didn't expect me to play gooseberry, did you? Barry's got a crush on you so watch your step.'

Lucy enjoyed her outing with Barry. He took her in his arms and she felt herself pressed against his strong body as they circled the dance floor and it brought back vivid memories of the times when she'd gone out dancing with Robert. It also made her realise that for the last eighteen months she had been so busy working and looking after Sam that she'd had no real life of her own.

When she told Barry how much she'd enjoyed their evening he looked pleased and said they should have gone out together before but he hadn't wanted her to think he was being pushy. 'Perhaps we could keep in touch,' he suggested. 'It would be nice if you wrote to me while I'm away; the only letters I ever get are from my mam.'

'Of course, I'd like to do that, but I don't want to upset your mam because she's been so good to us. Perhaps you'd better include a message for me in your letters to her at first so that she gets used to the idea of us keeping in touch.'

They all missed Barry when he went back to sea. Twice in one week Berky invited them in for supper. 'I forgot that young rascal had gone away again and I've cooked double the amount of grub

I should have done,' she told them.

'Never mind, you can always have a second helping or else keep it for tomorrow,' Lucy told her.

'Eat the same meal two days running? I'd sooner finish it all up at one sitting, so why don't you and Sam come and help me do that,' she said.

Even though Lucy knew Sam would have preferred to spend the evening in their own rooms, she agreed because she suspected that Berky was missing Barry so much that she was feeling lonely.

'My Barry seems to be writing to me a lot more than he ever used to do,' Berky told them a few weeks later, a twinkle in her bright blue eyes. 'This is the second time in about ten days that I've had a letter from him. There's a message at the bottom for you, Lucy. You'd better let me know what answer I'm to give him.'

At Christmas, Lucy sent a parcel to Barry and he wrote back to her to thank her, and this established a regular spate of letters from him directly to her.

If Berky noticed that the number of letters she received had dwindled, she said nothing apart from commenting that there were no messages for Lucy these days.

Lucy smiled and said nothing, though she knew Berky must have noticed letters were arriving addressed to her in Barry's handwriting and would know they were corresponding with each other. She hoped that she wasn't drawing the wrong conclusion. As far as she was concerned, she thought of Barry as a friend and nothing more.

Robert had broken her heart when he'd admitted that Patsy's baby was his and she still didn't think that she would ever trust any man again.

They spent Christmas Day with Berky. Lucy bought a large chicken and Berky roasted it along with potatoes and parsnips and served it with all the other trimmings to make it special. She'd also made a Christmas pudding and an iced Christmas cake and Sam added to the festivities with a bottle of wine, some Christmas crackers and a big box of chocolate-covered dates for Berky.

'This is one of the best Christmases I've had in years,' Berky enthused when she opened them later that evening and offered them around after they'd finished eating mince pies and Christmas cake. 'I only wish Barry was here to share it with us. Have you any idea when he is next coming on leave?' she asked, looking directly at Lucy.

Lucy felt her cheeks redden. 'No, he hasn't mentioned any dates to me, not as yet,' she admitted. 'You do know that he writes to me occasionally, then?'

'Of course I do, I'm not blind. I like the way you've kept it secret between the two of you,' she added quickly. 'You don't want any interference from me but I'll tell you this, Lucy, I couldn't wish for him to take up with anyone nicer.'

Lucy smiled politely. She wanted to tell Berky that there was nothing serious between them but she didn't think that this was the right moment to do so because it might put a dampener on the festive occasion. She thought of Barry as a friend, nothing more, and she hoped he felt the same way about her.

147

At the moment she didn't want anything to change. She and Sam had found a place to live that was comfortable; she enjoyed Berky's company and appreciated all the countless things she did for them that made their lives so much easier.

Sam was making a decent living from his shoe cleaning and she intended to look for a better job now that they were settled. In fact, it was her New Year resolution; the very first thing she planned to do in January 1923.

Later on when they were on their own, she mentioned what she had been planning to Sam and he seemed relieved. 'I agree that it's about time you stopped charring and washing up dirty dishes and found yourself an office job,' he told her.

'I don't know if I can manage that,' Lucy said dubiously. 'I thought perhaps I might get a job as a shop assistant or even work as a Nippy at the Lyons Corner House.'

'Becoming a Nippy is not much better than what you're doing now at the hotel; you would be on your feet all day, don't forget, and that can be very tiring.'

'I wouldn't be up to my elbows in scummy water, though. I rather fancy one of those smart little black and white caps and a black dress and white frilly apron.'

'It wouldn't suit you,' Sam teased. 'You look your best when you are sitting at a switchboard wearing headphones.'

'Those days are gone,' Lucy sighed. 'You can't turn the clock back, you should know that. We'd all be doing it if we could.'

'Since we moved in here we have become rather complacent, though, haven't we?' Sam sighed. 'The trouble is Berky spoils us. She does so much to make our lives comfortable that we're not making much effort to do better.'

Lucy frowned. 'I thought you were very happy with things as they are?'

'I am, that's the trouble. In the summer I was determined to extend my hours and I still haven't done so. I thought that if I went back again in the evening, say about six or seven o'clock, I might pick up trade from people coming over to Liverpool for a night out. Men who've dashed home from work and rushed to get ready to go out and completely forgotten about polishing their shoes.'

'It's possible,' Lucy agreed. 'Leave it until after Easter, when the nights are lighter and the weather's not so cold.'

Two weeks into January Lucy had a letter from Barry to say he would be on shore leave early in February.

He'd also written and told his mother, so all they could talk about in the evenings was his forthcoming visit.

'I wish he'd said how long he'd be home for,' Berky fretted. 'I wonder if he will be here for St Valentine's Day.'

'Why on earth does that matter?' Lucy asked.

'Well, you never know what might happen; it's the time when there's romance in the air, now isn't it?' Berky murmured, raising her eyebrows at Lucy.

Lucy smiled non-committally. She hoped Berky

149

wasn't getting silly ideas about her and Barry. Lately she had been talking a lot about how she was looking forward to Barry getting married. She'd even gone on about how lovely it would be to have grandchildren.

'As far as I'm concerned, Barry is simply a very good friend and there is no romantic involvement on either side and I intend it to stay that way,' Lucy told Sam.

As it turned out Barry's leave was a very short one. 'Don't worry,' he told them when his mother looked so woebegone. 'I'll be back again before you have had time to miss me. We are only going across to Holland this time so we should be back shortly after Easter, and I'll be home on leave again, probably before the end of April.'

'Well, I suppose that's something to look forward to.' Berky sighed. 'In some ways it would be nice if all your trips were short ones and we could count on seeing you a bit more. Don't you agree, Lucy?' she asked archly.

Chapter Fourteen

In the weeks leading up to Whitsun at the end of May, Berky regaled Lucy and Sam with details of all the Bank Holiday treats she and Barry had enjoyed in the past.

'One of his favourite outings was to go to Bidston Village. It's just outside Birkenhead and there is a lovely hill there; if you climb right up to the top, you can see all over Liverpool,' she told them, her blue eyes shining.

'So is that where you want to take him for a day out when he comes home at Whitsun?' Sam asked.

'He'd certainly love to go there but I know Lucy has set her heart on a trip to New Brighton.'

'Perhaps we could do both,' Lucy said quickly. 'On Whit Sunday we could go to Bidston Hill and then on the Monday go across to New Brighton.'

Berky could hardly wait to tell Barry what they'd planned when he arrived home. And her face registered disappointment when he shook his head.

'Sorry, Mam, but I have to leave on Whit Monday; we sail at midday. We can still have our outings, of course. We can go over to New Brighton on the Saturday, if that's all right with Lucy and Sam, and to Bidston Hill on the Sunday.'

'That's settled, then. On the Monday we can have a nice day at home. I'll roast a joint of beef so that you have some good food inside you before you sail.' She smiled. 'Sam and Lucy will come and eat with us and we'll give you a good send off.'

'That's our entire holiday weekend taken up with going out with them,' Sam grumbled when he and Lucy were alone. 'I was thinking of working on Saturday – it's all right, I'll come with you instead, if that's what you want me to do,' he added quickly as he saw the frown on Lucy's face.

'A couple of days off will do you good. All the offices will be closed so I don't suppose many people will be worrying about having their shoes shined,' she told him.

151

It was a bright sunny day on the Saturday and they set off for New Brighton around midmorning. Lucy was wearing a crisp, blue cotton dress with a scooped neckline and dropped waist and a wide-brimmed hat to keep the sun from her eyes.

'You'd better take a coat of some sort,' Berky told her. 'It can be quite chilly crossing the Mersey and it might get cold again before we come home. You can always carry it, if you get too warm.'

'Stop fussing, Mam,' Barry laughed. 'I can see you're well wrapped up, thick skirt and blouse and a scarf as well as a top coat, so you should be roasting,' he teased.

'It's better to be safe than sorry; I don't want to catch a chill and I can always take my coat off and carry it, if I'm too hot,' Berky told him as she pulled on her gloves ready to leave.

As they made their way down to the Pier Head the sun was warm but there was quite a keen breeze and Lucy was glad she had a coat. The crossing was choppy and as the *Royal* Iris ferry boat rolled, Barry laughed at the expression on her face and told her that she'd have to get some sea legs if she wanted to be a sailor.

'I prefer to be on dry land,' she told him. 'The sooner we get to New Brighton the better.'

'We'll be getting off any minute now,' Barry affirmed as the boat began to slow down and manoeuvre into position alongside the pier landing stage.

All four of them walked along the promenade and then when Berky felt tired they sat in one of the shelters watching people go by and admiring all the pretty dresses and smart hats that the women and girls were wearing. Lucy wondered how she would feel if Robert and Patsy sauntered by and if it would upset Sam at all if they did.

Barry took them to one of the cafés on the Ham and Egg Parade and they all had fish and chips and mushy peas for their midday meal, followed by a pot of tea.

'I thought you were going to take Lucy to the funfair,' Berky stated as they emerged on to the promenade again and made their way down on to the shore where there were deckchairs for hire. 'Go on, don't worry about me, I'll be happy enough sitting here watching all the folks in their finery parading by and the children having donkey rides on the sand.'

'Coming, then?' Barry asked, holding out a hand to Lucy who looked enquiringly at Sam.

'I'll stay here with Berky,' Sam told her, settling into a deckchair, stretching out his legs, and making himself comfortable.

Barry didn't give Lucy time to argue; taking her arm, he hurried her along King's Parade in the direction of the Tower Ballroom where there was a large fairground with countless rides and side-show attractions of every kind.

They even went on the Wilkie's Safety Aerial Railway and Lucy was so nervous that she kept her eyes tightly shut most of the time.

They had rides on the roundabouts, in tiny metal chairs that swung out right over the heads of the crowd, as well as in the swing boats until Lucy felt dizzy. Barry showed off his prowess in the shooting booths and they came away armed

153

with a large cuddly teddy bear which Barry had won on the coconut shy and which she insisted he must give to his mother.

He wanted to stay longer but Lucy was worried that Sam would be fed up and so she insisted they ought to get back and take Berky and Sam for a cup of tea.

'There's a live band and dancing at the Tower Ballroom tonight,' Barry said as they sat in one of the cafés on the promenade refreshing themselves with a big pot of tea and a plate of toasted teacakes. 'Would you like to go, Lucy?'

'Go on, my Barry's only got a couple of days' leave so he wants to make the most of it. Me and Sam will sit and listen to the band for a bit and then when we get tired of doing that we'll go home,' Berky said as Lucy shook her head.

Lucy was well aware that Berky was doing all she could to throw her and Barry together and although she enjoyed his company very much she didn't want things between them to become serious.

'I'm not wearing the right sort of dress or shoes for dancing,' she prevaricated.

Neither Barry nor Berky would accept this so, in the end, she gave in and said she would go dancing after they'd taken another stroll along the promenade. Berky and Sam said they'd decided not to stay on any longer but would go home, and they'd see them both later on. Lucy wished she could persuade Sam to come dancing so that perhaps he would meet someone.

'Now don't rush; if you're enjoying yourselves, stay until the dancing ends. There are bound to

154

be late boats to get folks back to Liverpool and I'll leave the door on the latch so you can stay out as long as you like,' Berky insisted.

It was Lucy's first visit to New Brighton's Tower Ballroom and she found the immense dance hall with its wonderful lighting, beautifully painted ceiling and sprung parquet floor impressive.

She felt she was in a dream as she circled the floor and wished she was in Robert's arms, not in Barry's. Finally, they danced the last waltz and left the ballroom and made their way to the pier to catch the ferry boat home. It was such a beautiful star-studded night that she found it hard to bring herself back to reality.

They went up on to the top deck of the boat and stood together by the rail watching the lights of New Brighton recede and then the lights of Liverpool gradually come into full view. When Barry took her into his arms and began kissing her, she found herself responding; it was all part of the magic of the night.

Berky was still up when they arrived home, her sharp eyes inquisitive as she studied their faces when they came in. Lucy declined the cup of tea she had waiting for them and quickly made her way up to her room. She didn't want to ruin her delightful memories of the evening by talking about it and she certainly didn't want to analyse the growing empathy between herself and Barry.

Lucy slept late; it was half past ten when she finally got out of bed and she would have stayed there even longer, only she knew Berky was looking forward to their trip to Bidston.

Berky already had a cold lunch on the table and

as soon as they had eaten they set off. They took the ferry across to Birkenhead, then a tram as far as Bidston Village.

'It's about half a mile from here to the hill,' Berky told them. 'Then it's a steady climb because it's almost three hundred feet high. It's the highest point hereabouts. There's an observatory up there, and a windmill and a lighthouse, although that hasn't been in use for years.'

All four of them were exhausted, especially Sam, by the time they reached the top so they sat down on the short grass to get their breath back and to admire the expansive view.

'I can understand why I'm out of breath,' Berky puffed, 'but you young ones shouldn't be.'

'It's all the dancing we did last night,' Barry laughed. 'We barely sat down all evening.'

Like Sam, Berky seemed to find going down more difficult than climbing up the hill. 'I think you'd better let me take your arm, Barry,' she said as her feet slipped and stumbled on the descent.

'Come on, then, Mam.' He stopped and waited for her but before she could reach him she slipped and, the next minute, she had collapsed in a heap on the ground and was crying out with pain.

Both Lucy and Barry rushed to her side but when they tried to get her up on to her feet again she shook her head and tears rolled down her cheeks.

'I can't stand, I can't put my weight on my leg,' she gasped.

Sam took off his jacket and made a cushion of it and they helped her to sit back down again. Very gently Lucy ran her hands down Berky's leg and looked concerned when Berky not only winced but cried out for her to stop.

'I think it might be broken.' Lucy frowned, looking up at Barry worriedly.

'Let me see.' He knelt down beside his mother and gently felt her leg and nodded in agreement.

'What are we going to do now? How are we going to get her home?' Lucy asked.

Barry shook his head. 'Her leg is going to need fixing so we'll have to take her to hospital.'

'How are we going to do that? We certainly can't carry her,' Sam pointed out. 'What we need is an ambulance.'

'I doubt if we will be able to get one of those on a bank holiday weekend,' Lucy murmured.

They looked at each other bemused. 'Perhaps one of us should go into Bidston Village and see if there's a policeman on duty and if he can arrange for an ambulance or something,' Lucy suggested.

'If there isn't one there, then it means going all the way to Birkenhead to find one,' Sam said, frowning.

'Perhaps I could phone for an ambulance from the village; there's bound to be a phone box there,' Barry murmured. 'Right.' He stood up. 'Can I leave you two here to look after my mam? It will be quicker if I go on my own,' he added firmly as Sam offered to go with him.

'Perhaps we should move her to somewhere a bit more comfortable; a spot where she can rest her back against a bank or something,' Lucy suggested.

'No, no, I couldn't stand the pain of you doing

that,' Berky protested. 'I'm all right as I am. Get going, Barry, and be as quick as you can,' she begged.

They waited for over half an hour and there was still no sign of Barry coming back with any help. Berky was moaning with pain and Lucy felt frustrated because there was nothing she could do to help her except sit beside her and hold her hand.

The brightness of the day had given way to an overcast sky and Lucy was concerned when it started to rain. Although it was only a fine misty drizzle, in no time at all they were quite wet and there was nothing they could do to shelter Berky.

By the time Barry returned to tell them that an ambulance was on its way from Birkenhead they were soaking wet and Berky was shivering with the cold.

It was almost an hour before two ambulance men arrived. They put a temporary splint on her leg and then there was a long discussion about how they were going to get her back to the ambulance.

One of them went back down to where they were parked at the bottom of the hill and came back with a canvas chair to carry her in. Once they had managed to get her into it, they strapped her in for safety before they set off down the hill.

Progress was extremely slow because they had to be cautious not to slip themselves. Each time they reached a particularly rough patch of ground Lucy could hear Berky whimper with pain as the ambulance men unavoidably jolted the chair.

When they finally reached the ambulance, the

men were reluctant to let Barry, Sam and Lucy ride with Berky, but after some arguing they agreed to do so.

Although she lived in Liverpool, Berky was taken to a hospital in Birkenhead because they were on the other side of the Mersey. Since it was a Sunday and quite late in the day, they were told that in all probability it would be the next day before they could operate on Berky's leg.

'The best thing you can do is go home and come back tomorrow,' the receptionist told them.

When Barry asked if she would be transferred to a Liverpool hospital or whether she would be sent home once her leg had been set, no one was prepared to say.

Barry was extremely worried. His ship sailed the following day and he knew it was impossible to stay on in Liverpool. He had no idea when he would next be coming home and he was in a dilemma about whether to forgo the trip and stay ashore or to leave it to Lucy to visit his mother and take care of her when she finally came out of hospital.

'I'll certainly do what I can, but I do have to go to work,' Lucy pointed out.

'I know, that's what worries me. I'm wondering if I ought to stay home until Mam is better.'

'What happens if you don't go back to your ship?' Sam enquired.

'I'll certainly be in trouble. I might get fined and, at the very least, I will be dismissed and won't be able to work for the same shipping company ever again.'

'Surely you don't want to take the risk of that

happening?' Lucy said worriedly.

'The way things are, I certainly don't. Once you're out of work then the chances of getting signed on again are not good, especially if you have a bad record. You have to produce a reference from your last captain so there's no chance of them not finding out.'

'In that case, then, you don't have any option but to rejoin your ship,' Sam told him. 'Don't worry, we'll do what we can for your mam; she's been very good to us so we'll take care of her one way or the other. There's no need for you to be concerned.'

Chapter Fifteen

As soon as she finished work the next morning Lucy went straight over to Birkenhead to find out what news there was of Berky. As she was entering the hospital she met Barry coming out.

'How is Berky?' she asked anxiously.

'The news isn't good,' he said worriedly. 'Getting wet and cold has added to her problems; she has some sort of chest infection as well as her broken leg.'

'Did they let you see her?'

'No, and there's not much point in you going in because they said she had been taken into the theatre to have her leg attended to and won't be out of the anaesthetic for several hours. They said to come back later but I won't be able to do that because my ship sails in just over an hour.'

'Don't worry, I'll come this evening and see her then, if they'll let me,' Lucy promised.

'That would be good,' Barry said gratefully. 'By the way, they won't tell you anything about how she is unless you are a relation so, since I won't be here, I've given your name to them as my mam's next of kin. I hope you don't mind,' he added quickly as he saw Lucy frown.

'No, I suppose that's all right, but what relation am I supposed to be to your mother?' Lucy asked.

'I've told them that your name is Lucy Mason and that you're my wife and you'll be acting for me while I'm away at sea.'

'What on earth made you do that?' Lucy exclaimed in dismay, her face reddening.

'It was the only way I could think of to make sure that they would tell you everything there was to know about my mam's condition.'

'What happens if they find out the truth, that I'm not even related to her?'

'They won't,' he assured her confidently.

'Your mam might tell them, or have you told her as well?'

'I haven't had the chance, have I? I told you they wouldn't let me see her.'

'She might think I've told them and she might be quite angry about it,' Lucy said worriedly, her dark eyes full of concern.

'Rubbish! She'll be delighted,' he laughed.

'Well, I'm not. I don't like telling lies and that's a whopper,' Lucy told him firmly.

Barry sighed and looked at his watch. 'I was doing it for Berky's sake. I can't stop to discuss it or they'll sail without me. We'll sort it all out as soon as I get home again.'

'You haven't told her and you are expecting me to do it, is that right?'

Barry kissed her lightly on the cheek, 'Thanks, Lucy, I knew I could depend on you. Don't worry about it; I'm sure my mam won't be upset by what I've said.'

'Well, that's something we won't know until I tell her,' Lucy said disapprovingly.

'Please look after her, Lucy; I'm depending on you.'

With another quick hug and a kiss on her brow, Barry had gone, leaving her standing there wondering what on earth she was letting herself in for and extremely annoyed with Barry for claiming that they were married even if it was the only way of making sure she would be allowed to see his mother.

It niggled away in the back of her mind for the rest of the day. She was on the point of mentioning it to the woman who was in charge at the hotel kitchen to see what she thought but then she decided that perhaps it was better not to do so, but she couldn't help feeling concerned about all the implications involved.

Later that evening when they sat down to eat and she told Sam what Barry had done, he didn't seem very interested.

'I don't understand what you are getting so worked up about,' he said as he loaded his fork with mashed potato and gravy.

'If someone at the hospital refers to me as Barry's wife, then Berky might believe it is true.'

'Does that matter?'

Lucy laid down her knife and fork. 'Of course it does. She's always dropping hints about looking forward to Barry being married and pushing the two of us together.'

Sam shrugged non-committally and went on with his meal.

'Don't simply dismiss it, Sam,' Lucy said, her voice laced with annoyance, 'tell me what I ought to do.'

'Not much you can do, is there?' Sam said laconically. 'Anyway, why all the fuss? What does it matter?'

'It matters to me,' Lucy told him hotly. 'Even though Berky must know it's not true, she's bound to think that there's something going on between us.'

'And isn't there?' Sam teased.

'I like Barry but only as a friend,' Lucy emphasised, 'and telling Berky that would probably upset her a great deal.'

'Then don't tell her. Let her think that one day you are going to marry Barry.'

'But I'm not!'

'All right, but don't shout.' Sam grinned, putting his hands over his ears.

'Then don't start surmising that one day I might marry Barry Mason,' Lucy said, her mouth a tight line.

'How can you say that for certain? You like him a great deal so if he asks you to marry him, why don't you?'

Lucy didn't answer. She gave her full attention to the food in front of her.

163

'You're not still carrying a candle for Robert, surely to heavens,' Sam exploded. 'He jilted you and double-crossed me with my girlfriend while I was too ill to do anything about it.'

He shoved his chair back so violently that it went crashing to the floor. 'I'll never understand women,' he said scathingly as he picked it up and pushed it under the table.

'You had that Percy Carter mooning after you for years. He'd have jumped at the chance of marrying you and look at the life you would have had then. You walked away from him and a good home to live in squalor until we came here. Now you are turning down Barry, a chap with a regular job who worships the ground you walk on, and whose mother has you up on a pedestal. What is it you want, Lucy? What sort of man is ever going to meet your expectations?'

Lucy sat stunned as he walked out of the room. She felt as if she was seeing herself in a new light and it utterly confused her. She knew Sam hadn't wanted to move away from Priory Terrace but she'd had no idea he felt so strongly about it all. It was almost as if he was blaming her for all that had gone wrong.

Perhaps in some ways he was right and she had done the wrong thing, but would marrying Percy Carter or any man she didn't love put matters right, or would it also end in tears?

When Lucy and Sam went over to the hospital later that evening they were told that Berky was still extremely ill and could not have any visitors, except close relations.

'We are close relations,' Sam stated, 'surely we can have a few minutes with her?'

'Wait here and I'll check with the sister in charge,' the receptionist told them.

When she came back she said they could visit but only for ten minutes.

'Who are you, exactly?' the sister asked when they entered the ward. 'Are you her son?'

'No,' Sam admitted, 'but my sister is her daughter-in-law. I've come with her because Mrs Mason's son is away at sea.'

'Very well, then, you can go in for ten minutes,' she said looking at Lucy, 'but I'm afraid you won't be able to,' she said turning to Sam, 'so please wait outside in the corridor.'

Lucy felt her heart pounding as she approached the screened-off bed. Berky was propped up against a mountain of pillows and she looked very pale and was having great trouble breathing.

Her eyes flickered open when the sister spoke to her. 'Your daughter-in-law is here to see you, Mrs Mason.'

'What? I haven't got a daughter-in-law,' Berky croaked in a puzzled voice. 'My son Barry's not married; it's him that I want to see,' she added in a pitiful whisper.

'She must have forgotten,' Lucy said quickly and managed a trembling smile when the sister looked at her questioningly.

Before the sister could intervene she picked up one of Berky's hands and gave it a gentle squeeze. 'It's Lucy,' she said softly, bending down and kissing Berky on the brow.

The older woman's face lit up. 'Lucy, my luv,

where's Barry? What's happened to me, what am I doing here in this bed? Take me home with you.'

'You had a fall while we were coming down Bidston Hill,' Lucy reminded her. 'You've hurt your leg and you are in hospital.'

'My leg? No, it's my chest that hurts. Terrible pain when I breathe. Tell Barry to come and take me home.'

'Barry has had to rejoin his ship,' Lucy told her gently. 'I'm afraid you will have to stay here until you're better. I'll take you home as soon as you are well enough.'

Berky sighed resignedly and closed her eyes.

'I think that is enough for today,' the sister said quietly, moving Lucy away from the bed. 'She needs to rest now. You might be able to stay longer tomorrow if she is feeling a little better,' she added in a reassuring voice.

'It's Barry she wants to see,' Lucy told Sam as they made their way back to the landing stage for the ferry boat that would take them back to Liverpool. 'I wonder if we can get a message to him through the shipping company?'

'We can try; he won't have gone far since they only sailed yesterday; perhaps they have some way of getting him home again.'

'He won't be able to do anything until they reach a port and then even if they do let him come back, he'll have to wait until there's a boat sailing to Liverpool.'

'Not necessarily. Any boat that is coming to England would do. He can always take a train from whichever port he disembarks at back to here.'

The shipping company were quite cooperative

166

when Lucy called in the next morning after she'd finished work and they promised to send a message by telegraph. 'It will be there waiting when they dock at Amsterdam tomorrow,' the clerk promised. 'I'll send a message to the captain explaining matters and he will inform seaman Mason.'

'Will they allow him to come home?' Lucy asked anxiously.

'Since his mother is so desperately ill I am sure they will. If you'd like to come back about this time tomorrow I should have an answer for you. That's unless he has already turned up on your doorstep,' he added with a smile.

'We've done all we can,' Sam commented as they went home. 'It's a pity Barry didn't ask for extended leave, but I don't suppose he thought his mother was as ill as she is.'

'It seems to be her chest and not her leg that is the main cause for concern,' Lucy mused. 'All we can do now is wait and hope that perhaps Barry is back in time to visit her tomorrow.'

'That's hardly likely if the ship doesn't reach Amsterdam until tomorrow.'

'I suppose not. I was thinking what that clerk said about his turning up.'

'He was trying to cheer you up,' Sam told her. 'We'll go back tomorrow like he said and see if he has any news. If we know that Barry is definitely on his way home, we can tell Berky when we go to see her tomorrow night and that will delight her.'

Knowing they were both too worried to sleep they sat up late debating what they ought to do about Berky's rooms until she came home.

'Locking the doors and leaving them as they are is probably the best thing,' Sam stated.

'Yes, I know that, but it was more about her duties here as landlady that I was thinking about,' Lucy told him. 'Apparently Berky collected the rents each week on behalf of the landlord and I don't even know who he is, do you?'

'No.' Sam shook his head. 'I never gave it a thought. She seemed to decide what we all paid and she made sure she collected the money on time. The sooner Barry gets back and sorts such things out the better.'

'That's if he knows the ins and outs of it all,' Lucy said worriedly.

'Well, if he doesn't, I'm sure the landlord will soon turn up if he doesn't receive his money and then we can tell him what's happened to Berky.'

'Do you think we should tell the other people who live here?'

'I don't know; I've not had much to do with any of them. I've passed the time of day when I've met them as I was coming in or going out but that's all.'

'Probably we should leave it until Barry comes home and let him handle all those sorts of things,' Lucy agreed.

It was almost midnight when they heard the sharp thud on the front door. They looked at each other questioningly.

'Could it be Barry?' Lucy asked.

Sam shook his head. 'He'd never manage to get home this quickly.'

'Shall we ignore it?'

'No, it might be important, I'll go and see who

it is,' Sam said, rising from his chair.

'Be careful,' Lucy warned as she followed him into the hall.

When Sam opened the door Lucy felt apprehensive when she saw two policemen standing there.

'Does Mrs Mason live here?' one of them asked.

'Mrs Mason is in hospital,' Sam told him.

'I mean Mrs Lucy Mason.'

Lucy gasped and retreated quickly back into their room. They must have found out that she'd been lying and impersonating Berky's daughter-in-law, she thought in alarm. She felt scared; surely, though, they couldn't arrest her for doing that, she told herself.

'I think you'd better come in and tell us what this is about,' she heard Sam say. 'Come through here,' he invited, leading them into their living room.

'Are you Mrs Brenda Mason's daughter-in-law?' one of them asked looking at Lucy.

She stared at them unable to answer and looked at Sam hoping he would take over.

'You have some news about Mrs Mason for us?' Sam asked.

'Are you Barry Mason?'

'No, I'm Sam Collins and this is my sister,' Sam told them, putting an arm around Lucy's shoulders. 'Barry is at sea but we have sent a message through the shipping line for him to come home because his mother is so ill. As a matter of fact, we thought that was who it was knocking on the door.'

'I see. When is he due?'

169

Barry explained about Barry's ship being due to dock at Amsterdam tomorrow and he would be coming straight home.

The police officer nodded. 'Well, I'm afraid he is going to be too late; we've come to inform you that Mrs Mason died at ten o'clock this evening.'

Chapter Sixteen

Lucy and Sam looked at each other in stunned silence after the policemen left. Then Sam hugged her and tried to comfort her as the tears rolled down her cheeks.

'What a terrible shock it's going to be for Barry when he gets home,' she snuffled.

'Let's hope he manages to get here fairly quickly so that he can take charge of everything,' Sam agreed.

'They said something about letting the hospital have details about her and the funeral arrangements, didn't they?' Lucy asked, moving out of his arms and wiping away her tears with a handkerchief.

'Yes, but I think we should wait for Barry to get home, don't you? He mightn't like us going through her private papers.'

'The trouble is, we let those policemen think that I was her daughter-in-law and Barry has said I'm her next of kin so we might have to be the ones to do so,' Lucy said worriedly.

'Well, we don't need to do anything about it

tonight and with a bit of luck Barry might arrive home tomorrow. We'll both be out at work so if anyone comes here looking for us in the morning they won't be able to find us.'

Barry arrived early in the afternoon the following day shortly after Lucy came home from work.

'I wasn't sure whether to come home first or go straight to the hospital,' he told her as he dropped his kit bag on to the floor and hugged her. 'How is Mam?'

Lucy bit her lip. She wanted to break the news to him gently but couldn't find the right words. He took one look at her face and shook his head in despair. 'I'm too late, aren't I?'

'I'm afraid so.' Lucy nodded. 'I'm so sorry.'

'When did it happen?'

'Last night. The police came to tell us. They said the hospital needed her personal details and information about the funeral arrangements.'

He nodded again but didn't speak.

'Would you like a cup of tea?'

The moment she'd asked the question she felt that it was a trite thing to say but, to her relief, he simply nodded, then walked over to the window and stared out unseeingly.

He was still standing there, his hands in his pockets and his shoulders hunched, when she had made the tea and poured him out a cup and she could see the grief etched on his face when he turned round to take it from her.

It brought back memories of when she'd lost both her parents in the car accident and it made her feel so sad that she wanted to put her arms

171

round him and comfort him. She hesitated, wondering if he would read more into it than she intended and the moment passed.

Barry drank his tea in silence, and then put the cup down on the table. 'I suppose I'd better go to the hospital,' he said.

'Would you like me to come with you?' Lucy asked.

He hesitated then shook his head. 'No, I think it might be better if I went on my own. You said they wanted to know about the funeral arrangements; you haven't done anything about that, have you?'

'Well, no. I wasn't sure what had to be done. I didn't like to go into her room and look for all the personal papers they said they would need.'

He frowned. 'Do you know where she kept them?'

'No,' Lucy shook her head. 'I have no idea at all.'

'I'd better go and see if I can find them. I suppose they'll want her birth certificate, wedding certificate, that sort of thing.'

'Yes,' Lucy nodded, 'I think that is what they want and probably any insurance policies, if she had any.'

'You mean to pay for her funeral,' Barry muttered and there was such unhappiness in his voice that Lucy threw caution to the wind and put her arms round him to try and comfort him.

He groaned and buried his face in her hair as he returned her hug then, with a great effort, he freed himself and went out of the room and downstairs to start searching.

Lucy respected his need for privacy. She wanted to help because she knew from her own experience how traumatic having to deal with all the officialdom could be. She suspected, though, that Barry wanted to do these things himself; it was a way of atoning for not being there when his mother died.

The funeral was a simple ceremony. Lucy and Sam attended, and one or two of the other lodgers in the house, but after the internment they all quietly went their own way. Barry went home with Lucy and Sam and they had a meal together. He stayed for a couple of hours before saying he was tired and, as he hadn't had much sleep lately, he thought he'd have an early night.

The next day he told Lucy that he'd only been given a few days' compassionate leave so he was clearing out his mother's rooms because he'd be rejoining his ship, which was still in the Albert Dock in Liverpool taking on fresh cargo, almost immediately.

'It seems senseless to go on renting them simply as a base for when I get leave,' he told Lucy. 'It would be different if I was planning to get married and needed a home for my wife,' he added looking pointedly at her.

Lucy didn't answer; she felt uncomfortable as the blood rushed to her cheeks.

Barry walked across to the door, then paused and turned round. 'I'm not much good at this sort of thing, Lucy, but I'm trying my damnedness to ask you to marry me.'

'Oh, Barry, I'm sorry, but the answer is no.'

Lucy laid a hand on his arm. 'I like you very much as a friend, but I can't commit further than that.'

'Ah well, I thought that was the case,' he muttered. He pulled out his cigarettes and Lucy noticed his hand was shaking slightly as he lit one. 'If you would like to have the rooms my mother had, I could always ask the landlord on your behalf,' he offered. 'Of course, it would mean that you would have to take over her duties as janitor and collect the rent from all the other tenants and be the one to interview new tenants when there were rooms to let.'

'I think all that responsibility might be rather too much for me,' Lucy said dubiously.

'Yes, you wouldn't have the right firmness in your tone when you said no to them; they might think that deep down you didn't mean it,' Barry said darkly.

Before Lucy could think of an answer he'd gone. She felt confused; surely he didn't think that she was playing hard to get, she thought angrily.

The minute Sam arrived home she related what had been said but to her annoyance he seemed to be surprised that she had turned down Barry's suggestion.

'Surely collecting rents would be far better than washing up dirty dishes and greasy pots and pans?' he pointed out. 'Barry was probably trying to make things easier for you; he's daft about you. I can't understand why you keep pushing him to one side. Marry him and your troubles will be over.'

174

Lucy decided not to argue with him.

She saw very little of Barry during the remaining few days of his leave. Once or twice she caught sight of him hurrying out of the house as though dashing to keep an appointment.

Sam said he had seen him going into Berky's room with a tall middle-aged man whom he thought was probably the landlord. When Barry finally popped in to say goodbye and tell them that he was sailing later that night, he said that the landlord was keeping all Berky's furniture so that he could let out her place ready-furnished to one of his relations who would also be collecting the rents and supervising the lettings.

'Have you any idea when you will next be coming home on leave?' Lucy asked.

'Home?' Barry gave her a wry smile. 'I don't have a home here any longer so I don't suppose our paths will ever cross again.'

'There will always be a bed and a meal for you here whenever you come ashore,' Sam told him as they shook hands.

Sam frowned as the door closed behind Barry and he turned to face Lucy. 'So you're happy to let him go without a word, are you?' he said bitterly.

'I don't know what you mean,' Lucy prevaricated, turning away and busying herself tidying some things on the table.

'Oh yes you do. What on earth is wrong with you, Lucy? Are you going to spend the rest of your days mooning over Robert? He was a first-class scoundrel who double-crossed you, so forget him and get on with your life.'

'I am getting on with my life,' she defended. 'We both are, if it comes to that.'

'That's utter rubbish and you know it,' Sam said angrily. 'You're not happy living here in a couple of rooms with only me for company. You have no friends; you earn your money charring. Heavens above, Lucy, you are worth far more than that. You make me feel a burden; it's as if I'm dragging you down and holding you back.'

'Why should you feel like that?' she asked in surprise. 'You're earning enough to pay your share. I would be much worse off if we weren't living together.'

'So you want to spend your life like this, do you, with no future to look forward to and struggling to make ends meet?'

'How else should I spend it?' she sighed.

'Well, you could have accepted Barry's proposal. He'd make a good husband.'

'Look, Sam, can you get it into your thick head that I don't love Barry?' Lucy told him angrily.

'No, you are still wearing your heart on your sleeve for Robert,' he said contemptuously.

'I don't dwell on what is all in the past,' she told him stiffly. 'I wish I could say the same about you.'

'What do you mean by that?'

'You still feel angry and hurt by what Patsy did; betraying you and having another man's baby.'

'And who was that other man?' he sneered. 'It was your boyfriend. The man you were on the verge of marrying – and would have done, if it hadn't been for the accident.'

Lucy walked over and put her arm round Sam's

shoulders. 'Don't let's keep going over it and stirring up the past. We've had some bad fortune but it's time to forget all about that. We've got each other and I'm happy enough if you are.'

He stared at her for a moment, his chin jutting out, then he relaxed and returned her hug. 'Don't take any notice of me. I'm happy enough and grateful for all you've done for me; it's just that I hate to see your life slipping by unfulfilled.'

'It's not. I'm far too busy to think about what might have been.'

'You're going to miss Berky. You haven't made any friends at all since we've been living here,' he said changing the conversation.

'No, and I didn't make any when we were living in Hans Court,' she reminded him. 'I think I am a loner; I'm happy enough with my own company and yours.'

Almost overnight, Lucy found that her life had suddenly taken a downward spiral. Joe and Madge Black, the middle-aged couple who moved into Berky's rooms, were intent on changes.

Lucy's first encounter with them was on their first Friday there. They didn't wait for her to take the rent money down but Madge came up to collect it. She was a thin, scrawny woman with frizzy red hair, green eyes and a very sharp voice.

When Lucy handed over the five shillings and sixpence, Madge held it in the palm of her hand, frowning. 'What's this?' she demanded. 'You've got three rooms, so it should be six shillings.'

'No, one of the rooms is only a box room; Berky agreed we need only pay one shilling and sixpence a week for it.'

'Berky's dead. We're in charge now. My husband said it was six shillings, so that's what I want.'

Lucy didn't like her tone or her attitude. 'My agreement is to pay five shillings and sixpence,' she said firmly and closed the door.

The Blacks were not content to leave it at that. Within minutes Joe Black was hammering on their door. Lucy almost felt afraid to answer it but knowing that Sam would be home at any minute and that Joe Black would undoubtedly face him with it, she felt she ought to deal with the matter.

The moment she opened the door Joe Black stepped inside. A big, untidy-looking man with receding dark greasy hair and a florid face with small dark eyes, he was an imposing figure.

His breath smelt of beer and involuntarily Lucy stepped backwards as he pushed past her into the living room.

'What's all this nonsense, trying to cheat us out of sixpence a week?' he demanded.

'I am not doing anything of the sort. The rent we fixed with Berky was for five shillings and sixpence a week.'

'That's your story. What proof is there of that now that Berky's dead and gone?'

'I'm hardly likely to lie to you over sixpence, now am I?' Lucy said hotly.

'I'm not so sure. You certainly don't want to pay it.'

'The room isn't worth two shillings a week. There's only space for a single bed in there. It was Berky's box room.'

'In that case, get your things out of there right this minute and we'll let it to someone else,' Joe Black ordered.

'I can't do that. It's my brother's room. I can't move his things without his permission.'

Joe Black chewed on the ends of his straggly moustache thoughtfully. 'Perhaps you'd better let me see the room for myself and just possibly I might reconsider.'

Reluctantly, Lucy took him along the passage to the small room at the far end. It was so small that there was barely room for the two of them to stand side by side once they were in there. As he turned to leave Joe pushed hard against her and Lucy found herself falling backwards on to the bed.

With a loud belly laugh he put out a hand to pull her upright. 'I suppose that's one way of making me agree not to change the rent,' he leered.

Lucy bit down on her lip to stop herself from saying anything as she drew back and shook his hand away from her arm, sickened by his suggestion and also by his beery breath.

'I'll take the five shillings and sixpence this week but I'll have to think it over and decide what to do before next rent day,' he told her as he ambled off back downstairs to his own rooms.

Chapter Seventeen

Even though Lucy was still shaking with fright when Sam arrived home he didn't at first seem to believe her when she told him about her encounter with Joe Black.

A few days later, however, when she answered the door to find Joe Black standing there and he forced his way past her and into their living room, Sam became aware of what a dangerous character he was.

Once again Joe Black was demanding they pay six shillings a week and his manner was so threatening that in the end Sam had no option but to accept his terms.

As soon as he had gone Sam agreed with Lucy that there was no doubt about it but they couldn't stay there any longer than they absolutely had to.

'The trouble is we can't afford to move, not right now. Paying him another sixpence a week is going to be bad enough, but if we want to move, then we will probably have to find a month's rent up front for the new place.'

'We didn't when we moved here,' Sam reminded her. 'But of course Berky was one in a million in every way.'

'Yes, Berky was an exception to the rule, wasn't she?' Lucy sighed. 'I doubt if we will ever find another landlady who was as good to us as she was.'

'True enough but, nevertheless, we don't want

to go on living here, not now that the Blacks have taken over the running of things. He seems to have designs on you and I don't like that; I don't think you're safe.'

'Don't worry, now that I know what he's like I'll be on my guard and make certain that I avoid any compromising situations with him.'

'Make sure you do. It won't be easy because I think he's a cunning old bastard and it would appear that his mind is made up about you,' Sam told her grimly.

'I'll try and find more work somewhere,' Lucy said thoughtfully. 'I have a couple of hours before I need to go to the hotel each morning and I'm usually finished there by three in the afternoon.'

'You have the cleaning and shopping to do for us, so don't go taking on too much other work,' Sam warned. 'You need some time for yourself.'

'No, I don't. If I wandered around the shops, I'd only spend money we haven't got.' Lucy chuckled.

'Window shopping is about all you ever do apart from buying food,' Sam said a trifle bitterly. 'It's a hard life for you, Lucy; you should have money in your pocket to spend on clothes and things like that, not work all day, every day like you do.' He shook his head sadly. 'I do wish you hadn't turned Barry Mason down; you would have had a much better life if you'd married him.'

'We'll have a much better life if I get some more work or else a better job with more pay,' Lucy told him crisply. 'Don't worry; we'll get away from here just as soon as ever we can.'

'You're not the only one who will be scheming,'

181

Sam promised. 'I'll see if I can think of some way of earning more money as well.'

Sam was as good as his word. The following week he announced that he had decided that in future he was not only going to work in the mornings but also see if he could expand his business. By working in the early part of the afternoon as well he hoped to entice people who arrived on the midday ferry boats and who had come over to Liverpool on business or to do some shopping to have their shoes cleaned.

On the Monday he had only three customers but, remembering how slow things had been the first time he'd started shining shoes, he was determined to stick it out for the rest of the week in the hope that things would improve.

On the Wednesday morning Lucy reminded Sam before she went off to her charring job that it was 12 July and Orangeman's Day.

'There will probably be huge crowds everywhere as well as men marching and a band, so it might be better if you stayed at home today.'

'The more people there are out and about the more chances I get of doing good business,' he argued.

'That may be true enough, but remember things can get nasty. The marches often end up in fights between the prozzies and the cat'licks before the day is out.'

Reluctantly, Sam agreed to take the day off but by the middle of the day he was so tired of being cooped up in their rooms and by the fact that he was losing money by not being at his pitch that he decided to go out.

The moment he reached the top of Water Street Sam found himself in a dense crowd of men, women and children as they waited for the marching bands that were making their way through Liverpool and were now heading for the Pier Head.

The crowd began shouting and waving flags and banners as the sound of the band approaching became louder and people began to surge forward to try and be the first to catch a glimpse of them.

Amongst the crowd were the two boys who had taunted Sam when he and Lucy had lived in Hans Court and the moment they spotted Sam they began shouting out rude names at him and taunting him about being a cripple.

As the band and the marchers came into view the crowds shuffled back on to the pavement to let them pass by. The two boys seized the opportunity to come up behind Sam and as he tried to move backwards they jostled him so hard that he stumbled forward right into the middle of the road and ended up directly in the path of the band, causing complete chaos as the men stumbled against each other desperately trying to keep their footing so as not to fall and damage their instruments.

Although they did their best to avoid Sam who was now lying prone on the roadway, one of the men accidentally trod on him breaking his right arm. The man marching immediately behind fell over the pair of them and landed directly on top of Sam and the impact left Sam unconscious.

The police who were escorting the marchers were immediately on the scene. None of the band or marchers was seriously hurt but an ambulance was called to take Sam to hospital. He was not only unconscious but also appeared to be having great difficulty breathing and they suspected that one or more of his ribs may have been damaged.

When, late in the afternoon, Lucy returned from her midday washing-up stint at the hotel which had taken far longer than usual due to all the extra customers they'd had that day, she felt annoyed when she found that Sam had not heeded her warning and had gone out.

Even so, she still wasn't unduly worried until a couple of hours later when he still hadn't put in an appearance and the meal she had prepared was still waiting to be dished up.

In the end she decided she might as well eat hers and warm his up again when he did get home.

As time passed and Sam still hadn't turned up she began to be seriously concerned. She had no idea where to start looking for him. She felt cross because he had ignored her advice about going out but, nevertheless, felt concerned in case he had become involved in some kind of trouble. However, she was reluctant to go to the police.

As the evening began to draw on Lucy's feeling of unease mounted. She kept remembering the rowdy crowds there had been in Liverpool earlier on in the day, waving flags and banners, and which she'd seen near the Exchange that afternoon when she'd been coming home. If, despite her warning, Sam had gone to his pitch as usual, then he might well have been involved in an incident of some kind.

Putting on her hat and coat Lucy decided to walk towards the Pier Head in case Sam had taken a walk that way first as he did every day now when he went off to work. If there was no sign of him, she told herself, then she would go the police station and explain that he was missing and that she was worried about him.

Before she even turned into Water Street she saw a placard outside one of the newsagent's in Scotland Road and as she read the headline her heart began to thud faster:
MARCHING TRAGEDY – YOUNG MAN SERIOUSLY INJURED.

Instinctively, Lucy knew it was Sam. It wasn't the police station she needed to go to but the hospital.

A thousand and one thoughts about what might have happened to Sam went through her mind as she hurried there. If only he had listened to her and had stayed at home today as she'd asked him to do, but it was too late to think about that. All she could hope for now was that he wasn't too badly hurt.

When she enquired at the hospital reception desk they informed her that they had no record of anyone by the name of Sam Collins being admitted.

As she turned away Lucy felt a wave of relief sweep over her. She'd been silly to panic; of course it wasn't Sam who'd been involved. By now Sam was safe at home and wondering where on earth she was at this time of night.

185

She was almost at the door when the receptionist called out, asking her to wait a moment.

'That chap you were asking about; how old was he?'

'Why do you ask?'

'Well, there was a young man brought in late this afternoon; he'd been involved in a scuffle of some sort with the marchers. The melee made headline news in the *Echo* tonight. He's still unconscious and we don't know his name, so I was just wondering...'

The woman stopped speaking as she saw the colour drain from Lucy's face. 'Oh, heavens, you're not going to faint, are you?' she gasped as she came round from her side of the reception counter and grabbed hold of Lucy's arm.

Lucy shook her head and took a deep breath. 'I'm all right. I think it might be my brother. Can I see him?'

'Sit down on a chair for a minute while I let the ward sister know what you've just told me,' the receptionist said as she went back to her desk.

Lucy tried to control her impatience as she sat waiting for what seemed to be an interminable time. When the receptionist finally came over and said she would take her along to the ward, Lucy found she was shaking so much that she could hardly stand up.

She tried to keep her wits about her as the sister asked questions about her brother's age, the colour of his hair and whether or not he was likely to have been in the Water Street area that afternoon.

'If you let me see him, then I can tell you right

186

away if it is my brother Sam,' Lucy told her.

The sister frowned uncertainly. She scrutinised Lucy for a moment before agreeing that she could do so.

'He's still unconscious,' she warned as she led Lucy towards a screened-off bed in one corner of the ward.

'Are his injuries very serious?' Lucy asked, her dark eyes anxious.

'I'm afraid you will have to wait until you have verified whether or not it is your brother before we begin to discuss his case,' the sister told her crisply.

As she drew back one of the curtains and indicated to Lucy that she was to approach the bedside, Lucy let out a gasp of distress. There was no mistaking that it was Sam's broad, stocky build beneath the covering sheet and even though his face was badly lacerated and there was a green shield over one of his eyes, she recognised him immediately.

'Oh, Sam, whatever has happened to you this time?' Lucy whispered, reaching out to take his hand even though the arm lying above the bedclothes was heavily bandaged.

'Careful, careful. Please don't touch him,' the sister warned, pulling her away.

'He is still alive, though, isn't he?' Lucy gasped in a trembling voice.

'Yes. Of course he is.'

'Then why doesn't he wake up and speak to me?' Lucy questioned when Sam had made no response whatsoever when she said his name.

'He has been unconscious ever since he was

brought in. We are not quite certain about the extent of his injuries. There is a possibility that as well as severe bruising he may have sustained several broken ribs because he is having considerable difficulty in breathing.'

'Can't you do anything for him? Surely there must be some way you can help him?'

'He is under constant supervision. There is no point in you staying. I suggest you go home and try and get some rest and come back again tomorrow afternoon.'

Lucy nodded; she was unable to speak because she was too choked by tears.

She knew it was useless to argue or ask for any more information. It was the same pattern as it had been after her parents had been involved in the car accident all over again. That time, though, she'd had Robert to support her; this time she was completely on her own.

Chapter Eighteen

As she left the hospital Lucy found a gaggle of reporters waiting outside and the moment they spotted her they surged forward, all of them eager for her story.

As she tried to walk past them they barricaded her path bombarding her with so many questions that she stood there dazed and trembling and shaking her head in bewilderment because many of their questions didn't even make sense.

'Was Sam Collins your husband or your brother?'

'Was he the shoeshine chap who had a stand in Water Street?'

'Where do you live, Miss Collins?'

'Are you one of them cat'licks?'

'Why did Sam Collins step out in front of the marchers?'

'Was he trying to stop the Orange Day parade?'

'Are you Irish or a Liverpudlian?'

Lucy clamped her hands over her ears to shut out their probing voices. When one of them moved closer and grabbed hold of her arm, she cried out in fright.

'Leave the young lady alone.' The voice was angry yet somehow familiar and Lucy looked around, startled, as a tall, broad-shouldered man dressed in grey flannels, a white shirt and a light-weight sports jacket rushed to her side and freed her from the reporter's grip.

As Lucy looked up to thank him she stopped in surprise. 'Robert!' she gasped.

For a moment they stared at each other, oblivious of the crowd. Then Robert took her by the arm and led her away down the road, looking back angrily when one of the reporters began to follow them.

'Come on, let's go somewhere quiet. You need a cup of tea or a coffee to settle your nerves,' he told her.

Lucy felt as if she was in a dream as Robert steered her towards a nearby milk bar. She said nothing until a steaming cup of coffee was in front of her and when she took her first sip it was as if her senses returned.

She stared across the table at Robert, wondering how on earth he had been there and what she would have done if he hadn't rescued her from the persistent reporters.

'Are you feeling better now?' he asked as he sipped his own coffee.

'Yes, much better.' She gave a wry smile. 'Thank you for rescuing me, I don't know what I would have done if you hadn't stepped in.'

He shrugged his broad shoulders. 'Glad to be able to help. It's a long time since I've seen you. In fact, I wasn't sure it was you until I heard some of the questions they were asking you. When they called you Miss Collins, it suddenly dawned on me that it must have been Sam who was involved in that accident because one of them mentioned that the chap injured was slightly crippled.'

Lucy flinched at the word cripple; it was one she hated hearing applied to Sam.

'So where are you and Sam living now and what are you doing these days?' Robert went on.

Lucy picked up her coffee cup. She felt uncomfortable about telling him that she was reduced to cleaning offices and doing washing up in a hotel kitchen.

'What about you? Are you still working at Carter's Cars?' she asked, trying to divert his interest from her.

'Yes, I'm still there. It seems a lifetime ago that you were working there as well,' he added with a grimace.

'Yes, and now you are a married man with a young child,' Lucy murmured trying to keep the sadness from her voice but she felt a lump in her throat as she said it.

'I married Patsy,' Robert said quickly, 'but she died in childbirth,' he added sadly.

'Oh, I didn't know,' Lucy said awkwardly. 'What about the baby, did it survive? Is it a girl or a boy?'

'A little girl called Anna. She was born on the thirtieth of July; she's almost a year old now.'

'Oh!' Lucy stared at him blankly. 'I never knew anything about that. I'm so sorry to hear that Patsy died,' she added in a low voice. 'How awful for you.'

'Patsy's mother was terribly cut up about it and she refused to have anything to do with the baby,' Robert went on in a matter-of-fact voice. 'She and Patsy's father moved up north to a village outside Edinburgh about six months ago.'

'So you are still living with your mother and she's bringing up the baby,' Lucy commented.

Robert shook his head. 'You obviously haven't heard about my mam either.' His face tightened. 'She died before Christmas from consumption.'

'Oh Robert! That's terrible news. I didn't even know that your mother was ill.'

'None of us did. It was very sudden. She was only really ill for a few weeks. Dad took it very badly. He couldn't bear to stay in the house any longer after the funeral, so he's gone to live with his sister up near Manchester.'

'So who is looking after the baby now?'

'That's the problem. I asked the woman who moved into your old house next door if she would look after her and she seemed to be quite keen but it's not working out. She has two children of her own and twice since little Anna has been in her care there's been an accident due to their pranks and Anna has ended up in hospital.'

'Oh Robert, that's terrible; the poor little mite.'

'That's how I came to be here at the hospital today. I brought her in last night with a broken leg. They're going to keep her in for a few days to give me time to find someone else to care for her.' He hesitated, looking directly at her hopefully. 'Would you consider doing it, Lucy?'

'Me!' she gasped in astonishment. 'I can't believe that I'm hearing this, Robert. You're asking me if I would look after Patsy's baby after all that happened.'

'No, I'm sorry, I'm so desperate that I'm not thinking straight. I suppose it is out of the question; you will probably have Sam laid up for weeks to come. I haven't even asked you how he is,' he added contritely.

'Sam is still critically ill. He has a broken arm but they also think that he has some ribs broken and that has affected his breathing.'

'It sounds pretty serious. Do you know how long he will be in hospital?'

'No, I haven't any idea. They said a lot depended on whether his lungs have been damaged in any way by his broken ribs. They haven't X-rayed him yet, but will be doing so either later tonight or first thing tomorrow morning. The nurse said she hoped to be able to tell me more when I visit tomorrow.'

'So will you be here again around this time tomorrow evening? I will be coming to see little Anna, so if you're visiting Sam, then perhaps we could meet up again afterwards for a cup of coffee?'

Lucy hesitated. It had been a shock bumping into Robert and it had stirred up so many emotions that she wasn't sure if she wanted to see him again. She'd missed him so deeply when they'd first parted and meeting him again was far more distressing than she had ever imagined it would be.

'Don't worry, I won't try to cajole you into looking after little Anna,' he said grimly. 'I'm sorry about that, it was thoughtless; I should never have mentioned it in the first place.'

'I'm not too sure what time I will be coming tomorrow night,' Lucy said evasively.

'No, I understand.' He pushed back his chair and stood up. 'Do you want me to walk you home?' he asked as she preceded him out of the milk bar.

Lucy shook her head. 'No. Thanks for the coffee. It was just what I needed but now I'd like time to think over what's happened to Sam,' she said, attempting a smile.

'I hope you find he's much better when you visit him tomorrow,' Robert said as they stood for a moment outside on the pavement. Then, with a brief nod of his head, he turned and walked off.

Lucy remained standing there, feeling desolate as she watched his tall, broad-shouldered figure disappear into the distance. She wanted to call out to him to stop but felt that it would be foolish to do so because it would be opening up the old wound all over again.

193

Lucy couldn't put Robert out of her mind as she walked home; she kept thinking about Patsy's baby, Anna, and wondering how on earth Robert was going to manage to take care of her. Even though she felt sorry for the little mite, the thought of looking after the child sent shudders through her.

She didn't think she could bear recognising features and perhaps even mannerisms that could be attributed to either Patsy or Robert as the little girl grew up. It would be like a knife turning constantly in her heart.

She had loved Robert so much that when she found out that, unknown to either her or Sam, he'd been carrying on with Patsy, she'd felt betrayed and bitterly hurt. She knew that Sam felt much the same about Patsy's behaviour.

He'd always known Patsy liked to flirt, but he'd always laughed about it and said that he knew it was never serious because she always claimed she only did it for fun. Sam had always believed her because he loved her and trusted her. He'd even accepted her explanation that she had only been visiting Percy Carter after the bonfire incident because it meant getting time off from work.

What made it even more despicable was that Sam had been so worried at the time because he knew that it might be quite a long time before he could complete his apprenticeship because of the state of his hands.

Her doubts about looking after Anna didn't have anything to do with all this, Lucy reminded herself. That was all in the past and until she had bumped into Robert today she had managed to banish it to the back of her mind most of the time.

The reason she was so unsure about helping him was that a child needed love and she didn't feel she could give that to Patsy's baby, even though Robert was the father. Perhaps it was because Robert was the father, she mused unhappily.

She'd had such high hopes and plans about the family she and Robert would have, and the sort of home they would live in. There would be a boy for him and a girl for her. She sighed. She'd never make plans again.

It sometimes seemed to her that dreams weren't meant to come true; in fact, that it was the opposite. She'd never thought that one day she'd have to go out cleaning offices and trying to make every penny she earned do the work of two.

At least she had her full health and strength to do that, she reflected as she reached Horatio Street. Poor Sam didn't even have that, not since the car accident, and now this second accident was bound to make his life more difficult than ever.

That was another reason why she was feeling so guilty about turning down Robert's request. If they moved back to Priory Terrace it would give Sam a far better life although she was worried about how some of the old neighbours might treat them seeing that they had left under a cloud.

Ever since Joe Black had moved in to Horatio Street, they'd been planning to move as soon as they could afford to do so, but now that Sam would probably not be able to work again for several weeks at least, they'd have to forget all about doing that, Lucy reflected as she let herself into the house.

Before she could reach the stairs to go up to her rooms, Joe Black came out of the kitchen. He was wearing only a singlet and although a cigarette was dangling from his lips he looked as though he was about to go to bed.

'Aah, the wanderer returns,' he quipped. 'The rozzers have been here twice this evening looking for you,' he leered, coming closer and breathing beer fumes and tobacco smoke into her face. 'So what sort of trouble are you in now?'

'They probably wanted to speak to my brother, not me, about the accident he was involved in with the marchers, but I'm afraid he's in hospital.'

'So that means you're going to be here all on your own, does it?' Joe Black smirked. 'Well, if you should get lonely and find you can't sleep, then you know where to find me. Perhaps you'd like me to come upstairs with you now and keep you company,' he said suggestively, trying to put an arm round her.

Lucy pulled back quickly. 'I'd like to go up to my room, so will you please stand aside and let me pass,' she said stiffly.

'Oh come on,' he held on to her arm so tightly that she couldn't free herself. 'There's no hurry; no one is up there waiting for you.'

Lucy jerked her arm free and scuttled up the stairs as fast as she could. Once inside her room she shut the door and stood with her back against it. She felt so afraid that she wished she had let Robert come back with her.

It was too late to think like that, she told herself as she pushed one of the chairs up against the door to try and stop anyone coming into the room. Robert didn't even know where she lived.

Perhaps, if they happened to meet the following evening, she ought to let him walk her home; if Joe Black saw them together then maybe he would leave her alone in future.

Chapter Nineteen

The following weeks had a nightmare quality about them for Lucy. Each time she visited Sam she hoped to bump into Robert, but she was never fortunate enough to do so. She even began to wonder if she had imagined their meeting.

Finally, in desperation, she asked one of the nurses if she knew whether a small child called Anna Tanner had been a patient there.

The nurse promised to make some enquiries and eventually told Lucy that there had been a little girl of that name but she'd now gone home.

Sam was making very slow progress. Each time she visited him Lucy hoped that they would say he could come home. She hated living at Horatio Street without him because of Joe Black.

She often wondered whether she should mention his unpleasant behaviour to his wife, but Madge Black was always so hostile towards her that she didn't think it would do a lot of good.

It was the middle of August before Sam was fit

enough to be discharged from hospital.

He had lost quite a lot of weight and he looked far from well. His threadbare jacket hung from his shoulders as if it was suspended on a hanger and his grey trousers flapped against his thin legs as he walked.

A crowd of curious neighbours gathered in Horatio Street as the taxicab bringing them home from the hospital drew up. Several people called out to ask what was going on as Sam, leaning heavily on Lucy's arm for support, was helped out of the taxi.

Hearing the commotion, Madge Black came to the front door and stood there, arms akimbo, and, for one minute, Lucy thought she wasn't going to let them in.

'What's all this about, then?' she asked aggressively. 'He's not had a skinful, has he?'

'No, Mrs Black, my brother isn't drunk; I'm bringing him home from hospital.'

Madge Black's mouth tightened and she made no move to stand to one side so that they could enter. 'Been in a fight and got himself beaten up, has he?' she questioned.

'No, of course he hasn't.'

'My Joe told you when we moved in here that we didn't like having people who cause trouble living in the house.'

'My brother's hardly trouble. And he's not likely to spread a broken arm and a lacerated face to anyone, now is he?' Lucy retorted sharply. 'Furthermore, he wouldn't be in this state if it wasn't for those two young hooligans who live in Hans Court who pushed him into the roadway.'

Madge Black's mouth dropped open. 'Gerr-away! Are you talking about young Tommy and Billy Sparks?'

'Yes, I am,' Lucy told her.

'Well, they're friends of ours and this is the first I've heard that they had anything to do with what happened at the Orange Day parade,' Madge Black commented, her eyes narrowing.

'I'm quite sure you know all about it,' Lucy stated, struggling to keep her voice steady. 'There was a full account in the *Echo*. Now, if you'll let us pass, I'd like to take my brother up to our rooms so that he can have a rest.'

Although she put a brave face on things and tried to remain calm, inwardly Lucy was trembling as she heard the babble of comments that broke out all around them.

Some of the people were condemning the action of the two boys; others were siding with Madge Black about sick people spreading their illnesses.

'If your brother isn't well enough to stand on his own two feet, then he should still be in hospital,' someone stated.

'Made a right mess of his face; have a job finding anyone to take him on when he looks like that.'

'He hasn't got much to say for himself,' one woman commented. 'If you ask me, he's got more bum than brains.'

'No, he's right enough in the head even though he's a cripple; the trouble is, he's uppity, the same as she is,' Madge Black pronounced. 'They think themselves too good for round here. Don't know why they came to live here in the first place, not unless they're running away from the rozzers.'

Sam said nothing but Lucy could feel him shaking as he clung to her arm and she wasn't sure whether it was from weakness or anger because of what was being said about them both.

Determinedly she pushed past Madge Black and, ignoring the many remarks called out after them, helped Sam down the narrow passage and up the stairs.

The window of their living room overlooked the street outside and for a good half-hour afterwards a bunch of women were gathered there. Lucy could hear them talking volubly either to each other or to Madge Black who was still out on the doorstep, but Lucy shut her ears to their carping comments.

In the days that followed Sam was so weak and despondent that Lucy was concerned about leaving him on his own for very long. If only they could turn the clock back to when they were still living in Priory Terrace, she thought over and over again. In those days she could have asked one or other of the neighbours to pop in and keep an eye on him while she was out at work.

Even there, she reflected, things had changed. In the old days Robert's mother or even Patsy's mother, June, would have been willing to come in and make him a cup of tea and then stay for few minutes to have a chat and make sure he was all right.

There was no one in Horatio Street whom she could ask to do that, not even Madge Black. Perhaps she should have tried to make friends when they'd first arrived with some of the others who had rooms in the same house or even people living in the street instead of avoiding them. It was the same at Hans Court – they just didn't fit in.

Sam needed so much attention that Lucy found it was impossible to cope with both her jobs. There wasn't time after her office cleaning job finished to come home and make Sam a hot drink because she now went straight to the hotel kitchen to prepare the vegetables each day before she started the washing-up.

When Lucy explained her predicament to Martha West, the woman in charge of the kitchen, and asked if she could go back to simply coming at midday to do the washing-up, she was most indignant.

'I'm not going to be messed about like that,' she stated. 'If you can't do both then there are plenty of other girls who can.'

Lucy tried to protest but Martha West wasn't interested and at the end of the week Lucy found herself dismissed.

Reduced to only the money from her office cleaning Lucy found that she was dipping into their precious savings; the money they had both worked so hard to put aside so that they could move out of Horatio Street.

She didn't tell Sam but pretended that she was managing well enough and that it had been her decision to give up the hotel job so that she could spend more time with him.

He was so weak that she had insisted that he

must be the one to sleep in the larger bedroom while she made do with the pokey little box room.

The room was so stuffy that she didn't find it easy to sleep and, night after night, she lay there wondering what she could do to make things better for them both.

Sam didn't seem to be improving in any way at all. He was still pitifully thin and there were black shadows under his eyes. He looked as though he'd had no sleep for weeks yet he spent the greater part of the day in bed with his eyes closed.

When she did manage to persuade him to get up, have a wash and shave and come through into the living room, he was so listless and depressed that she was seriously worried about him.

He hadn't been outside the house since he'd come home and he never even mentioned going back to work. He blamed himself for all the bad luck they'd had and he even went as far as to say that it would have been far better if he had never recovered after the accident with the marchers.

When she tried to make light of his remarks, telling him that he'd have more energy once the weather was cooler, he said he would never feel better. He was sure that there was something terribly wrong with him and he wished he was dead.

Lucy refused to listen to such talk but, as she saw him growing weaker every day, she began to feel almost as depressed as he did. Constantly she blamed herself for not listening to his advice after their parents had been killed. She had ignored his suggestions because of her own pride. Now, she could see how very wrong she'd been

202

and wished there was some way she could put matters right.

Two weeks later, early in September, when she came home from her office cleaning, Madge Black intercepted her as she was about to go upstairs.

'There's been a well-dressed bloke here today asking after you. He looked like a debt collector; are you in some sort of scrape?' she asked inquisitively.

'No, I most certainly am not,' Lucy told her flatly.

'There's no need to be so hoity-toity,' Madge Black sniffed. 'Anyway, he's coming back later on today. He looked too well dressed to be your fancy man,' she added as she turned to go back into her own part of the house.

Her cheeks flaming, Lucy went on upstairs without answering. She had no idea at all who it could be and she racked her brains to see if there was any debt outstanding that she had overlooked but she was pretty sure there wasn't, not unless it had something to do with Priory Terrace and she felt sure that had been forgotten.

Lucy was clearing away the remains of their midday meal when there was a rap on the door and she heard Madge Black shout, 'Keep on knocking, I know she's in there.'

'Robert!' Lucy gave a gasp of amazement when she opened the door and saw who was standing there. He was wearing a lightweight grey suit and he looked so smart that she could understand why Mrs Black had thought he might be a debt collector.

Her hand went up to smooth down her hair and

she was conscious of how bedraggled she must look because she was still wearing her oldest skirt and blouse which she always put on in the morning when she went out to her cleaning job. The look on Robert's face as he looked around their room registered his surprise at what they had been reduced to and she felt uncomfortable.

'Hello, Lucy. May I come in?'

'Yes, of course.' His warm smile made her heart beat faster. She opened the door wider and at the same time, to hide her nervousness, called out, 'Sam, you'll never guess who's come to see us.'

Sam didn't even bother to reply; he simply glanced towards the door and, when he saw who it was, he looked away again as if not interested.

'Perhaps you'd like a cup of tea, Robert?' Lucy asked quickly, in an attempt to cover up the uncomfortable moment caused by Sam's hostility. She wished now that she had told Sam that she had met Robert at the hospital, but as she hadn't seen Robert again, she'd thought it was pointless to do so, especially as Sam was so ill.

'No, not really.' Robert removed his cap and twisted it awkwardly in his hands.

'Do sit down. You may as well have that cuppa as it's freshly made because we were just going to have one.'

He nodded and did as she asked. He was obviously as much on edge as they were and Lucy hoped the tea might help to put them all at their ease.

'How are things now? Is Anna quite well again?'

'Her leg has healed but otherwise things are pretty much the same as when I spoke to you at the hospital,' he murmured as Lucy put the cup on the table in front of him. 'That's why I'm here, really; there's something I want to ask you.'

'Well, I might have known that you hadn't come here to ask us how we were getting on,' Sam muttered.

'How did you know where we were living?' Lucy asked, ignoring her brother's comments.

'It wasn't easy.' He smiled. 'They wouldn't give me your address at the hospital so I checked up at the *Echo* about what happened to Sam. I managed to speak to the chap who'd reported the incident and to persuade him to tell me where you were living,' Robert told her.

'Bloody well taken you long enough to come; that all happened a couple of months ago,' Sam stated.

Robert didn't answer; he took a mouthful of tea and was silent for such a long time that Lucy became both impatient and uneasy because she suspected what it was that he wanted to ask her.

Sam, too, sensed the tension. 'Come on, then; spit it out, let's hear what it is you have to say that is so important that you've taken the trouble to find us after all this time.'

Robert took a deep breath. 'I've already mentioned to Lucy the problem I'm having looking after Anna. I saw her the day you were admitted to hospital, Sam. Perhaps I should explain,' Robert said awkwardly. 'You knew Patsy was expecting–'

'Too bloody true I did,' Sam cut in. 'You pinched my girlfriend and now I suppose you've come to tell us that you want us to be bloody godparents to your kid.'

'It's a little girl and she's called Anna,' Lucy told Sam quickly. 'She was born several months after we left Priory Terrace, but Patsy died in childbirth.'

Instinctively, Lucy rose and went over and put an arm round Sam then drew back as he roughly shook her hand away.

'Is that all you wanted to tell us?' Sam demanded.

'No. It's not everything,' Robert said in a low voice. He looked directly at Lucy, 'Can we go somewhere private to talk? I think I'm upsetting Sam.'

'Don't worry about me,' Sam said in a bitter voice. 'You didn't do so when you stole my girlfriend from me while I was lying ill in hospital, so why consider my feelings now?'

'Look, Sam, I'm sorry about what happened; I know how cut up you must feel, but I've really come to talk to Lucy and to ask her to do me a favour, not to start a row with you.'

'Ask Lucy to do you a favour? You've got a bloody nerve. You jilted my sister and now you come here asking her to do you a favour! Who the hell do you think you are?'

Lucy waved both her hands between the two of them. 'Shush!' she ordered her brother. 'I bumped into Robert when you were in hospital. He was visiting Anna who had a broken leg and he told me then about the hard time he was having bringing her up. The woman who moved into our old house was looking after her while he was at work but she has children of her own and it seems they play rather roughly with Anna.

Now, can we listen to what Robert has to say?'

'It is about Anna,' Robert agreed. 'I asked you then if you could look after her for me; help me to bring her up. Now I'm not simply asking you but begging you to consider doing so, Lucy.'

Sam stared at him for a moment in stunned silence. 'Can't your mother or Patsy's mother do that?' he asked in a strained voice.

'Lucy obviously hasn't told you that my mother is dead. She died before Christmas from consumption.'

'Surely, though, Patsy's mother–'

'June Tanner was so upset when Patsy died that she wouldn't have anything at all to do with the baby. Patsy's father was pretty cut up about it as well; she was their only child. In the end they decided to move right away from Liverpool to try and make a fresh start and forget all about what had happened. They were adamant that they didn't want anything at all to do with Anna.'

'That's so unnatural,' Lucy protested sadly. 'They're her grandparents.'

'I know, I was counting on their help but that's the way it is,' Robert said grimly. 'I don't want to put Anna up for adoption but I can't raise her on my own.'

'I do understand, Robert, but I couldn't possibly take care of a baby, not here, even if I wanted to do so,' Lucy told him. 'It's a terrible place to live; I'm sure you wouldn't want your child growing up here and mixing with the children who live here. Anyway,' she went on quickly before he could answer, 'I have my hands full looking after Sam. This last accident has put him right back; so far he isn't able to even consider going back to work.'

'I wasn't thinking of bringing Anna here,' Robert said quickly. 'Like I said before when I mentioned it to you, I thought you could both come and live in my house.'

'Move back to Priory Terrace?' Lucy's heart beat faster. It was what she had dreamed about doing, but not like this.

'I'm living there on my own. My dad has gone to live with his sister in Yorkshire. He says he can't stand having a young child in the house,' he added ruefully.

Lucy shook her head uncertainly. 'I'm not sure if that would work, Robert; you'll have to give me time to think about it and to talk it over with Sam.'

'It would be a much better life for both of you,' Robert persisted as he looked around the shabby room.

Lucy clenched her hands into tight fists at her side. 'I'm not at all sure.'

Robert looked bemused. 'Why ever not, Lucy?'

'I'm not sure that I could take to a child that was yours and Patsy's,' she said with a tremor in her voice.

'Please, Lucy. Give it some further thought ... for Anna's sake,' Robert pleaded. 'I know I acted foolishly by having a fling with Patsy but I never meant to hurt you. I acted on impulse because at the time I was so frustrated because you never seemed to have any time to spare for me.'

Lucy wiped away a tear from the corner of her eye. 'I don't know, Robert, I really don't know,' she murmured indecisively.

'You heard what she said, now bugger off,' Sam told him angrily, struggling out of his chair and pulling open the door.

Chapter Twenty

In the days that followed Lucy could think of nothing but Robert and little Anna. It was obvious from what Robert had told her that the child wasn't being looked after properly and she couldn't help feeling that she ought to do something to help. After all, she told herself, it wasn't little Anna's fault; the poor little mite hadn't asked to be born and she certainly wasn't to blame for the past indiscretions of her parents.

She wished she could talk about the situation with Sam, but he refused to discuss it further. Remembering the anger in his voice when he had shown Robert the door, she was quite sure that he wouldn't want to be involved in any way with Patsy's child.

The problem was going round and round in her mind as she left Old Hall Street and started to walk home. She almost jumped out of her skin when she heard someone calling out her name, and she turned to find Robert hurrying to catch up with her.

'What are you doing here? How did you know where I worked?' She knew she was gabbling almost incoherently but she was worried in case he had been round to Horatio Street and she knew that would upset Sam yet again.

'I managed to find out where you worked – never mind how, but it wasn't from Sam,' he told her hurriedly as he saw the anxious look on her face. 'That's not important. I wanted to get you on your own so that I could talk to you and find out if you had managed to come to any sort of decision yet about looking after Anna.'

Lucy bit down on her lower lip. 'It's too difficult, Robert; I don't feel that I can do it.'

'Look, let's find a milk bar and have a drink and talk this over,' he pleaded.

'No, I can't.' Lucy shook her head emphatically. 'I must get back. Sam will be up and dressed by now and he waits for me to come home to get his breakfast.'

'Ten minutes isn't going to make much difference,' Robert insisted, taking her firmly by the arm and heading towards Tithebarn Street. 'We'll find a milk bar on the way back to Horatio Street.'

The feel of Robert's hand holding her arm sent a shiver through Lucy. Her knees felt weak and she felt powerless to argue. She couldn't stop thinking about how many nights she had lain awake remembering the touch of his hands on her body, his lips pressed against hers; the sweet words of love being murmured in her ear and now, once again, they were walking side by side.

Silently she let him take command and it wasn't until they were seated inside the milk bar and the coffee was on the table in front of them that again she tried to explain her feelings about bringing up Anna after what had happened between them all.

Robert listened in silence, his eyes studying her face, nodding now and then as he listened to her reasons. 'I understand what you are saying but I am sure you wouldn't let it make any difference to the way you cared for Anna.'

'I'm not sure,' Lucy said worriedly.

'Perhaps we should give it a try,' he suggested hopefully.

'It wouldn't be fair on Sam to do that; not without him agreeing, because he would think you were offering us charity by letting us move back to Priory Terrace,' she said lamely, staring down into her coffee and avoiding Robert's gaze.

'Then talk to him about it.'

'He refuses to discuss it and I don't want to upset him,' she added uneasily.

'I do understand,' Robert said gravely. 'Look, if it would make matters easier for you, I am quite willing to move out of the house and live somewhere else. I'm earning good money so I can afford to do that.'

'Even if you did that it would still be so complicated because it would be such a long-term commitment for me to make,' Lucy murmured, shaking her head.

'I will take care of the rent and all the other household expenses as well as paying you for your time and trouble, so you'll be better off in every way,' Robert went on quickly. 'I promise you that I will arrange it all so that you don't even have to see me or speak to me unless you want to do so for any reason.'

'That all sounds fine but what about your visits to see Anna? As her father, surely you would

211

want to see her regularly so that you could watch her growing up.'

'True.' Robert nodded thoughtfully. 'Even so, if my coming to the house to do that would upset Sam and make things difficult for you, then I am willing to meet you and Anna somewhere right away from Priory Terrace.'

'No,' Lucy shook her head, 'that might be all right at the moment while Anna is too small to understand, but what about when she is old enough to know what is going on? Don't you think she would think it odd that she is taken to meet this strange man called Daddy every week and that it is always in the park or somewhere like that and that he never comes to the house?'

Robert shrugged. 'I don't know, you are probably right about that, but surely we can work something out. Once Sam is back to full health and starts to make a new life for himself he may not feel so antagonistic towards me. Remember, Lucy, in time Sam might even want to get married and have his own home.'

'So then you would feel you were free to come and visit Anna whenever you wanted to do so. You might even want to move back into your house again?'

'Lucy, I can't think that far ahead. Let's deal with what is happening at this very moment. I desperately need someone I can trust to look after Anna and bring her up. You need a better place to live for Sam's sake, if not for your own well-being.'

Lucy drank the remains of her coffee and made to leave but Robert laid his hand on her arm to stop her.

'I am willing to be as accommodating as I possibly can,' he said earnestly. 'You name your terms and I will gladly make any compromises that are necessary.'

Lucy looked at him with tears in her eyes. 'I don't know, Robert,' she whispered. 'I really don't know what to say. There are so many things to be considered.'

'Perhaps if you met Anna you will feel differently,' Robert murmured. 'I could bring her to meet you both next Sunday,' he suggested.

'No, no, that might upset Sam even more. I would like to see her,' she added quickly as she saw Robert's jaw tighten. 'Perhaps we could meet in St John's Gardens?'

'Very well. About two o'clock?'

Lucy could think of nothing else all week. Several times she was on the point of mentioning it to Sam and even asking him if he wanted to come along as well, but caution made her hold her tongue.

There was no point in antagonising him any more, she decided. She would meet Robert and Anna and make sure she wanted to be involved before she talked to Sam about it again.

It wasn't cold on the Sunday but it was blustery and, as she made her way to St John's Gardens, Lucy was glad she'd put on a thick jacket over her blouse and skirt.

The gardens were almost deserted and most of the summer flowers were looking tired and straggly as if they sensed that winter was not very far away.

Robert was already there. As she walked towards them Lucy's heart thudded as she looked at the child in his arms. She wasn't at all like Patsy; instead, she had straight light-brown hair like Robert and she was extremely thin.

What struck Lucy most about little Anna was that she looked very unkempt. Her face had a smear of jam around the edges of her mouth; her hair was greasy and uncombed. She was wearing odd socks and the hem of her dress had come unstitched so that it hung unevenly around her spindly little legs.

'Are you going to say hello to Lucy?' Robert prompted as they drew nearer.

'Come on, you're not shy,' he persisted as Anna shook her head and buried her face in Robert's shoulder.

'She'll come round,' he murmured as he fell into step alongside Lucy.

After a few minutes Lucy suggested that perhaps if they sat down on one of the park benches for a few minutes she would be able to talk to Anna.

They found a sheltered spot and sat down with Anna seated between them. When Lucy handed her a little bag of Dolly Mixtures she'd brought along for her, the barrier between them was broken immediately. Excitedly, Anna shared the little sweets with both of them before tucking into them herself and in next to no time was smiling happily.

Ten minutes later when, once again, they resumed their walk, Anna insisted on holding Lucy's hand as well as Robert's as she trotted along between them.

Lucy was completely captivated. There was now no doubt at all in her mind that the child needed far more love and care than she was getting at the moment and deep down she knew that she wanted to be the one to give her that.

She was tempted to take them both back to Horatio Street and let Sam see the child for himself, confident that he would be won over just as she had been. Common sense prevailed; she knew it would be better to prepare him in advance.

Before they all parted, as she hugged Anna goodbye, Lucy promised Robert that she would think it over yet again and that she would give him a definite answer in a few days.

'Sam is the stumbling block, isn't he?' Robert said harshly. 'Talk to him, Lucy. Point out the better life he could have away from that slum where you're living now. He'll never get better while you stay there, not with all that foul air and dreary surroundings. You said yourself that he is very depressed; well, you're the one who can do something about it.'

'I'll think it over and try to talk to Sam about it,' she promised. 'By the way, who is looking after Anna at the moment?'

'Jenny Wood, the woman I told you about, who is living in your old house. She has a husband, three kids and half a dozen cats and she's good hearted, but she is slapdash. The other thing that worries me is all the cats. She lets them sleep in the cot alongside Anna and I don't think that's healthy.'

215

There were tears in Lucy's eyes as she walked home after they parted. Her thoughts were in turmoil. It wasn't only the problem of placating Sam and persuading him that living back in Priory Terrace again would be far better for his health that worried her, but also that she had to convince herself that it was the right thing to do.

Robert's attitude worried her. She knew he was concerned about Anna and it was easy to see that he loved her dearly and was desperate to do the best he could for her. But never once, Lucy reflected, had he expressed any feelings for her. It was almost as if she was a mere acquaintance; someone he thought could prove helpful to him in his time of need.

Did he still have feelings for her, or were they completely dead? she wondered. She still felt an overpowering love for him and she wasn't sure she could tolerate the close relationship with Robert that taking care of Anna would involve.

She would have to talk it all over with Sam, perhaps that would help to clear her mind and help her to make a decision, she resolved as she reached home.

'You're late, I was worried in case something had happened to you,' he greeted her as she walked in.

'Sorry about that, I forgot the time. I'm pleased to see you've made yourself a cuppa.' She smiled.

'Not before time,' he said ruefully. 'I rely on you doing things for me far too much.'

Lucy didn't answer. As she busied herself making a meal for them she wondered if perhaps this might be a good time to talk about Robert's suggestion. Sam seemed to be in a better frame of mind than he usually was. Would talking about the future of Patsy's baby spoil all this? she wondered.

She waited until they had eaten then, instead of clearing away their plates and starting on the rest of the chores that were waiting to be done, she poured them both another cup of tea.

'Have you got something on your mind that you want to talk about?' Sam asked, noticing that she seemed distracted.

'Yes, as a matter of fact I have,' Lucy told him as she stirred some sugar into her tea and then pushed the sugar basin across the table towards him.

'Well, go on, then, spit it out; let's hear what it is. Has it got something to do with that business Robert came here asking you about the other day?'

'Yes, it has. I saw him again this afternoon and he wanted to know if I'd made my mind up yet about what I'm going to do.'

'And have you?'

'No, Sam, I haven't. I've given it a lot of thought but it's not simply my decision, is it?'

Sam drained his cup and pushed it to one side. 'As far as I'm concerned, it is. You do whatever you think is best.'

'That's what I'm trying to do. I want to do what's best for us as well as for him. I know how desperately you want to move away from here and moving back to Priory Terrace would give us a chance to do so.'

217

'Go and live with that bugger! You can go if you want to; I'd rather stay here until I die.'

'Patsy was as much to blame for what happened as Robert was,' Lucy reminded him quietly.

'I trusted her.'

'I know you did, and I trusted Robert, but it's all water under the bridge. We can't undo what has already happened but perhaps we can all make a fresh start by looking after Patsy's baby.'

'Robert's baby, you bloody well mean. Every day I'd have that thrust under my nose,' he muttered morosely.

'Oh Sam, it's not little Anna's fault; she didn't decide who her parents should be,' Lucy said softly. 'I'd dreamed that one day I'd have a family and that Robert would be the father of my children but it was not to be, was it? Now that I've met Anna I am convinced I could love her and care for her.'

'So you think that by sacrificing what's left of your life by looking after his kid you'll put matters right,' Sam said, his voice laced with sarcasm.

'Not altogether. I hoped it would be a fresh start for us as well. We'd get away from this horrible place, and you'd recover your health and strength.'

'Don't you think you've already made enough changes because of me? I've dragged you down into the gutter and been a load round your neck for years now.'

'Sam, don't talk like that. You're my brother and I care about you a great deal; I've only done what any sister would do.'

He ran his hands through his hair despairingly.

'I've no prospects; no hope, if it comes to that. I wish I had died in that car accident along with Mam and Dad and then it would all have been over and I wouldn't have put you through years of misery. In fact, none of this would have happened.'

'Stop right there,' Lucy told him fiercely. 'Yes, all right, I admit I have made sacrifices for you and I don't intend to see them all thrown away. If you don't want me to take on the responsibility of bringing up Patsy's child, then I won't, but don't add to all my problems by having such a defeatist attitude.'

'I'm not being defeatist, I'm being realistic,' Sam stated angrily. 'Do you really want to move back to Priory Terrace and have all our old neighbours gossiping and sniggering about us? They certainly will do when they find out that we're living with Robert and that you're caring for his kid. I thought you'd got more pride than that,' he added bitterly.

Lucy stood up and began to stack up their dirty plates and carry them away. How on earth did Sam think they were going to survive on the money she earned cleaning offices? she thought despairingly. Why couldn't he accept what Robert was suggesting as a means of paying their way and living in reasonable comfort at the same time?

As she washed up and put away the dishes they'd used she let her mind dwell on what Sam had just said. Pride might come into it for him, but did she really care about what the neighbours thought or said? Would it be any worse than having to go on living where they were and being scared of what Joe Black might do if he ever managed to get her on her own?

Perhaps if Sam saw Anna and realised what a lovely little girl she was, then he might reconsider the idea of the two of them bringing her up.

Lucy thought about it for the rest of the day and she knew she had to clear the air before she went to bed that night. She waited until evening before she broached the subject again.

Sam listened in silence as she expounded both the good points of their moving back to Priory Terrace and the drawbacks that there might be.

'Your mind's made up, isn't it?' he said dryly.

'No, I think it is what we ought to do but I won't do it unless you are in agreement.'

He was silent for such a long time that Lucy began to think he wasn't going to give her an answer. Then, with a long-drawn-out sigh, he said, 'All right, if you think you can handle it. I want to make a couple of things clear, though.'

'What are they?'

'Don't expect me to be friendly with Robert and never ask me to keep an eye on his child. Is that understood?'

'You will be civil to him, though?' she asked anxiously.

'I suppose I will have to be if I'm living under his roof but tell him he'd better keep out of my way as much as possible if he wants this arrangement to work. As soon as I am able to do so I'll pay my way because I don't intend to be beholden to the man.'

Chapter Twenty-One

A week later Lucy wrote a letter to Robert to let him know that they would consider moving back to Priory Terrace. She explained that Sam was not totally in favour of what they were doing but he'd agreed to give it a fair trial.

Robert replied that he understood and that he would keep out of Sam's way as much as possible. He suggested that it might be a good idea if she came round one evening on her own so that she could see what arrangements he had made for them and change anything that didn't meet with her approval.

Lucy went there the following evening and she was surprised at how nervous she felt to be walking down Priory Terrace again after such a long time away. She wondered if she would meet any of their old neighbours and, if so, how they would react. As it was she met no one she knew but, nevertheless, her heart was thudding as she knocked on Robert's front door and cast a covert glance at the house next door where she had grown up.

It seemed very strange to be back once again inside a house that she'd visited so often and which was almost identical to the one she'd grown up m.

'Let me show you how I've planned things so far and then we'll have a cup of tea and talk it over and you can tell me if everything is to your liking,' he suggested when she arrived.

'That sounds like a good idea, but where's little Anna? I'm looking forward to seeing her again.'

'She's in bed and fast asleep.'

'Oh, I was hoping she would still be up,' Lucy said, her voice tinged with disappointment.

'You can still go up and see her if you really want to.'

'I would like to; I promise to be very quiet and not waken her,' Lucy said, smiling.

As she stood beside the cot looking down at the tiny figure curled up with her thumb in her mouth, Lucy's heart turned over. She wished Sam was there; if he took one look at Anna, she was sure his antagonism would melt because she was so utterly irresistible.

She looked nothing at all like Patsy; she was just a very small child needing love and affection and in that moment Lucy knew she was determined to give it to her, even if it jeopardised her own chances of happiness in the future.

Very gently she moved away a damp tendril of hair that had fallen across Anna's cheek, and then she bent over the cot and kissed her lightly on the brow.

As she did so Anna stirred and opened her eyes. Lucy looked across apologetically at Robert who was standing on the other side of the cot but he merely smiled.

As she turned back to the child, Anna stretched and opened her eyes wide and stared up at them; first at Robert and then at Lucy. Then she raised both her arms, as if asking to be picked up, and

Lucy's breath caught in her throat because Anna was looking directly at her, not at Robert.

Hesitating for only the briefest moment, Lucy bent over and picked the child up. Anna was warm and sweet-smelling from sleep and as her arms held on tightly round Lucy's neck and she buried her little face in Lucy's shoulder, Lucy felt an overwhelming flood of love for the child flow through her.

She wanted to go on cuddling Anna, but when she saw Robert straighten the bottom sheet in the cot she took it as a hint that he felt Anna should be put back down to sleep. Very tenderly Lucy kissed the child and lowered her back into the cot and tucked the covers in around her.

There was a tiny smile on Anna's face as she closed her eyes and once more drifted into sleep. Taking a last look to make sure she was comfortable, Lucy very quietly tiptoed out of the room.

Robert said nothing as he led her towards the stairs. Neither of them spoke until they were downstairs.

'Right, shall we do the grand tour first?' Robert pronounced, his voice and manner brisk and formal. 'If I go on living here as well, then we'll have to share the kitchen, of course, but I thought I could use the middle room and keep all Anna's toys and paraphernalia in there and you and Sam have the front room as your sitting room.'

As he led her in there to show her what he meant she saw that what had been the Tanners' best room when she was a child remained exactly as she remembered it all those years ago. The sofa and two big armchairs, all upholstered in red and green multi-patterned plush, were still in pristine condition. As children, she recalled, they had never been allowed even to sit on them in case they left finger marks on the highly polished wooden arms and framework.

When she and Robert had been courting they had often found solace in this very room, knowing that it was unlikely that anyone else would come in there. Even so, she'd always felt guilty as they'd sat on the sofa with their arms around each other in case either Robert's mother or father came in unexpectedly and caught them together and voiced their disapproval.

She looked at Robert, wondering if he remembered those occasions, but there was nothing on his face to indicate that he did. Yet she couldn't believe that he didn't recall the magic of those precious moments, the promises they'd made to each other and the wonderful future they'd planned.

Her eyes were blurred by unshed tears as she studied the Turkish carpet square that almost covered the entire room and the piano that no one ever played still standing against one wall.

'I'm planning to get rid of the piano and replace it with a table and chairs, if you think that would be more suitable,' Robert assured her when she said nothing.

'Why do that?' Lucy frowned. 'We'll all be eating our meals together in the kitchen, won't we?'

His face lightened. 'I would like that, but are you sure that it will suit Sam?'

Lucy hesitated. 'If it doesn't, then he can have his on a tray in here, but I most certainly will be sitting down with you in the kitchen. How else can I teach Anna table manners and make sure she eats all the right things?' she said firmly.

'Well, perhaps we should wait and see what happens when you move in,' Robert cautioned. 'If it doesn't suit Sam, then we can change things around to suit him.'

'I don't think you should get rid of the piano. Anna might want to learn to play one day.'

'We can't expect everybody to fall in with what is best for Anna, you know,' Robert said dryly. 'There'll be grown-ups living here as well as Anna and they have to be considered as well.'

'Anna is the reason we are moving in here and I intend to do everything possible to make her life a good one. As far as the piano goes, we never had one, but I rather think Sam might like to try and play it and an interest of that sort might be good for him as well.'

'Right, in that case, I'll leave the room as it is for the present but I do want you to know that you are free to make any changes you feel necessary,' Robert insisted as they went back out into the hallway and he closed the door behind them.

'Up here is more of a problem,' he went on as they went up the stairs again. 'I want you to have the big front bedroom and I will have to take the middle bedroom. That leaves Sam with the small back bedroom which is rather unfortunate because I'm sure he needs more space. I would have taken that one myself except there's only room in there for a single bed and I have to get Anna's cot in.'

225

'Why don't you and Anna have the large bedroom, then?' Lucy suggested.

'That's not fair on you. You'd be far too cramped in that smaller middle bedroom.'

'Another solution would be for me to have the large bedroom and to move Anna's cot in there too. In next to no time she will be ready for a bed of her own and it is probably the only room that is big enough to take two single beds.'

They argued amicably about the set-up as they went back downstairs and into the kitchen. Robert made a pot of tea and eventually agreed to try out Lucy's idea.

'You must tell me if it doesn't work out,' Robert told her emphatically. 'I never expected you to look after Anna at night as well as all day. She does sleep fairly well most of the time but you might get some disturbed nights.'

'Once she's in a regular routine I'm sure she will sleep right through; anyway, you're a working man and can't afford to lose your sleep. As I'm going to be at home all day it won't matter quite so much if I have a disturbed night,' she added with a smile.

'So if all the arrangements I've made so far are acceptable and meet with your approval, then can I assume that you and Sam will be moving in?'

Lucy's heart sank. Robert sounded so formal, almost as if he was letting the rooms, and she was merely a tenant; or else that he was hiring a housekeeper. Had every trace of the feelings he had felt for her not all that long ago vanished for ever? she wondered.

Trying to keep her voice as unemotional as his she said, 'As soon as you like. It's a bit late to do so tonight, so what about tomorrow evening? We haven't much to bring apart from our clothes and a few bits and pieces of personal stuff. Also, it will give me time to let my present employers know that I've left.'

'That sounds great! Would you like me to come round after work tomorrow and help you move?'

'No, I think it might go more smoothly if you aren't there, Robert, because Sam is still rather touchy about what we are doing,' Lucy said a trifle awkwardly.

'That's fine; I do understand.' He laid his hand on her arm. 'Give it time, Lucy, and I'm sure it will all work out as you want it to.'

'Well, I do hope you're right.'

He reached into his inner pocket and drew out his wallet and took out a five-pound note. 'Take this and get a taxi; don't try carrying everything yourself.'

She tried to refuse but Robert was insistent. 'Please, Lucy, if you won't let me come and help you pack and move, then this is the least I can do.'

'Thank you.' Reluctantly Lucy took the money. From now on, she told herself, she was going to have to get used to taking money from Robert each week since looking after Anna was now going to be her source of income.

'It will all work out,' Robert told her, patting her shoulder as she went through the door. 'Sam will see that what you are doing really is the best for all concerned.'

Lucy pondered Robert's words all the way home. Was she doing the best for Sam or was she simply thinking of herself? Anna had won her heart and more than anything else she wanted to look after her. The child had had a rough start in life and had been pushed from pillar to post but from now on she would make sure that Anna was surrounded by love and security.

Sam still hadn't met Anna but Lucy was confident that when he did he would understand why she felt so strongly about looking after the little girl.

Before she'd left Horatio Street that evening to come and see Robert she'd told Sam to start gathering together all the things they would be taking with them.

He'd said nothing, merely nodded, but she couldn't help noticing how his mouth had tightened into a grim line. Even so, Lucy felt that if she arrived home and found he'd done as she'd asked, then surely it meant that he really was in agreement with her decision and was prepared to accept the situation.

The house in Horatio Street was in darkness when she reached it. She went in as quietly as possible, not wishing to meet either Joe Black or his wife, and quickly made her way upstairs.

She intended to wait until the very last minute to tell them that they were leaving; perhaps as they went out of the house with all their belongings.

As she opened the door of the living room she was surprised to find that it was also in complete darkness and for one stark moment a frisson of fear went through her in case Sam had taken it into his head to clear off somewhere on his own.

As she went in she stumbled over something on the floor. For a moment she thought it must be one of the cases that she'd left out ready so that Sam could pack some of their stuff but then she realised it was too soft for that.

In the dim light coming in through the window from the street light outside she realised it was someone lying there.

'Sam?' She bent down and touched him. 'Sam, what's happened, why are you lying on the floor?'

With shaking hands she lit the gas light and then gasped in dismay. Sam was not simply lying there, he appeared to be unconscious and, to her horror, she could see that blood from a gash on his head had seeped into the carpet.

'Sam?' Lucy knelt down and felt his pulse; it was so faint that she wasn't sure if there was one or not and his chest was barely moving, his breathing was so shallow.

She hesitated for one moment, wondering whether she should leave him lying there while she went to call an ambulance or whether she should ask the Blacks to do it for her and instinctively she knew that it was better to do it herself.

Chapter Twenty-Two

Lucy sat on a chair in the hospital corridor outside the room where they were administering to Sam for the rest of the night, waiting to hear news of how badly hurt he was. She found it hard to believe that this was happening all over again just as they were about to get back on their feet at last.

It was eight o'clock the next morning before they would let her in to see him. His face was ashen and his head so heavily bandaged that he was barely discernible against the white pillow.

She knew she was trembling as she moved to the side of the bed. She picked up one of his hands and murmured his name, but there was no response.

She sat there for another couple of hours. Whenever a nurse came to check on Sam or on one of the pieces of equipment he was attached to, she asked them if they would tell her what was happening but they told her nothing.

When it was mid-morning, a pleasant youngish nurse in a different-coloured uniform came over to speak to her. 'I think it might be better if you went home and got some rest and then came back tomorrow. Your husband will have regained consciousness by then.'

'Sam is my brother, not my husband,' Lucy told her. 'Couldn't I come back this evening?'

'Of course you can if you wish to do so. Your brother should be conscious by then but he still may not be well enough to talk; he might not even recognise you,' she warned.

'Is he really that bad?' Lucy said worriedly.

'Head injuries very often give rise to various problems of this sort but in most instances, with careful nursing, the patient recovers completely,' the nurse explained gently. 'It does take time, though,' she added cautiously.

'I'll come back this evening; would seven o'clock be all right?'

'Very well, I'll tell the night nurse to expect you.'

'I was rather hoping I would see you; you're the first person who has explained anything to me.'

'Well, if you can make it earlier, say half past six, I'll still be on duty then.'

Lucy returned to Horatio Street in a daze. Although she'd been up all night she knew she wouldn't be able to sleep; not until she knew that Sam was out of danger.

As she went into their living room, the first thing that met her was the dark stain on the carpet where Sam had fallen and his head had been bleeding. She stood for a moment looking down at it, wondering what had happened.

About a foot away from the stain was a suitcase. The lid was open and some of the contents had spilled out on to the floor. He must have been in the middle of packing it and been attacked, she mused. Else how on earth could he have hit the back of his head when he had fallen? He'd been lying face down when she'd found him. It didn't make sense.

Bending down she put the clothes back in the case and closed the lid. As she did so she saw the bottle. A heavy, dark-brown glass bottle. She picked it up and noticed that it was a beer bottle and frowned. The mystery deepened. Sam didn't drink beer, so what was an empty beer bottle doing in their room? she asked herself.

As she picked it up she felt something sticky down one side of it. At first she thought it must be beer that had trickled down there when the beer was being poured out. When she looked at her hand, though, she saw that her fingers were covered with stale blood. The bottle must have been used to hit Sam on the head.

She felt frightened. Who would do such a thing and for what reason? She suspected that it might have been Joe Black, but she couldn't understand why.

She was still debating whether or not to go and confront Joe Black and ask what had happened when there was a thunderous knocking on her door. Before she could answer it Joe Black's voice shouted from the other side of it, 'Come on, open up. I know you are in there because I saw you come in.'

When she opened the door the merest scrap he slammed it back and was inside the room before she could stop him.

'Planning to do a runner last night, were you, you and that brother of yours? Well, I'll soon put a stop to that. Nobody cheats me out of any ackers that are due to me.'

'No one was intending to cheat you out of anything, Mr Black,' Lucy told him hotly. 'Yes, we are planning to leave, but we had every intention of letting you know when we were ready to do so and, let me remind you, we are paid up to the end of the week.'

'Don't you come that hoity-toity act with me, luv, or I'll belt you one the same as I did him.'

'So you were the one that knocked him unconscious with a beer bottle?' Lucy said scathingly. 'I've been sitting at his bedside in the hospital all night and he hasn't come round yet. If he dies, then I'll make sure that you're hung for murder.'

'Oh will you, indeed? In that case, I'd better shut you up the same as I did him.'

Lucy retreated back into the room and as she did so her foot caught against the suitcase that was still lying there and before she could save herself she was sprawled on the floor.

With a derisive laugh Joe Black stuck his boot hard into her side, making her cry out with pain.

'At last I've got you right where I want you,' he leered. 'You won't be quite such an uppity little bitch after I've finished with you,' he sniggered as he undid his braces and then began to unbutton his trousers.

Fearful of his intentions as he bent over her, Lucy let out a wild scream.

'Shut your bloody gob, you silly little cow, or else we'll have Madge rushing up to see what's going on,' Joe hissed, clamping one of his hands roughly over her mouth.

Lucy felt her senses reeling and she was so scared that she was afraid that at any moment she

233

might black out. Making a tremendous effort she bit down on one of his fingers as hard as she could, making him yelp with pain.

'You soddin' little bitch,' he growled. 'I'll make you damn well pay for doing that.'

'Oh no you won't.'

Lucy almost fainted with relief as the heaviness of Joe Black's body was pulled off her and she was able to breathe freely. Then a feeling of shame washed over her that Robert should see her lying there in such a dishevelled state.

He was holding Joe Black by the collar of his shirt and pulling it so tight that the man could hardly breathe.

In vain Joe struggled to free himself and pull up his trousers which were now around his ankles, but every movement he made only tightened the restriction round his neck and the edges of his mouth started to turn purple.

He was no match for Robert who was younger and stronger. By the time Lucy had scrambled to her feet, straightened her clothing and smoothed her hair back into place, Robert had thrust Joe Black out on to the landing. In a voice that brooked no argument he threatened to push him down the stairs if he ever came up there again while Lucy was living there.

Robert slammed the door shut then turned and took Lucy in his arms. 'I was worried when you didn't turn up,' he said. He hugged her and tenderly stroked her hair back from her brow while whispering words of comfort.

Lucy shuddered as she nestled against him. The feel of Robert's arms around her and the soft murmur of his voice brought a feeling of safety and comfort as well as reviving memories of the days when they had been close.

Deep in her heart she knew she still loved him as much as ever and for a moment she hoped that his show of concern and tenderness meant that he felt the same.

'I don't know what has been going on here but you can tell me about it later,' he said, as he released her. 'As soon as we've finished packing your things we're getting out; you're not staying here another night. Where is Sam?'

'Sam's in hospital.'

'Hospital?' Robert frowned. 'Why, what's happened? Has it something to do with that fellow who was attacking you?'

'Yes, I'm afraid so. He knocked Sam over the head with a beer bottle. I found Sam lying on the floor when I came home from your place last night. I've spent all night at the hospital waiting for him to wake up but he still hadn't done so when I left there. The nurse said to come back about six o'clock.'

'Right. The best thing we can do, then, is to take all your belongings to my place, grab a bite to eat and then go back to the hospital. I'll come with you.'

'What about little Anna?'

'We'll have to leave her where she is, next door with Jenny, until we get back. I'll pop in and let Jenny know what's happened; she'll understand.'

'It's a terrible start,' Lucy said apologetically.

Robert shook his head dismissively. 'Don't worry about that; let's get you settled in and see how Sam is.'

'His head was bleeding pretty badly when I found him,' Lucy said worriedly. 'Look, Robert,' she pointed to the dark stain on the carpet, 'that was where he was lying when I came home and I've no idea how long he'd been there.'

'And you think that this was what he was hit with, do you?' he asked, picking up the heavy glass beer bottle.

'I'm sure it was, because there was blood on it. Sam doesn't drink beer, so it couldn't have been his; Joe Black must have brought it up here with him.'

'Why on earth would he attack Sam?'

'I think it was because he found out that we were leaving and they had words about it. Until Sam wakes up and is able to tell us what happened, it's all guesswork.'

'Well, it's a good job I decided to take a couple of hours off this afternoon and come and find out why you were late,' Robert commented. 'Come on, we haven't any time to spare if we are going to be at the hospital for six o'clock. You collect up what has to go and I'll pack everything into the suitcases.'

An hour later and they were back at Priory Terrace. Despite her concern for Sam, Lucy felt happiness flood through her as she walked in through the door of Robert's house.

The incident with Joe Black had frightened her a great deal more than she'd realised. Now, knowing that she would never have to see or avoid him and his wife ever again was a tremendous relief. It gave her such a sense of liberation that tears of sheer joy started trickling down her cheeks.

'Hey, what's all this?' Once more Robert's arms were round her, reassuring her that everything was going to be all right.

'I know it will be.' She dabbed at her eyes and struggled to smile through her tears. 'I feel so safe and happy that I can't help crying,' she whispered. 'You must think me an utter idiot.'

'No, of course I don't. You've been through a lot in the last twenty-four hours,' he reminded her. 'Come and sit down for a minute,' he said as he led her towards an armchair.

'I'll put these suitcases up in your bedroom and you can sort everything out later,' he told her. 'We'll have something to eat and then we'll go to the hospital. Have you had a meal at all today?'

'No.' Lucy shook her head. 'I'm not hungry so...'

'So you'll sit down and eat whatever is put in front of you and no argument,' Robert told her firmly.

'Can I freshen up first?'

'Very well. Go and do that while I get the food ready,' Robert agreed with mock severity.

To her surprise, when she came back down, Lucy found that the appetising aroma of the plate of hot scouse that Robert put in front of her stimulated her appetite and she tucked in with relish.

'I must say, that was extremely tasty,' she commented as she laid down her knife and fork on her empty plate. 'I had no idea that you could cook.'

'I can't. I asked a neighbour to prepare it and

then leave it in the oven to keep warm. It was intended for the three of us after we'd moved your belongings back here. As everything has changed and since we have no idea how long we will be visiting Sam, I thought it made sense for us to have it now.'

Half an hour later they were at the hospital. Lucy felt very apprehensive as they waited for admission to the ward. She hoped the young nurse who had been so friendly the night before was still on duty because she felt confident she could be relied upon to tell them the truth about Sam's condition.

Chapter Twenty-Three

The young red-headed Irish nurse was still on duty when they arrived and she greeted Lucy with a reassuring smile.

'How is my brother tonight, may we see him?'

'To be sure you can. He's a great deal better than he was when you went home,' the nurse told her. 'He's awake, but remember, there's just the chance that he mightn't recognise you, so try not to be upset if that happens. I'm afraid it does sometimes happen with head injuries. The poor old brain gets bumped around a bit and it takes time for it to settle down again.'

'So it's not anything serious or ... or per-manent?'

'No, there's nothing for you to worry about,'

the nurse assured her. 'I'm afraid the rule is that only one visitor at a time is allowed at the bedside while a patient is in intensive care,' she added, looking apologetically at Robert.

Robert nodded in acceptance. 'Will it be all right if I wait out here?' he asked.

'Yes, yes, of course.' She smiled and indicated a chair in the corridor.

Sam still looked ashen and appeared to be asleep when the nurse took Lucy along to his bedside. As Lucy spoke his name, however, he opened his eyes and stared up at her. The look was so blank that Lucy wanted to cry.

'Sam, it's me, Lucy,' she said in a low voice. 'How are you feeling?' she asked, lifting up one of his hands and holding it gently between both of her own.

He didn't reply, but merely made a guttural sound and pulled his hand free and then closed his eyes again.

'It's possible that he'll be more responsive to-morrow,' the nurse told her. 'At the moment it appears that he is unable to remember anything about his accident; or, indeed, anything at all,' she explained. 'Now try not to worry, he's in good hands and we're doing all we can for him. Come again tomorrow and you'll see a vast difference in him, I promise you.'

'Would you mind if Robert came in? He might recognise him,' Lucy suggested. 'I'll wait out in the corridor,' she added quickly when she saw the nurse hesitate.

'Did Sam recognise you, Robert?' Lucy asked,

the moment Robert came out of the ward.

'No.' Robert shook his head. 'Well, I don't think so. He certainly opened his eyes and looked at me, but he didn't speak.'

'Well, now, like I said, there's no need to be worried. When you come back tomorrow, you'll see a great improvement in him,' the nurse assured them.

It was all very well saying not to worry, Lucy thought as they left the hospital, but she couldn't think of anything else. Although she was quite sure the nurse knew what she was talking about, she still felt upset.

Robert said very little as they made their way home and she suspected that he was every bit as concerned about Sam's condition as she was, and also worried about whether Lucy would be able to care for both Sam and Anna at the same time.

'Do you want to go indoors and have a cuppa first or shall we stop and collect Anna on our way home?' Robert asked as they approached Priory Terrace.

'I think we ought to pick up Anna,' Lucy agreed. 'I'm sure it's well past her bedtime.'

'She's possibly already asleep,' Robert admitted.

Anna wasn't asleep but she looked very tired and from her tear-stained face it was obvious that she had been crying. She held up her arms to Lucy the moment she saw her.

'No, I'll carry her,' Robert said. 'She's too heavy for you.'

'It'll be all right; it's only a few yards,' Lucy assured him.

Anna clung on to her neck so tightly that by the

time they reached Robert's house Lucy could barely breathe. When she stepped over the doorstep, however, the child's hold slackened and she gave Lucy a big wet kiss on the cheek as if she was relieved that Lucy was not going to leave her.

While Robert made some tea Lucy undressed Anna and put on her night clothes. As she did so she was once more aware of how painfully thin the child's body was. Her mouth tightened as she noticed the number of bruises there were at the top of Anna's arms and legs; it worried her because they were places which were not normally exposed, so no one would ever know they were there.

She wondered whether to mention it to Robert, but they were both so tired after the events of the day that she thought perhaps it was better to keep her own counsel for the moment. She would be looking after Anna from now on so there would be no more bruises and, given time, the ones she already had would fade and be forgotten.

Lucy was acutely aware that after Anna was in bed and they'd eaten their evening meal there seemed to be an uneasy tension between herself and Robert. Neither of them seemed to know what to do next. It had been a long day and she felt worn out by all that had happened so she decided to have an early night.

There was a look of relief on Robert's face when she said goodnight. He immediately picked up the newspaper and settled down to read it.

As she undressed for bed Lucy wondered if she should have gone off to her own sitting room after they'd eaten, but she'd felt so worried about

Sam that she'd stayed, hoping to have the opportunity to talk things over with Robert.

Although she was desperately tired Lucy found sleep eluded her for quite a long while. She heard Robert come upstairs to bed and it seemed strange to be lying there so close to him and yet feeling that the distance between them was as great as ever.

She hoped that in the days to come, once the strangeness of living together wore off, they would be more at ease with each other. She knew things could never return to what they had once been and she couldn't expect him to feel the same over-powering love for her as she still felt for him. In the past they had wanted to spend every waking moment in each other's company. In those long ago days they'd also shared their thoughts and dreams and often talked about the day when they would set up home together.

They had never anticipated that, when the day came and they were living under the same roof, it would be in the sort of circumstances they were encountering now, she thought sadly.

Anna didn't settle either; she tossed restlessly and whimpered from time to time. She was so restless that in the end, although she knew it was a bad start and possibly would cause trouble in the future, Lucy took the child into her own bed.

Comforted by the warmth and closeness, little Anna fell asleep almost immediately. Lucy lay in a semi-dream state, feeling an overpowering attachment for the child which she wouldn't have thought was possible a week or so ago.

Anna was no longer Patsy's child; she was

Robert's little daughter and Lucy felt as protective of her as she would have done if she'd been Anna's mother herself.

Lucy felt desperately worried about Sam's future. It was all very well saying that, given time, he would regain his memory but, forgetting about the traumatic event he'd been through in the last few days was surely very important.

If he didn't regain his memory, then possibly there would be changes in his personality and whether that would be for the better or not remained to be seen. It was a relief to know that Robert would be there at her side to help deal with whatever problems lay ahead.

If only they could all obliterate those years since the car accident, she thought ruefully, but there was no turning the clock back. They'd all changed and they'd all made irrevocable mistakes, and now they had to deal with the consequences as best they could and look to the future.

Her heart ached as she recalled exactly what had happened in those traumatic days. Losing Robert – and to Patsy of all people – had been heart-breaking for her but equally so for Sam. She could understand why there was animosity between them but she hoped that, for all their sakes, it could now be forgotten and that it wouldn't flare up and cause rows in the future.

The past was over; it was time for all of them to build a new future for themselves.

In the weeks that followed Lucy found that looking after Anna was a full-time job. The little girl was lively but Lucy discovered that she clung on to her like a limpet, almost as if she was afraid she might disappear.

She stood watching as she made the beds, stayed by her side as she washed the dishes, and followed her around the house as she did the rest of the housework and prepared the meals.

The moment Robert came in from work each evening Lucy went to visit Sam. His progress was slow and although he recognised Lucy, he seemed to be unconcerned about the changes she had made in her life. In fact, it sometimes seemed to Lucy that he was actually enjoying being in hospital and had forgotten all about the outside world.

When she mentioned this to Nurse Kelly, the pretty red-haired nurse who was so friendly, she merely smiled. 'Perhaps you should have a talk with the doctor about your brother if you are worried about his progress,' she advised.

In order for Lucy to do this it meant Robert taking time off work but as soon it was possible they arranged it.

Lucy found the doctor's prognosis was worrying. He said they were almost ready to discharge Sam but that he thought she ought to be aware that although his physical health was quite good there was a slight brain defect.

'It is nothing to worry about. It's possibly a cumulative effect of all that has happened to him recently and shouldn't in any way interfere with him leading a normal life,' he assured her.

When Lucy asked for more details the doctor admitted that Sam's memory had been affected.

'It would seem that he has no recollection of

what has happened to him in the past few years. You mentioned that you were living in Horatio Street when this accident happened. Your brother has no recall at all about such an incident. He tells me that he was born in Priory Terrace and has lived there all his life.'

'Does he remember what he did for a living?' Lucy asked.

'He says he's an apprentice mechanic at Carter's Cars,' the doctor stated, reading from the case notes he was holding. He frowned and studied the papers in his hand again. 'Judging from his age I think he must have progressed to something else since then,' he said as he looked up.

As briefly as possible Lucy told him about the car accident in which their parents had both been killed and that Sam had been the driver. 'Does he remember anything at all about that and being so badly injured?' she asked.

'He's certainly never mentioned it, nor that he had been injured and in hospital himself for quite a long time.'

'Will he regain his lost memory?' Lucy asked.

The doctor rubbed his chin thoughtfully. 'It's very difficult to say. The brain is extremely complex. Although it has been damaged it may over a period of time recover. On the other hand, there may be a chunk of his memory, the years between his previous accident and now, that are gone for ever.'

'When will we know if this is so? Is there any way of helping him to remember?'

'You'll have to be patient, Miss Collins. There is no point in pressurising him. If he doesn't under-

245

stand or remember something from his past, then ignore it. He may remember it later on; if he doesn't, then it is better not to press the issue.'

'Apart from that, would you say he is quite all right and there is nothing to worry about?'

'Yes, he is physically fit and well now and can go home. We will want to see him again in three months' time, to check on his progress, but there is no reason to think that there will be any other problems. If there are, then you must get in touch with us. You will be given a number to call should there ever be an emergency.'

They arranged to take Sam home the next day and it was agreed that they would collect him at about five o'clock. Robert insisted that he ought to be there in case Sam needed support of any kind, although Nurse Kelly assured them that Sam was fit enough to walk from the ward to a waiting taxi with the help of his walking stick.

When Robert, Lucy and Anna walked into the ward the next afternoon Sam greeted them enthusiastically. With Nurse Kelly's help he had already packed up all his belongings and was waiting impatiently to leave.

Lucy was on tenterhooks wondering what Sam's reaction to Anna might be but he smiled and said hello to her as though he'd known her all her life.

'I've forgotten your name,' he told her, 'are you going to tell me what it is?'

Anna pulled back and then slipped her hand into Lucy's. 'Mummy?' she questioned, looking up at Lucy.

Lucy hesitated, looking questioningly at Robert

who gave an imperceptible shrug as if to imply that he was leaving the decision to her.

'My name is Uncle Sam,' Sam told Anna. 'Can you remember to call me that? And this is Aunty Brenda.' He held out his hand to Nurse Kelly.

'Hello, Anna, are you going to give me a kiss?' Brenda Kelly said smiling, crouching down and holding out her arms.

Anna hesitated for a second then ran towards Brenda Kelly and kissed her on the cheek and received a warm hug in return.

'You're a real little darling, so you are,' Brenda Kelly told her as she stood up.

'Would you mind if I asked Brenda to come home with us tonight so that she knows where Priory Terrace is?' Sam asked as they prepared to leave. 'She needs to know so that she can find her way when she comes to visit me,' he added.

'Are you sure that's all right with you two?' Nurse Kelly questioned, colour rushing to her cheeks.

'Yes, of course it is.' Lucy smiled. 'You'll be welcome at any time. I may be glad of your help with Sam in the days to come.'

'Good! Well, I'll be off duty in ten minutes,' Brenda Kelly told them with a beaming smile, 'so if you will give me time to change out of my uniform then I'll join you by the main entrance.'

As they waited, Lucy mused on how different Brenda Kelly was to Patsy. She was so much more caring and seemed to be genuinely fond of Sam and there was certainly a light in his eyes when he looked at her.

Chapter Twenty-Four

As the taxi pulled up outside Robert's house and they helped Sam out, Lucy sensed there were going to be problems when he headed straight for their old home.

'Wrong house, Sam,' Robert told him, grabbing him gently by the arm and guiding him towards the adjoining front door;

Sam looked confused. 'Why are we going to Robert's house?' he asked, turning to Lucy.

'It's where we're living now,' Lucy told him.

'You might be, but I want to go to my own place,' he muttered.

'This will be your home from now on, Sam, you're living with us,' Robert told him.

Sam stood there frowning, a belligerent look on his scarred face.

Although she obviously had no idea what the problem was Brenda Kelly took Sam's arm and squeezed it. 'Let's go along with what they're asking and sort it out later, shall we? They might give us a nice cup of tea and I could certainly do with one.'

For a moment Lucy resented the way Brenda spoke to Sam; it was almost as if he was a child who needed to be coaxed but she said nothing, merely smiled at Brenda and followed them through the front door which Robert was now holding open.

She left Robert to settle them down in the living room while she hurried through into the kitchen to make the promised tea. As she did so she couldn't help wondering whether bringing Sam back there had perhaps stirred up forgotten memories for him and she wondered how she was going to deal with them. On the pretence of needing some help she called Brenda into the kitchen and briefly acquainted her with what the situation was and how they had come to be living with Robert.

As soon as they'd finished drinking their tea Brenda said she must be going.

'You'll come back again soon?' Sam asked anxiously as she stood up to leave.

'Of course I will, Sam.' She looked questioningly at Lucy and Robert. 'I'll come round tomorrow night right after I finish work, if that is all right with you?'

'Of course. Come and eat with us and then you can see how well Sam has settled in and he can tell you what he's been doing on his first day at home,' Lucy told her.

After Brenda left the trouble really started. Sam was adamant that he wanted to go next door and see his parents. He looked at Lucy in stunned disbelief when she broke the news to him that they were both dead.

'When did that happen?' he asked in a bewildered voice. 'Was it while I was in hospital?'

Lucy looked helplessly at Robert, undecided about giving Sam a direct answer.

'Yes, Sam. It happened while you were in hospital,' Robert said quietly.

Sam was not easily appeased. 'Is that why you married Robert and moved in here, Lucy?' he pressed.

'Moving in here seemed to be for the best,' Lucy said awkwardly.

'Where are your own mam and dad, then, Robert? I haven't seen anything of them since we got here.'

'Mam died and Dad's gone up North to live with his sister,' Robert told him.

Sam nodded and said no more but he still looked perplexed and it was obvious that he was deep in thought and trying to puzzle out how so much could have happened in such a short time without him knowing anything about it.

When Anna toddled over to him, clutching her favourite doll and trying to give it to Sam, he shook his head and pushed her away impatiently.

Anna burst into tears and it took Lucy several minutes to comfort her. After that Anna wouldn't go near him but stared at him from a safe distance, ready to run to Lucy if he spoke to her or even looked in her direction.

Robert didn't seem to be too concerned. 'He's a stranger to her. Give her a few days and she'll come round.'

'She was talking to him when we were in the hospital and he was quite friendly towards her and told her to call him Uncle Sam,' Lucy reminded him. 'Now she says she doesn't like Uncle Sam and he's a bad man,' Lucy sighed.

'As I said, once she gets used to him being here she'll be friends with him if you give her time.

'Anyway, I'm more concerned about Sam than

about Anna,' Robert went on. 'I think bringing him back here must have brought back memories that would have been better left buried; things we all thought he'd forgotten. I wonder if we should sit him down and tell him everything that has happened in his life from the time of the car accident right up to the present day.'

'Don't you think that might be too much for him to grasp? Perhaps we should leave it until we see Brenda again and ask her what she thinks. She'll be coming to see him after she finishes work so I'm sure it can wait until then.'

When they discussed it with Brenda she didn't think it would be a good idea because it might be too much of a shock for Sam especially if they told him the truth about how his parents had died.

'I tell you what I can do if you think it might be of any help,' she offered. 'I can talk to the psychiatrist who has been handling Sam's case and see what he thinks would be the best way of dealing with it.'

In the weeks that followed Lucy found that every minute of the day was busy. Anna was awake by six each morning and full of life. She was not only a chatterbox but was also continually asking questions as she followed Lucy around.

Sometimes in sheer desperation Lucy was tempted to ask Sam to play with her for an hour so that she could concentrate on what she was doing. She was reluctant to do this, though, because she wasn't too sure about what his reaction would be or even how Anna would behave if she left them together. Anna was still wary of him and usually pulled back or hid her face in Lucy's skirts if Sam spoke to her.

Sam seemed to take it for granted that Anna was Lucy's and Robert's child. He never mentioned Patsy at all and seemed to have no recollection of what had happened; it was as if that part of his memory had been wiped clean.

In the same way he seemed to assume that Lucy and Robert were married. From time to time this caused slightly embarrassing situations but they both agreed that it was better to let him continue thinking they were rather than to confuse him with the truth.

Sometimes Lucy felt that it was almost as if she and Robert were married and that made it all the more heartbreaking for her because it was something she wanted more than anything in the world. They had a happy family life together and so far Sam had not realised that they slept in separate rooms. Or, if he had noticed, he probably assumed it was so that when Anna woke in the night she didn't disturb Robert who needed his sleep because at the moment he was the only bread-winner in the house.

Sam was now fully recovered physically but his memory still had a large gap; the years between leaving Priory Terrace and returning there still seemed to be rather hazy.

Lucy waited for him to ask again about their parents but he seemed to take it for granted that they were dead; just as he accepted that Robert's mother had died and his father had moved away.

In some ways Lucy felt it was all for the best

that Patsy's parents had also moved out of Priory Terrace so there was no risk of Sam ever bumping into them.

Brenda Kelly was now a regular visitor and it was plain to see that the bond between her and Sam was a strong one and Lucy had accepted that Brenda's influence on him was good.

Lucy had grown to like her and found her lilting Irish voice pleasant, but she still wished that Brenda wouldn't treat Sam as if he was a child. She put it down to the fact that Brenda was a nurse and Sam had been her patient, so she said nothing.

Sam had been at home about six weeks when he started to become restless. The weather had improved and he wanted to go out walking on his own but Lucy was afraid to let him do so in case he got lost. When she spoke to Robert about it he said that it was a risk she must take otherwise Sam would never regain his independence.

'Why don't you put a card in his pocket with his name and address on it and then if he does get lost, he can ask someone to direct him back home?'

'Yes, that is a good idea,' Lucy agreed. 'If he has an accident of any kind, then it would also mean that they'd know where to bring him,' she said thoughtfully. 'The only thing is it does make him sound rather like a parcel,' she added with a smile.

'Well, it's far better than us having to spend hours looking for him. You could try telling him where to go for a walk but the chances are he won't remember five minutes after he's through the door.'

Sam seemed to enjoy his walks. For the first few days he was only out for about half an hour and said he had walked round the block. As time passed he ventured further and claimed that he felt so much better for getting out and about.

Lucy welcomed the freedom it gave her. She was able to concentrate her attention on Anna and listen more patiently to her prattling on about things. The little girl was developing fast and loved to help Lucy no matter whether it was with the dusting or baking a cake.

Often the two of them were so absorbed that they hardly noticed Sam's absence until they heard him coming back in again. Then Lucy would interrupt what she was doing to make him a cup of tea and talk to him about where he'd been.

A couple of weeks later on a bright sunny spring morning in April, Sam took matters into his own hands. Of his own volition he went off to Carter's Cars to tell them he was quite well again and ready to come back to work.

He reported to the manager of the showroom who was at a loss about what he ought to do because he was pretty sure that there was no job waiting for Sam.

Having heard from Robert about Sam being in hospital and how his memory had been affected, he didn't want to be the one to tell him in case he reacted badly, so he went in search of Robert and asked him to come and take Sam home.

'I don't think that is the way to deal with it,' Robert stated. 'I think that perhaps Mr Carter should be the one to speak to Sam and tell him whether or not there is a job here for him.'

The showroom manager didn't see the point of doing that, not until Robert pointed out that unless it was Mr Carter who told him there was no job, Sam wouldn't believe it.

'Well, I suppose it makes sense,' he agreed, 'but I don't want to be the one to ask Mr Carter.'

'Then I suppose I'll have to go and explain the situation to him,' Robert said reluctantly.

Mr Carter himself was not in that day but Percy was and when Robert told him Sam wanted his job back he shook his head. 'I can't do anything without speaking to my father first of all and I hardly think that he will want to take him back. He never finished his training and, as you know, he was sacked.'

'All his troubles started with the bonfire incident,' Robert reminded him quietly.

Percy looked uneasy. 'Yes, I suppose they did, but that was quite some time ago. Look, Robert, you'd better leave it with me. Tell Sam to go home and come back tomorrow and I'll talk it over with my father and see what he thinks can be done.'

'Very well.'

Robert himself went to the showroom to tell Sam this. Sam seemed quite happy about it and agreed to go straight home and come back again the next day.

Robert said nothing to Lucy about it until later that evening after Sam had gone to bed and the two of them were sitting having a cup of cocoa together.

'Sam never mentioned it to me so he must have forgotten all about it once he came home,' she said sipping her hot cocoa. 'What do we do? Is it best to forget about it?'

'No, I think he should go along and see Mr Carter. Who knows, he might find him work of some kind.'

'Yes, but if he does, will Sam be capable of doing it? If he's told something he forgets it five minutes later.'

'We can explain that to Mr Carter and perhaps he can be given a job where he's under constant supervision and someone is on the spot to tell him what to do all the time.'

'Do you think Sam would accept that?'

'Well, he seems willing to do whatever you tell him and he was certainly happy to do whatever Brenda told him when he was in hospital.'

'It means someone ought to go with him to see Mr Carter, can you do that?'

Robert looked dubious. 'I don't think it would be right for me to be the one because I work there and I don't want to stir things. Perhaps it would be better if you went with him.'

'And took Anna with me?'

'I don't see why not. It might make them realise that Sam isn't your only responsibility.'

Lucy didn't answer. She drained her cup and held out her hand for Robert's empty cup and then took them both through to the kitchen to wash them up.

'You don't like the idea very much, do you?' Robert commented as he followed her out into the kitchen and picked up the tea towel to dry their cups.

'I don't like the idea of facing Mr Carter. He sacked me, remember, for taking time off to look after Sam.'

'That happened a long time ago; in fact, it might even stand you in good stead because he might still have an uneasy conscience about doing that.'

'Mr Carter has a conscience! I very much doubt it,' Lucy said scathingly.

'Think about it and let me know before I go to work in the morning,' Robert told her.

'No, there's no need. I'll do it,' she said resignedly. 'I'm doing it for Sam's sake because I think it would be good for him to go back to work,' she added.

'I agree with you,' Robert said quickly. 'Don't build your hopes too high, though, because there may not be any opening for him,' he cautioned as he headed for the stairs.

Lucy stayed on down in the kitchen brooding over what was to happen the next day. She'd vowed that she would never go back to Carter's Cars and she didn't like the idea of Sam asking them for work; she wished he'd never approached them in the first place.

Yet, she mused, the very fact that he had gone there must mean that his memory was improving. He obviously remembered that he'd once worked there.

She still didn't think he would be able to hold down a job and hated to think that if he couldn't, and ended up being sacked, it would mean that once again he would be humiliated by the Carters.

257

Chapter Twenty-Five

The appointment to see Mr Carter was timed for ten-thirty and Lucy was up early to make sure that Sam was ready in good time. She also wanted to make sure that he had a good breakfast and that he was wearing the white shirt she'd washed and ironed ready for him. She had sponged and pressed his one and only suit the night before and had done the same to her own skirt and jacket as well as ironing her white blouse in readiness.

She thought Sam ought to go to the meeting with Mr Carter on his own but Robert argued that if they left him to do that, then he might forget all about it and not turn up.

'Nonsense,' Lucy laughed. 'He must be really keen to go back to work for him to have gone along there on his own in the first place.'

'You don't have to go in with him, you can wait in the general office while he has his interview,' Robert pointed out. 'You might enjoy the chance to have a chat with some of your old colleagues.'

His words had sent a shudder through Lucy. How could Robert be so insensitive? she wondered. She would have Anna with her and everyone in the office would know that she was Patsy's baby.

If they didn't already know then they were bound to wonder why she was looking after little Anna. If they already knew that she was living back in Priory Terrace and had moved into Robert's house, then no doubt they'd be speculating and gossiping about what her relationship was with Robert.

Still, she decided she'd put on a brave face. So far she'd been fairly lucky in that she hadn't bumped into many people she'd known in the old days. Even in Priory Terrace the neighbours were surprisingly cordial.

Well, there was one thing for sure, Lucy thought grimly as she started to get ready, they would be bound to recognise her in the office because she was wearing the same white blouse and dark skirt as she'd worn when she'd worked there.

She sighed as she brushed her hair and put on her hat; she'd enjoyed those days when she'd operated the switchboard so much, even though it seemed to be a lifetime ago.

Sam seemed to be quite positive that the interview with Mr Carter would go well and he talked about how pleased he would be to get back to work. Remembering that he had left under a cloud, Lucy wasn't nearly as confident about what the outcome would be but she said nothing; she didn't want to make him nervous.

As they approached the imposing showrooms of Carter's Cars Lucy felt her own resolution to face her former colleagues ebbing away. 'It might be best if I wait for you out here, Sam,' she told him, stopping by the side door which opened on to a flight of stone stairs that led up to the offices above.

'You'd better come in and show me where Mr Carter's office is,' he mumbled and her heart went out to him because she could see that in the last few moments his courage had waned and he seemed to be as nervous as she was.

'It will mean taking Anna out of her pushchair and carrying her,' Lucy prevaricated. 'You can always ask someone in the general office,' she added.

The sound of approaching footsteps as someone came up behind them wanting to go into the office part of the building made them move to one side. Lucy felt frozen to the spot when she saw that it was Percy Carter.

For a moment she thought he was going to walk past them, and then he paused and stared at them. 'Lucy ... Lucy Collins,' he said, his face beaming. 'I knew I was interviewing Sam this morning but I didn't think I'd have the pleasure of seeing you as well.' He opened the door wide. 'Come along in.'

'Well,' Lucy hesitated. 'I thought I'd better wait here for Sam because of the pushchair.'

'Nonsense. Here,' he pushed his briefcase into her hands, 'you carry that and I'll carry your little girl and her pushchair upstairs with no trouble at all.'

It all happened so quickly that Lucy found herself following behind as they all made their way up the stairs and into the general office. As the usual morning chorus of 'Good morning, Mr Percy' broke out Lucy felt that all eyes were on them. As Percy placed the pushchair with Anna in it down on the floor and then stood aside to let her take it, Lucy wished the floor would open and swallow her up.

From the other side of the room she saw Miss Yorke staring across at them, a look of astonishment on her tight-lipped face. It quickly changed to one of disapproval as, accompanied by Sam, Lucy pushed Anna across the room and into Percy's office.

Once they were inside and Percy had closed the door behind them Lucy felt her self-confidence returning. She studied Percy as he took off his dark trilby and black Melton overcoat and hung them on the coat stand near the door.

He'd changed quite a lot since she'd last seen him. His untidy mousy hair was now cut in a sharp, short style and his heavy-framed spectacles had been replaced by lighter horn-rimmed ones. He had filled out and was no longer thin and gangling.

'Right, would you like to take this chair over here, Lucy?' he pointed to an armchair in the corner of the room, 'and you take a seat here, Sam,' he said in an authoritative voice, indicating a chair on the other side of his desk.

'Is this Patsy's little girl?' he asked looking at Anna, who gave him a smile and giggled.

'Yes, we've moved back to Priory Terrace and I'm looking after her,' Lucy said in a low, stilted voice while at the same time giving Percy a warning frown. She was conscious of Sam listening to their conversation and she wondered what his reaction would be if he remembered how in the past even though Patsy had been his girlfriend she had often flirted with Percy but to her relief he didn't seem to take any notice at all.

'I had heard something of the sort.' Percy's

voice was clipped, almost as if he disapproved. He looked at Anna speculatively. 'She looks more like her father than her mother,' he murmured.

Lucy nodded but said nothing.

'I was hoping when I saw the name Collins against the timetable that you were the one who was coming for an interview,' he commented as he moved to his desk and sat down in the imposing high-backed leather chair.

'I didn't know I would be seeing you, I thought I was seeing Mr Carter himself,' Sam interrupted.

'My father only comes in three days a week now to check on what we are doing and to deal with anything he feels needs his attention. For quite some time now I have been dealing with all the day-to-day matters,' Percy explained.

'So are you the one I have to ask if I want my job back again?' Sam asked.

Percy frowned as he picked up a file and began to look through it. 'You left us in September 1921,' he murmured. 'That's almost three years ago.'

'Sam didn't simply leave, he was sacked the same as I was,' Lucy intervened.

'Yes, you're quite right; the details are all here,' Percy affirmed, tapping the folder.

'Sorry, I didn't mean to interrupt, but Sam sometimes has difficulty in remembering things that happened around that time and I didn't want you to get the wrong impression,' Lucy said, the hot blood rushing to her face.

'I understand it has something to do with his accident? Now which accident are we talking about?' Percy frowned.

'The very last one,' Lucy told him.

'I see; not the accident when he was driving one of our cars but the one he had on Orangeman's Day in July last year. I read in the *Echo* all about that; it seemed to be quite serious and caused a lot of commotion.'

'Well, yes it was. Sam was trampled underfoot by the marchers and was in a coma for a while. He's fully recovered from that incident, though,' Lucy added hurriedly.

'So which accident has impaired his memory?' Percy persisted.

'It was an incident since then. Sam was hit over the head with a heavy bottle several months ago when we were living in Horatio Street,' Lucy explained. 'I know when you read the list it sounds like a catalogue of disaster but he's just been unlucky,' she added wryly.

'I see. But you are saying he has fully recovered and is fit enough to work now,' Percy commented. He selected a sheet of paper from the file on his desk and studied it. 'It appears that you never completed your apprenticeship as an engineer, Sam.'

'He was unable to do so after the bonfire incident because both his hands were so badly burned; surely you must remember that,' Lucy said sharply.

'Oh, I do. Very vividly. I don't think I will ever forget the ordeal I went through or the time I had to spend in hospital. That was followed by the dreadful car accident and I recall the dressing down I had to take from my father because I was the one who had suggested that Sam should become a driver–'

'Do we have to go over all those painful details again?' Lucy interrupted. 'Sam doesn't remember anything at all about the car accident and so we never mention it.'

'Very well,' Percy agreed hastily. He shuffled the papers together and put them back inside the folder. 'So what sort of work are you able to do now, Sam?'

Sam looked confused. 'I was hoping for my old job back, as a mechanic.'

Percy shook his head frowning. 'I don't think that's possible because you aren't qualified.'

'He had nearly completed his four-year apprenticeship,' Lucy reminded Percy. 'I'm quite sure that Robert Tanner would keep an eye on his work and I understand that Robert is your head mechanic and in charge of the workshop.'

Percy pursed his lips and looked uncertain. 'You'd better leave it with me for a couple of days, Sam, so that I can discuss the idea with my father,' he prevaricated. 'I'll get in touch with you again as soon as we reach a decision.'

He pushed back his chair and came round to the other side of his desk, then opened the door to show them out. Lucy felt bitterly disappointed on Sam's behalf. He had been so convinced that the interview with Mr Carter was merely a formality and that he would automatically be reinstated.

'Would you like me to carry the pushchair down the stairs for you?' Percy offered.

'There's no need,' Lucy told him stiffly. 'I can bump it down them quite easily.'

'That won't be a very comfortable ride for the

little one, though,' Percy said gravely. 'No, if you carry her, then I'll take the pushchair down for you.'

The moment she had lifted Anna out the pushchair he picked it up and strode across the general office and through the door leaving Lucy and Sam to follow.

Conscious that all eyes were on them as she walked through the office with Anna in her arms, Lucy wondered what they would say about them after they'd left.

When they reached the street outside Percy waited until Lucy had settled Anna into the pushchair, then held out his hand to her to say goodbye.

'I didn't know you were living back in Priory Terrace,' he told her in a low voice. 'I've tried several times to find you. What about meeting me one evening to give us a chance to catch up properly?'

'I don't think that's possible because my time is taken up looking after little Anna,' she told him.

'Surely Robert can look after her for one evening; you must have some free time and a life of your own, even if you are living in his house.'

Lucy was conscious that he was watching her closely as he said this and her lips tightened. 'Of course I get time to myself,' she said quickly. 'Robert usually looks after Anna when he gets home from work and he often puts her to bed.'

'There you are. I'm glad we've sorted that out and that there's no problem at all about us meeting. Shall we say tomorrow night? By then I will have had time to talk things through with my father and be able to tell you what decision has been made about Sam coming back to work for us.'

Lucy hesitated. She didn't want to go out with Percy Carter. He had asked her to do so many times in the past but she had always refused and he'd never argued about it.

She hadn't had a night out for so long that it suddenly seemed to be an attractive idea. If it was going to help to make sure that Sam was re-instated, then perhaps it would be diplomatic to accept Percy's invitation on this occasion.

'Thank you, Percy, but I'm not sure,' she pre-varicated, hoping he would let the subject drop.

'Good. I'll pick you up at seven o'clock and we'll go to the Paradise Club. A nice meal and a spot of dancing afterwards, how does that sound?' he asked in a jovial voice.

Although she smiled and nodded her accept-ance, inwardly she was perturbed about what he would expect from her afterwards. Also, what on earth would she wear to the Paradise Club? She had nothing remotely suitable for such an exotic occasion; except a summer dress and that would hardly do justice to such an occasion.

Chapter Twenty-Six

Lucy found that she kept going hot and cold all over as she walked home with Sam and Anna. What on earth had made her accept an invitation to go out for the evening with Percy Carter? she asked herself over and over again.

She wasn't at all sure what Robert would think when he heard; in fact, she decided that it might be better not to mention it yet. She hadn't even made up her mind whether she would be going or not. She had nothing suitable to wear and she suspected that everybody there would be dressed to the nines.

Sam was jubilant about the prospect of working again but she only half listened to what he was saying; her own problem made it impossible for her to think of anything else.

She decided to take Anna out in her pushchair in the afternoon because she couldn't stand listening to Sam talking about working at Carter's any longer. She hoped Anna would fall asleep so that she could sort out in her own mind what she was going to do, but Anna chattered so much that it was impossible to think.

Instead of their usual walk to the park Lucy went into the centre of Liverpool and it seemed to her that although it was still only the beginning of spring all the stores were displaying the sort of dresses that would be just right to wear to the Paradise Club.

Over their evening meal to Lucy's dismay Sam related every detail about his interview that morning with Percy Carter. He even added that Percy had carried the pushchair down the stairs for them and then asked Lucy to go out with him.

'Really; so what did you say to that?' Robert asked, looking across at her.

She felt the hot colour flooding her cheeks as she tried to avoid his direct gaze. 'I thought it was diplomatic to say yes because Percy said that it would be an opportunity to tell me what had been decided about Sam,' she added hastily.

'I would have thought that his decision about whether there was a job for Sam or not should be discussed with Sam, not you,' Robert said sharply.

'Well, yes, I am sure you are right and of course he'll talk to Sam about what has been decided, but I thought it would be nice to know as soon as possible. Otherwise it might mean having to wait several days before a letter arrives,' Lucy explained lamely.

'Mmm! Or was it the idea of a night out somewhere glitzy with Percy Carter that appealed to you?' Robert asked dryly.

'No, most certainly not, but I didn't know how to refuse without causing offence,' Lucy said hotly. 'In fact, I'm not at all sure that I will go because he said we would be going to the Paradise Club and I have nothing suitable to wear to a place like that.'

'You'll probably look as good as any of the others there whatever you are wearing,' Robert said dismissively.

Lucy didn't argue with him because she thought it was pointless to do so; what did a man know about such things? It was so easy for them, all they had to do was put on a clean shirt and a fancy tie and they could go anywhere.

Nevertheless, she couldn't put it out of her mind and she tossed and turned most of the night wondering whether she should brave it out and wear her summer dress or send a message to Percy to say she wouldn't be coming.

If she turned down his invitation, she reasoned, it might jeopardise Sam's chance of a job and she knew it meant so much to him to be back in work.

She was hollow eyed and still tired when it was time to get up the next morning. In silence she prepared Robert's breakfast and placed it on the table in front of him before pouring herself a cup of tea and sitting down to drink it.

'Did you have a bad night?' Robert asked piling his fork with egg and fried bread.

'Yes, I'm afraid I didn't sleep very well,' Lucy admitted, desperately trying to stop yawning.

'I suppose it was Anna who kept you awake and now it's time to get up she's sound asleep.'

'No, Anna was as good as gold, she didn't keep me awake,' Lucy admitted.

'Oh, I see,' Robert said grimly. 'In that case, I suppose you were thinking about your date tonight and what you should wear to impress Percy.'

'I haven't even decided whether or not to go. I'll have to wait and find out if Brenda is off duty this evening and if she can come and babysit first.'

'Brenda? What has Brenda got to do with it? I can look after my own daughter.'

'I wasn't sure if you were free to do so or not; you never offered when I mentioned about going out.'

'You knew perfectly well that I would be here and that you are free to go out in the evening any time you wish to do so,' Robert told her huffily.

When she made no reply Robert fished out his wallet from his back pocket and took out a five-pound note. 'Buy yourself a new dress; something to show him that you are as smart as you ever were,' he said as he put it down on the table beside her cup and saucer.

Lucy's mouth tightened. 'Thank you, but I don't want that; I'll wear what I've got.'

'And ruin your evening by feeling out of place? Don't be daft, go out and buy something new; a dress to knock spots off all the others there. Afterwards, when you get back, try and get an hour's sleep otherwise you'll be falling asleep in Percy's arms on the dance floor and making a laughing stock of yourself.'

Before she could answer he'd stood up from the table, reached down his cap and top coat and was walking out of the house, leaving her looking questioningly at the money he'd left lying on the table.

Robert was so right in what he had said but she wished he hadn't seemed so angry and cynical. She didn't like the idea of taking his money to buy a new dress when it was to go out with Percy. She wondered if perhaps Robert was jealous and if so did that mean that he still had feelings for her and resented the fact that Percy was showing an interest in her again?

Robert Tanner was in a very bad mood when he arrived at Carter's that morning. He hadn't slept well because he couldn't put the thought of Lucy going out with Percy from his mind. What on earth did she want to do that for? he kept asking himself.

It stirred up so many memories that he'd thought were buried and gone for ever. He'd tried to move on after Patsy died and he thought he'd done so. He'd been quite proud of the way he'd dealt with all his problems and life had started to look good again but suddenly it seemed to be all turning to ashes.

What made it worse was the way he'd handed her the five-pound note and told her to buy a new dress almost as if he was condoning their outing.

His reasons for doing that had been because he didn't like to think of her turning up at the Paradise Club in one of her old frocks and being the laughing stock of the hoi polloi who went there. Deep down he did want her to enjoy her night out because she had worked so hard that she deserved it.

Why he hadn't thought to take her out one night himself he couldn't understand; well, he knew the reason but he didn't want to admit it. His feelings for Lucy were as strong as they'd ever been. Never a day passed when he didn't wish that he could turn the clock back to the time before things began to go haywire. There would have been no Patsy in his life, for a start, he thought grimly.

That would have meant that there would have been no little Anna either, he reminded himself and there was no doubt about it that she meant a great deal to him and always would, even though he still loved Lucy.

Loving your child was different and something very special, he told himself. She was part of him and he felt responsible for her welfare and happiness.

It was one of the reasons why he'd wanted her to be brought up by someone he could trust to care for her properly and even love her. Lucy filled the bill perfectly.

Even as he told himself this, he knew that deep in his heart he also hoped that perhaps one day, if he was sure that Lucy had the same sort of feelings for him that he still had for her, the three of them might become a proper family.

So far they had treated each other with tremendous caution as if both of them were afraid of saying or doing something that might be wrongly construed. They both seemed to be taking great care not to reveal their true feelings. At least he had, but he wasn't sure about Lucy. Did she still have feelings for him or was she finding it onerous to be living with him and regretting her decision to do so?

In the olden days they had never wanted to be out of each other's sight for a minute. They'd walked home from school together talking over the day's happenings and helping each other with their homework. At the weekends they'd gone for walks together and, in the summer, over to New Brighton on the boat.

In fact, in those days they'd spent every moment they could in each other's company. They'd shared their thoughts and dreams for the life ahead of them and had taken it for granted that they would be together for ever.

It was all Percy Carter's fault that it had all gone wrong, he told himself. It had started with the stupid incident when Percy had fallen on the bonfire. That had started a chain of events that within a very short time had churned up all their lives.

After Sam's car accident, Robert reflected, Lucy had been so busy grieving for her parents and then looking after Sam after he came out of hospital that he'd felt pushed into the background. Patsy had been so dependent on him helping her with Sam and so willing to keep him company when he'd felt miserable that at the time she had filled the yawning gap in his life.

Before he realised what was happening Patsy was pregnant and there was no turning back. He'd done the only thing he could in the circumstances; he didn't love Patsy, but he had married her because that was what was expected of him.

He knew that both Lucy and Sam had been bitterly hurt and angry; Lucy because he had jilted her and Sam because he'd lost Patsy.

Looking back, Robert could see how selfish he'd been. Still, he told himself, there was no point in dwelling on that now. In his estimation, simply because of what happened then was certainly no excuse for Lucy to accept a date with Percy.

If she thought going on a date with Percy would make any difference as to whether or not Sam was given a job at Carter's Cars, he could have told her that she was wasting her time. Percy had no real say in matters of that sort; those decisions were made by old man Carter himself and he brooked no interference from anybody.

Lucy cleared away the breakfast dishes and washed up after Robert went to work but she left the five-pound note lying on the table where he had put it. Each time she walked through the room it seemed to draw her eyes towards it and stir up the argument that was trying to battle itself out in her mind.

She had to admit that she was tempted. She knew exactly the sort of dress she would like to have. It would skim her knees, have a dropped waist and the skirt would be box-pleated. As she danced the pleats would flare out prettily as she twirled around. She wasn't sure about the colour but she thought perhaps a dramatic red or else a pretty pastel colour, so that she could enjoy wearing the dress to go out in all through the summer.

When she'd finished dressing Anna and done all the housework the money was still lying there, tempting her to go on a spending spree. As she strapped Anna into her pushchair ready to go shopping she picked it up and slipped it into her purse. It would be safe there, she told herself. Perhaps she'd use it to buy something special for their meal tonight.

It was a crisp, sunny morning and as she set out for the shops she decided that for a change she would go as far as St John's Market. It was quite a long walk but because it was such a nice day they would enjoy it and she might pick up a bargain.

She hadn't meant to walk through the town centre and look in all the shop windows again but when she did so she couldn't help thinking of the money tucked away in her purse. Before she knew what was happening she was inside Frisby Dyke's and was making her way to the ladies' dress department.

She had already seen the sort of dress she wanted in their window but it wasn't in a colour she liked. Inside the store there was a whole rail of similar styles.

As she looked through them one in a gorgeous shade of turquoise seemed to jump out at her. She studied the label: it was her size and it would fit her perfectly.

'Would madam like to try it on?' a posh young voice asked.

Lucy backed away from the slim, elegant young woman who stood at her side. 'Thank you, I was only looking.'

'It's a colour that would suit you,' the well-modulated voice told her. 'Do try it on. I am sure you will look perfectly lovely in it,' the girl added persuasively.

'I ... I'll think about it; I want to have a look around and see what else there is first,' Lucy told her.

Quickly she moved away, accidentally bumping the pushchair into the nearby counter which made her feel all the more gauche and uncomfortable.

Determined not to be rushed into buying, she walked around the entire dress department. There was nothing at all that seemed more suitable and, instinctively, she made her way back to where the turquoise dress was hanging. She needed to see the price tag before she committed herself.

The moment her fingers touched the soft, silky fabric she knew she must have it; the price was four pounds, nineteen shillings and eleven pence. She could afford it but it would mean she had spent the entire five pounds; she had never paid that much for a dress in her life.

She stood there trying to convince herself that it was the right thing to do because it was to help Sam.

'Perhaps madam would like to try it on now?' the salesgirl suggested hopefully.

'No, I haven't time to do that,' Lucy said hesitantly. 'It is my correct size, so I am quite sure that it will fit me perfectly,' she added quickly, the colour rushing to her face.

She would have liked to try the dress on very much and to study her reflection in one of the full-length triple mirrors in the well-appointed changing room. It was impossible to do so, though, because it would be far too embarrassing to let this immaculate-looking young assistant see her shabby underwear.

'My little girl is tired and she might prove rather fractious,' she said lamely.

The salesgirl smiled superciliously. 'Very well, madam, I quite understand. If you'll accompany me over to the counter I'll pack it up for you.'

As she handed the five-pound note over Lucy

wondered what Robert would think of it. It seemed to be such a lot of money to spend on one dress, even such a lovely one. Nevertheless, as the girl folded it meticulously in white tissue paper before carefully putting it into a carrier bag with the shop's name printed on it, she couldn't wait to get home and try it on so that she could see what she looked like in it.

On the way home Lucy kept thinking about her new dress and hoping Robert wouldn't feel that she had been extravagant in spending so much money on it. She also hoped he would be in a better mood when he came home from work because he'd certainly seemed to be so very put out about her going out with Percy that, for a moment, she'd wondered if he was jealous.

Anna was asleep when they arrived home so Lucy left her in the pushchair while she unpacked her new dress. As she took it out of the smart carrier bag and removed the layers of tissue paper, she drew in her breath in delight. It looked even better than it had when it was hanging in the shop.

Quickly, right there in the living room, she took off her blouse, stepped out of her skirt and slipped the new dress over her head. It fitted perfectly.

Excitedly she dashed upstairs to her bedroom to see if she could get a full-length view in the mirror in her room. As she twirled, the pleats at the bottom of the skirt swirled out attractively exactly as she had thought they would.

She couldn't help thinking how wonderful it would have been if she was going to wear it for a night out with Robert.

A plaintive cry from downstairs signalling that

Anna was awake brought her back to reality. Why was she indulging in such foolish fantasies? she asked herself. Robert had moved on and they'd lost their chance of having a future together long ago. Taking the dress off she laid it carefully on her bed before going back downstairs and putting on her everyday skirt and blouse again.

Chapter Twenty-Seven

Lucy was ready well before seven o'clock but she stayed in her bedroom until the very last minute. She hoped that she wouldn't bump into Robert as she was going out because she was afraid that he would say something critical about her going out with Percy and that would spoil the occasion for her.

At five minutes to seven, though, she decided that perhaps she had better go downstairs because if there was a knock on the front door Robert might go and answer it and she didn't want that to happen. If she waited on the stairs then she could make sure she was the first to reach the front door.

Although she went down as quietly as she possibly could Robert heard her and came out into the hallway. For a moment they simply stared at each other in silence.

'Ready, are you?' he said at length. 'Well, have a good time. Your new dress, or what I can see of it under your coat, looks nice,' he added rather awkwardly.

'Thank you.'

She felt embarrassed by their encounter and wondered if he expected her to take off her coat so that he could see her dress properly. To her relief, at that moment there was a knock on the door signalling Percy's arrival.

'Come on, then, you'd better not keep him waiting,' Robert commented as he opened the door. 'He's taking you in one of Carter's smartest cars, I see.'

It wasn't very far to the Paradise Club which was near Lime Street Station. Lucy felt nervous because she'd never been there before. As they drew up outside they were greeted so effusively by the doorman who dashed forward to open the car door for her that she realised Percy must be quite well-known there.

After they'd handed in their coats she noticed that Percy looked extremely smart. Like many of the men there he was wearing evening dress but because he was so overweight there was an air of pompousness about him that was out of keeping with a man so young. Lucy couldn't help thinking how extremely handsome Robert would look if he was dressed like that.

Percy straightened his bow tie before he escorted her into the dining room. As they were shown to their table she was again aware that he was given a very cordial greeting not only by the waiters but also by some of the other diners.

Lucy felt butterflies inside her as she sat down and saw the vast array of glasses and silver cutlery on the table in front of her. When she was handed the enormous glossy menu card she had no idea at all about what to order. Uneasily she scanned the long list of dishes, desperately trying to work out what some of them were, but the names were all in French.

Percy saved her from embarrassment by selecting what they would have and merely asking her if she liked prawns and lamb. She smiled and nodded and then tried to locate the dishes on the menu but found it impossible to do so.

Percy also chose the wine and Lucy breathed a silent sigh of relief when their waiter came and collected up the menu cards and took them away.

While they waited for their first course Lucy felt overawed by the magnificence of the room with its glittering chandeliers, highly polished dark wood-work and the floor-length dark red velvet curtains. The round tables with their gleaming white napery sparkling glass and silver were of varying size. There were three very large tables seating six or more people.

Percy put her at ease by chattering away about trivial everyday matters until their food arrived. She was anxious to ask him what had been decided about Sam but felt that she would have to wait for him to bring the subject up.

She found that the dishes he had ordered were delicious and so was the wine. Normally she never drank wine, except the occasional small glass of sweet sherry or a port and lemonade at Christmas time or on her birthday. She was too afraid to do more than take tiny sips in case she started talking silly. Percy, she noticed, let the waiter fill up his glass over and over again.

At the end of their meal Percy suggested they

should have their coffee and a liqueur at one of the little tables in the ballroom where a live band called The Five Aces was playing and then, when they were ready to do so, they could dance.

Lucy found the rest of the evening was rather stressful. When she'd been younger she'd always enjoyed dancing but it had always been with Robert as her partner and their steps had always seemed to match perfectly.

Dancing with Percy was quite another matter. His hands were hot and clammy and he held her far too tightly; his movements were clumsy and half the time he was out of step with the music. He trod on her toes so often that they felt bruised and sore. Added to which his breath was unpleasant and he insisted on dancing with his face pressed up against hers.

Lucy found it quite exhausting and knew she had made a mistake in accepting his invitation even though she'd done it for Sam's benefit. After two dances she rather timidly suggested they sat the next one out. To her relief, Percy agreed and after they had returned to one of the tables at the edge of the dance floor he called a waiter over.

'I would much sooner have a glass of lemonade,' Lucy told him when he asked for two cognacs.

'Nonsense. You need a few drinks down you to help you relax before we take to the floor again,' Percy told her with a laugh as the waiter hovered ready to take their order.

When she insisted that she didn't want any more strong drink because she was already feeling woozy the waiter gave an imperceptible lift of his eyebrows and suggested, 'Perhaps an orange cooler?'

'A good idea,' Percy agreed. 'Make it a special one,' he emphasised with a broad smile.

Lucy found her drink extremely refreshing. She didn't know what else had been added apart from the cubes of ice that clinked enticingly, but she had certainly never had orange juice that tasted anything like this one did, she thought, as she took another long drink.

She would have been content to sit listening to The Five Aces and enjoying her drink for the rest of the evening but Percy was soon restless. After about ten minutes he ordered another cognac and the moment it arrived he drained his glass and stood up saying he was ready to go back on to the dance floor.

'I haven't finished my drink yet,' Lucy demurred, ignoring the hand he was holding out to pull her up from her chair.

'Never mind, leave it there on the table and we'll come back again later and you can finish it then, or have a fresh one,' Percy told her impatiently.

Once again she found herself being pressed firmly against his bulky body and held far too tightly but she didn't know how to make this known to him. When he began nibbling at her ear as they circled the room she felt that was going too far and pulled away from him quite sharply and shook her head firmly.

Far from it making him stop, he began nuzzling her neck with hot kisses and she felt his hands wandering up and down her back in such an intimate way that she wanted to scream.

Lucy felt that it was almost like being caught up in a bad dream from which there was no escape. She felt tired and exhausted and her feet were sore and Percy's behaviour was becoming more and more obnoxious.

He insisted on dancing until the very end of the evening. Lucy breathed a sigh of relief when the band finally played 'God Save the King' and brought the evening to a close.

As he helped her into her coat, Lucy tried to ignore what was happening as she felt his hands fondling her breasts. As he turned her round and made a pretence of fastening her coat she felt him slip one of his hands inside the neck of her dress so that she had to step back to be free of his touch.

In the car on the way home she thanked him politely for a pleasant evening and then summoned up the courage to ask what was happening about Sam.

'We don't have to talk about that now, do we?' Percy muttered. 'Tell him to come to my office tomorrow around ten o'clock and I'll discuss it with him then.'

'So you are going to give him a job?' Lucy breathed thankfully. 'I'm so glad, because it means so much to him. He seemed to lose all confidence in himself for a long time after that driving accident and he was just managing to get his life together again when there was this other incident on Orangeman's Day and, more recently, the blow to his head has ruined everything for him again...'

Percy didn't answer; instead he took his left

283

hand off the steering wheel and placed it on her knee and began to slide it up and down, getting higher and higher up her thigh each time. Lucy pushed his hand away and moved as far away from him as it was possible to do in the confines of the car.

He pulled up in Priory Terrace a short distance from her front door and switched off the car engine. Quickly she thanked him again for a nice evening and fumbled with the door to open it.

When he leaned across her, she thought it was to help her to open the car door but, instead, he caught her by the arm, pinioning her to the seat and preventing her from moving.

'Don't I get a goodnight kiss?' he asked, breathing heavily as he tried to pull her into his arms.

She pulled back and smiled dismissively. Again she tried to open the car door. This time he grabbed her quite roughly and forced her back into her seat. His abruptness left her completely breathless and his mouth covered hers before she could say anything. When he thrust his tongue inside her mouth Lucy felt like gagging. Desperately she tried to fight him off but he was so much bigger and stronger than she was that her efforts were in vain.

He pinned her against the seat, his mouth covered hers again and at the same time he began running one of his hands up her leg. As it moved up to her thigh she managed to twist her face free and let out a scream. She didn't want him touching her at all and certainly not in the manner in which he was trying to do so now.

The more she struggled and protested the more

it seemed to excite Percy. Lucy began to feel utterly degraded and humiliated by his behaviour.

'So you like a fight, do you?' he muttered in an exultant tone. 'Well, so do I. I'll master you so you may as well give in. I intend to have you and nothing you can do will stop me.'

Finally she managed to jab him hard in the stomach with one of her elbows and as he doubled up in agony she succeeded in pushing him away. As she forced open the car door he managed to grab hold of her again and tried to stop her. Somehow the hem of her dress got caught on the gear stick and there was a sickening tearing sound as some of the stitches gave way.

In a blind panic she scrambled out of the car and ran along the pavement, tears spilling down her cheeks, praying that he wouldn't try to follow her. She heard the car engine start up and was aware that he had drawn level with her and had slowed down so that he was keeping pace with her as she hurried to her front door.

He kept the car moving so close to the pavement that she thought that at any minute it would mount the kerb and run her over. She heard him shout something and hoped none of the neighbours had heard. All she wanted to do was to get inside the house and bolt the front door; to be somewhere where she knew he wouldn't be able to follow her. Then and only then would she feel she was safe.

Her hand was trembling so much that when she pushed open the letterbox to reach for the door key that they kept there on the end of a piece of string, she had difficulty in grasping it. When she

285

did manage to withdraw it she was so blinded by tears that she could hardly see to fit it in the lock.

Once she was safely inside and the door was securely bolted she leaned against it and stood there in the dark for a minute trying to get her breath back.

Knowing what a near escape she'd just had, a feeling of relief flooded over her and before she could stop herself she was sobbing out loud.

She knew she wouldn't be able to sleep after such an ordeal so she decided to make herself a cup of tea before going up to bed and quietly opened the door to the living room.

Chapter Twenty-Eight

As Lucy went through the living room on her way to the kitchen she was taken aback to find Robert sitting there in one of the armchairs. She was immediately conscious of what a mess she must look with her torn dress and blotched cheeks.

'You've had a good evening, then,' he commented dryly, looking up and staring at her appearance from over the top of the newspaper he was reading.

'You startled me,' she said in a shaky voice. 'What are you doing up so late?'

'I thought I'd better wait up and make sure you managed to get home safely.'

Lucy stared at him for a moment, saying nothing. She had been trying to bolster up her courage but she was suddenly aware of how frightened she was by the horrible time she had endured and burst into sobs once more.

Immediately Robert discarded his newspaper and was out of his chair and had taken her in his arms. 'Don't take on so,' he comforted. 'I didn't mean anything by it.'

'It wasn't what you said,' Lucy snuffled, 'it was what happened while I was out. Percy Carter's behaviour was revolting and it was a waste of an entire evening because I didn't find out anything at all about what is going to happen about Sam's job.'

'You mean that's the only reason you went out with Percy?' Robert asked in disbelief.

'Of course it was; what other reason would there be?'

'I thought you must like him,' Robert said glumly. 'I know he's always fancied you.'

'Every minute of it was utterly horrible,' Lucy sniffed as she wiped her eyes.

'Even going to the Paradise Club?' Robert asked in surprise.

'Well, no. The food there was delicious and the band was tremendous,' she admitted. 'It was Percy who ruined what could have been a nice evening.'

'Sit here in the armchair and toast your toes in front of the fire while I make us both a drink and then you can tell me all about it,' Robert said.

Lucy tried to calm down but she still felt frightened and when Robert brought in their cocoa she was still shivering and tears were trickling down her cheeks.

Robert put their cups down on the table and sat on the arm of the chair. Then he put his arm round Lucy's shoulder and murmured words of comfort to try and console her as if she was a child.

In minutes she felt so safe and reassured that she was gradually able to relax. They sat like that for quite a while; they didn't talk but sipped their cocoa in companionable silence until her trembling gradually subsided.

Their closeness brought back memories to Lucy of happier times when they had always been close like this. It was something she had missed so much and, not for the first time, she wished she could turn the clock back.

As Robert took her empty cup from her and moved to put it on the table along with his own she felt a tremor of deep affection for him run through her.

When he turned round and held out a hand to pull her to her feet she was aware from his touch that the cool reserve that he'd shown ever since she had moved into his house seemed to have disappeared. The next moment they were in each other's arms.

For the briefest moment Lucy stiffened, wondering if it was foolish to try and recapture what had once been something so memorable between them. Then her overwhelming longing and need for the closeness they'd known overcame her qualms and with a sigh of pleasure she relaxed in his arms.

His passionate words as he kissed her were at first gentle and soothing then his increasing ardour stirred her own feelings. As she submitted to his kisses and sensitive touch it was as if all the old magic was restored.

Once again she was being transported into realms of delight but this time it was far more intense than anything she'd ever experienced before in the whole of her life.

Robert was gentle and considerate, but far more passionate than she had ever known him to be. As they clung together in the flickering firelight, their lovemaking surpassed all her memories. She wanted their reunion to go on for ever but Robert, whispering how very late it was, brought her back to reality.

For several minutes they lay entwined, enjoying their closeness to each other. Robert's sweet whispers expressing how he felt filled her with happiness. Then a plaintive cry from Anna shattered their bliss.

Once she stood up and his arms were no longer round her, the feeling of anxiety returned. Shivering uncontrollably she hurried upstairs. Automatically she checked on Anna and found that she was sleeping and that the blankets were tucked in around her. Still shivering she crept into her own bed and huddled there, hugging her knees in an effort to stop herself from shaking.

Seconds later she felt a movement and then Robert's arms were round her once more as he slipped in beside her. Within a few minutes she was asleep.

When she woke next morning she was alone and for several minutes she lay there wondering if he really had been lying there alongside her the night before or whether that and their love-making had all been a dream.

Anna's whimpering aroused her and, realising that she had overslept, Lucy hurriedly washed and dressed. She felt annoyed that it had happened today of all days, when it was important to make sure that Sam was up and ready to go along to Carter's Cars.

All the time she was dressing Anna, Lucy kept asking herself if she and Robert really had made love the night before or not. If they had, then how would he react today?

To her immense relief Robert had already left for work by the time she arrived downstairs with Anna. Sam was up and he looked elated when she told him that he had to be at Carter's Cars that morning by half past ten.

'That must mean that they're giving me back my job,' he said confidently.

Anna was still fretful and Lucy assumed it was because she was hungry and so as quickly as possible she prepared breakfast for the three of them.

As she put it on the table Anna pushed her plate away saying that she didn't want it and Lucy realised that she was looking flushed as if she was unwell.

'Come on, now, eat it all up and then you'll feel better afterwards,' Lucy encouraged.

Anna sat at the table with her head propped up on one hand looking very dejected all the time Lucy and Sam were eating their breakfast. The moment Sam finished he stood up anxious to leave so as not to be late for his interview.

This time he was going on his own so Lucy wished him good luck and he smiled his appreciation. The moment he'd gone Lucy turned her attention to Anna who had hardly touched the food she'd put in front of her.

As she lifted her down from the table and sat down in the armchair to cuddle her, once again Lucy's thoughts went back to the previous night and how she and Robert had sat in this very same chair. Then she had been seeking solace from Robert just as Anna was now snuggling into her arms for comfort and consolation.

It was so peaceful sitting there nursing the child and singing gently to her that before Lucy knew what was happening they were both fast asleep.

Lucy awoke with a start; she had no idea what time it was or how long they had both been sleeping. Very gently she transferred Anna from her arms on to the armchair before going into the kitchen to check the clock. She could hardly believe her eyes when she saw that it was after three o'clock.

She looked around her in dismay. She hadn't even cleared away the breakfast things. Robert would be home in a couple of hours and she wondered how she was going to face him after what had happened; or had it all been a dream? she asked herself.

She scurried around as fast as she could, all the time hoping that Anna would go on sleeping long enough for her to wash the dishes, tidy up and prepare some vegetables.

Suddenly she remembered Sam and his interview and stopped what she was doing to go to the bottom of the stairs and call up to him to know how he'd got on. When there was no answer she ran up the stairs to his room and was puzzled to find that he wasn't there.

As she got on with her chores she wondered if he had already started work. Surely not, she told herself. They wouldn't want him to do so there and then. He'd be expected to report first thing Monday morning at the very earliest.

Her thoughts were diverted by Anna waking up and calling out to her. Knowing by now she must be really hungry because she had not eaten any breakfast Lucy stopped what she was doing and boiled an egg for her then buttered a slice of bread and cut it into thin strips before sitting her up at the table.

To her surprise Anna didn't seem very interested although normally she loved eggy soldiers, as she called them. She did drink the cup of milk that was on the table by her plate but then she wanted to get down. Immediately she climbed back into the armchair and curled up again and closed her eyes.

'Come on, sleepy head, you mustn't doze off again or you won't sleep tonight,' Lucy told her. 'I need you to help me lay the table,' she added, holding out her hand.

Anna shook her head and stayed where she was, putting her thumb into her mouth and cuddling up to a cushion.

Lucy was so behind with everything that she decided that as long as Anna was quiet then she might as well leave her where she was and get on with all the jobs that needed doing.

The next couple of hours seemed to flash by and she didn't think about Sam again because she was too concerned about Anna. The child was flushed and far from well and in the end she decided she might be better off in bed.

When Robert arrived home and asked her how Sam had got on at his interview she looked at him blankly.

'You mean he's not with you?' she asked in surprise. 'He went off at half past nine this morning and he hasn't been home since. I thought perhaps he had started working already.'

'Probably making the most of his freedom before he has to join the world's workers,' Robert laughed. 'Anna's missing as well, she hasn't gone to look for a job, has she?' he joked.

'Anna's not feeling too well,' Lucy told him.

'Oh, what's wrong with her?' he asked, his voice full of concern.

'She has slept most of the day and I think she must be sickening for a cold or something so I popped her back into bed just before you came home.'

'So it's only Sam who's missing. I'm sure he'll walk in any minute now; he knows what time the food is on the table.'

Sam didn't walk in, though. The two of them finally sat down to their meal and at Robert's suggestion Lucy put Sam's meal on a plate over a pan of hot water to keep warm.

'I can't think where he can be,' Lucy said worriedly as she cleared away their dishes.

'No, it is strange,' Robert agreed. 'You say he

293

hasn't been home at all since the interview?'

'Not as far as I know,' Lucy admitted.

'You could have missed him; he could have come home while you were out shopping and then gone straight back out again when he found that there was no one here.'

'I haven't been out shopping today. Mind you,' she added a trifle shamefacedly, 'I did fall asleep. I was nursing Anna because she wasn't too well and we both nodded off.'

'Surely you would have heard him if he'd come in, wouldn't you?' Robert frowned.

'I would have thought so, although I must admit we did sleep rather soundly.'

'You mean you went back to bed?'

'Oh no, certainly not. I was sitting down here in the armchair nursing her.'

As she said it, memories of the previous night when she and Robert were sitting there came flooding back and she felt her colour rising but Robert didn't seem to notice and for a fleeting moment she felt piqued that he hadn't said anything at all about their passionate lovemaking the night before.

'So if he hasn't been back at all, then where is he?' he pondered.

Suddenly Lucy felt alarmed. Sam had been feeling very depressed about not being able to find a job and had built up such great hopes on going back to work at Carter's Cars that, if he hadn't been offered work, he would be feeling devastated. It would be the last straw and she felt worried about how he might react.

'Perhaps I should go and see if I can find Brenda

and see if he is with her,' Robert suggested.

'Brenda is working nights this week so I suppose they could have been together all day.'

'It's possible,' Robert agreed. 'They could even have been out celebrating because he now has a job.'

'Of course! Why on earth didn't I think of that earlier?' Lucy exclaimed in relief. 'Surely, though, Sam would have come home first to let me know what happened because he knows how anxious I was,' she added frowning.

'Well, let's assume they spent the day together celebrating,' Robert affirmed.

'Even so, he should be home by now if Brenda's on nights,' Lucy said.

'Have you any idea what time she would be going on duty?' Robert asked.

'I think it's seven o'clock but I'm not too sure.'

'Well, if I go along to the hospital, she should be there by now so I can find out if she's seen him at all today.'

'It's not like Sam to be so inconsiderate unless, of course, he simply forgot,' Lucy said lamely.

'I'll probably meet him halfway,' Robert laughed. 'You attend to Anna and make sure that she is all right and by that time we'll both be back home again.'

Lucy was surprised when Anna said she wanted to stay in bed even though she'd been sleeping for most of the day. She still seemed to be rather weepy and her brow was hot to the touch as if she were coming down with a cold.

As she came back downstairs Lucy felt on edge; she kept looking at the clock expecting the front door to open at any minute and Robert and Sam to walk in.

She topped up the water in the saucepan to make sure that Sam's meal was ready for him when they did come home. She laid up a tray with three cups and saucers then filled the kettle and put it on to boil in readiness to make a pot of tea for them all.

The minutes dragged by and became hours and she was still waiting for news. It was well after nine o'clock before Lucy heard the front door opening. Her spontaneous welcoming smile faded as Robert came in alone.

'Where's Sam? Haven't you found him?'

Robert shook his head. 'Neither sight nor sound of him anywhere,' he said wearily. 'I've walked miles; I've visited both the places off Scotland Road where you lived and I've walked down to the Pier Head and walked along by the river as far as possible.'

'What about Brenda, hadn't he been with her?'

'No, she's not seen him all day. I did promise to let her know he was all right but it's a bit late for that now.'

'If you don't, she'll worry all night,' Lucy pointed out.

'And if I do, then she'll worry even more when she hears that none of us know where he is.'

'Yes, that's true. So what are we going to do?'

'There's not much we can do. He's obviously gone off somewhere on his own.'

'I know that, but where? And, what is even more to the point, why has he gone without a word to any of us?'

They stared at each other for a long moment in silence.

'If it was any other chap then I'd say he'd gone on a bender to celebrate getting a job but that's not what Sam would do,' Robert said running his hand through his hair.

'I suspect that he didn't get a job, and that's why he's disappeared,' Lucy said worriedly.

'We don't know that for sure,' Robert told her. He pulled her into his arms and kissed the top of her head. Lucy felt confused; she knew he was worried about Sam, they both were, but his caress had been almost brotherly and once again her thoughts went back to the previous night and she wondered where all the passion had gone.

'Don't worry, Lucy, he'll come home. I've looked everywhere I can think of even back at Carter's Cars so we will just have to be patient and wait for him to turn up.'

Chapter Twenty-Nine

Lucy couldn't sleep for worrying about what had happened to Sam and where he might be or if he had met with an accident. She tossed and turned as all sorts of dreadful images kept going through her mind. She wished they had checked with the hospitals and alerted the police that Sam was missing and she was determined to do it the very first thing next morning.

Anna didn't sleep well either and kept wriggling

around and throwing off her covers and occasionally whimpering in her sleep. Lucy went over to her several times and replaced the covers and noticed that Anna was still very hot and flushed and that she seemed to be having trouble breathing.

Several times she was tempted to take Anna back into bed with her, knowing that she would gain comfort from cuddling the child, but she felt it wasn't right to disturb her and she didn't want to get her into the habit of their sleeping together.

A couple of times she padded along to Sam's bedroom to check whether he had come home, though she hadn't heard him come upstairs, but each time she did so she found his bed empty.

Lucy was up and dressed well before first light; Anna was sleeping and she wondered if she dared go out for half an hour to see if she could locate Sam.

Carrying her shoes in her hand she tiptoed down the stairs and was putting on her outdoor hat and coat when Robert appeared. He looked weary and unshaven.

'What's up? Where are you going?' he asked, his voice heavy with sleep.

'I thought I'd take a quick walk round and see if there was any sign of Sam; Anna's still sound asleep. I'll be back before you have to leave for work.'

'I'm not going in to work until we've found Sam,' Robert told her. 'You stay here and put the kettle on so that he can have a hot drink when I bring him back.'

'No,' Lucy shook her head, 'you really must go

to work, Robert, so you need to get washed and dressed. I'll go and look; I've already got my coat on.'

She made for the door before Robert could argue with her. Some inner instinct told her Sam might be down at the Pier Head and she went straight there.

It was quite a cold morning and a keen wind was blowing in off the river. As she approached the floating roadway she saw the *Royal Daffodil* was about to dock and she spotted a lone figure standing on the top deck leaning over the rails and staring down into the dark turbulent waters of the Mersey.

Fear gripped her like a giant hand; she was sure it was Sam. Terrified that he was going to jump she screamed his name. The sharp wind lifted the sound as if it was the cry of one of the many gulls circling the boat and carried it away.

She almost knocked over the seaman who was lowering the gangplank as the boat ground against the quayside. It was so early in the morning that there were only half a dozen passengers coming off the boat and she rushed past them, muttering her apologies as she pushed them out of her way in her eagerness to reach Sam.

'Come on home, your breakfast is going cold,' she screamed at him trying to make herself heard above the combined sound of the wind and the noise of the boat's engines.

She wasn't sure if he'd heard her or not but when he turned his head she sensed that he'd seen her.

'Keep away, Lucy, you shouldn't be here,' he

299

rasped, backing away from her. 'Leave me alone.'

'Why, where are you going?' She tried to keep the fear out of her voice but it was impossible. She knew even before he told her that he intended to jump.

'Don't do it, Sam; think of me and Brenda. You've got all your life ahead of you.'

'Life, what life? I have nothing to look forward to. Brenda will be better off without me and so will you. I'm nothing but a burden; I'm an out-of-work-down-and-out,' he added bitterly.

'Oh dear, you didn't get the job at Carter's Cars, then?' she commiserated.

'Percy Carter didn't even take the trouble to see me,' he told her bitterly. 'He sent one of the office girls down to tell me that there was no job for me after all.'

Lucy felt her stomach churn. Was that her fault? she wondered. Had she jeopardised Sam's chances by rejecting Percy's advances the night he'd taken her out?

'So where have you been since then? Why didn't you come home? We've all been so worried. Robert even went to the hospital last night to ask Brenda if she had seen anything of you.'

Sam gave a wry laugh. 'Brenda won't want to see me again, not when she hears I don't have a job. All our dreams and plans for a future together are as far away from coming to anything as they've ever been,' he said bitterly.

'There are other jobs; Carter's Cars isn't the beginning and end of the world, you know.'

'It is for me. I haven't got qualifications on paper so they are the only ones who know what I am capable of doing. What other employer will take my word for it when I tell them that I almost completed my apprenticeship? I can't see Percy Carter or his old man giving me references, can you?'

Lucy didn't know what to say but as Sam turned away and stared down into the murky Mersey once again she felt desperate. Somehow she had to persuade him to come home with her.

'Standing there looking down into the water isn't going to solve anything,' she said sharply. 'Come on, let's go home and when you've had a meal, we can start to plan what to do next. Perhaps you could start your shoeshining business up again,' she suggested.

'I've stopped thinking about the future; it ends right here. If you don't want to watch me jump, then go but, whatever happens, don't feel sorry for me. This is the best way out; I'm a failure and a burden and I always have been.'

'Come on, whacker, you've been riding back and forth on this boat all night, haven't you got a home to go to?'

The jovial voice of a deckhand startled them both. He'd come up on top deck without either of them noticing, they'd been so engrossed in their own problem.

'If he's your boyfriend, love, now that he's sobered up, why don't you forgive him and kiss and make up?' the deckhand told Lucy with a broad grin.

'We are just leaving,' Lucy assured him. Stepping forward and firmly taking hold of Sam's arm she added, 'I hope he hasn't been too much of a nuisance.'

'We get used to it; most nights there's someone who's had a skinful who'd rather stay on board than go home and face the music.'

'Come on!' Lucy pulled on Sam's arm. 'I've left Robert keeping an eye on Anna, which means that he's already late for work so we'd better get back as quickly as we can.'

For a moment as he tried to resist, she thought he was going to refuse to go with her. Then with a resigned sigh he walked with her towards the gangplank.

They walked home in silence. They found Robert was nursing Anna when they went in. 'She seems to be a bit flushed and unhappy,' he said as he passed her over to Lucy. 'I've tried giving her a drink of milk and a biscuit but she doesn't seem to want them.'

'She's been restless most of the night,' Lucy agreed as she took Anna from him. 'Don't worry, I'll sort her out, you get to work.'

'You all right, Sam?' Robert asked as he shrugged on his coat and pulled his cap out of the pocket and put it on.

'Yes, you don't need to worry about me,' Sam told him gruffly. 'You'd better get a move on, though, or you'll find yourself out of a job the same as me.'

'Brenda will probably be here any minute now,' Robert said as he headed for the front door. 'She said she'd be dropping in as soon as she came off duty to see if you were all right, Sam. She was very worried about you the same as the rest of us were when you didn't come home last night.'

'I'm off to bed,' Sam stated the moment the

door closed behind Robert.

'Aren't you going to wait and see Brenda? You heard what Robert said,' Lucy asked in surprise.

'No. I don't want to talk to her. Tell her that it's all over between us,' Sam said flatly.

'Over between you? What on earth are you talking about, Sam? Only a couple of days ago you were both talking about getting married quite soon.'

'That's when I thought I was getting a job and would be able to support a wife,' Sam said bitterly. 'There's not much point in her wasting any more time with me, is there, when I haven't got a job and I'm not likely to get one in a hurry.'

'Perhaps you should let Brenda be the one to decide that,' Lucy told him.

Before Sam could reply there was a knock on the front door and Lucy, carrying Anna in her arms, opened it and welcomed Brenda into the hallway.

'He's just this minute come home and he's in the living room,' Lucy told her. 'I'm just going to take Anna back upstairs for another sleep; that's if I can pacify her.'

Lucy stayed upstairs singing softly to Anna until she was asleep then she covered her over before going back downstairs.

Brenda was on the point of leaving but she stayed long enough to ask what was wrong with Anna.

'I think she is tired because none of us slept well last night,' Lucy explained.

'I understand that. I'm off now to catch up on my own sleep but I'll try and pop back later before I go on duty, if that's all right.'

Lucy nodded and smiled and then left Sam to say goodbye to Brenda while she went into the kitchen to make Sam something to eat and a pot of tea for the two of them.

'I hope you didn't say any of that silly nonsense to Brenda that you were spouting to me earlier on when we were on the boat,' Lucy commented as she placed some toast in front of Sam and picked up the teapot and filled both their cups.

'Not much point, she probably wouldn't have listened to me,' Sam said sullenly.

'Well, that's lucky for you and shows she has more common sense than you have. She knows the same as I do that you will get a job given time.'

'Given time,' he mocked. 'What sort of time are we talking about? Do you mean this year, next year or when?'

'Sam, try and be patient. You've had a run of bad luck and you are still not completely fit. Another few months will make all the difference.'

'By then I'll be too old to be considered for a job,' he said in a bitter voice.

Lucy stirred her tea thoughtfully. 'You're only a couple of years older than me, Sam.'

'I'm twenty-two, I have no qualifications and the only work I've ever really done is to shine shoes.'

'Don't belittle yourself. It was very successful and you were doing a good trade until that unfortunate incident on Orangeman's Day,' Lucy pointed out.

'You can hardly call it much of a job,' he

304

muttered. 'I can't see Brenda wanting to marry a shoeshine boy, can you?'

'If you were making a living wage, then I don't think she would mind,' Lucy argued.

'She mightn't, but I would; it's not a proper job for a married man, now is it?'

Before they could discuss it any further there was a plaintive wail from upstairs indicating that Anna was awake again and that by the sound of things she was far from well.

'Can you clear away these dishes for me?' Lucy asked as she went back up to try and comfort Anna.

A few minutes later she was back down again with Anna in her arms. 'I'm sure there is something more than having a bad night wrong with her,' she said worriedly. 'Her head is burning; she must have a temperature.'

'When I've finished doing these dishes would you like to go round to the doctor's and ask him to call?' Sam asked.

'I suppose I could walk round there with her,' Lucy murmured hesitantly.

'Not a very good idea; there's a cold wind blowing outside, remember,' Sam cautioned. 'It might be best if you stayed here with her and I went and asked him to call.'

It was almost two hours before the doctor arrived. By then Anna was struggling to breathe and Lucy was at her wits' end trying to pacify her.

The doctor was middle aged and authoritative. His face became grave after he'd examined Anna and listened to her breathing through his stethoscope.

'This child has diphtheria and needs to be in hospital and properly looked after,' he stated. 'I'll arrange for an ambulance; it should be here to collect her within the hour.'

'Can I go along to the hospital and stay there with her?' Lucy asked hopefully.

'You can certainly go as far as the hospital with her but once there she will be put into an isolation ward and you won't be allowed anywhere near her after that.'

'We will be able to visit her?' Lucy said anxiously.

'They may let you see her through a window, but you won't be allowed into the ward. Surely you are aware that diphtheria is a highly infectious illness? It's most fortunate that none of you have caught it.'

'Yes, I do know that, but she needs me there to comfort her,' Lucy argued.

'No,' he shook his head, 'we are wasting valuable time; she is far too ill to know whether you are there or not. What she needs at this moment is skilled nursing and the sooner she gets it the better will be her chance of pulling through.'

Lucy stared at him in disbelief. 'Are you saying that Anna might die?' she gasped.

'It's an extremely serious illness and quite a high percentage of children do not recover,' he stated.

'Please don't say that,' Lucy pleaded.

'Try not to worry,' he said placatingly. 'I'm going to make the necessary arrangement now so will you have her ready when the ambulance arrives?' he added returning his stethoscope to his black bag and snapping it shut before picking up his bowler hat and making for the door.

Chapter Thirty

For the next few days all Lucy's thoughts were centred on little Anna. Even Sam's disappointment over not getting a job paled into insignificance as they waited for news.

Brenda had warned them that the real testing time would be in a couple of days when the fever reached its peak. If she survived that then she would get better although it might be a very long time before she was completely well again.

Lucy and Robert were at the hospital on the night of the crisis and whenever Lucy peered through the small viewing window and saw how grey and lifeless little Anna was, she dreaded what the news might be.

It was shortly after midnight when a nurse emerged from the isolation ward and came over to speak to them. Lucy felt sick with anticipation as she clutched at Robert's hand, wondering what they were going to be told.

'The crisis has passed,' the nurse said quietly. 'Anna has pulled through. She will have to stay in hospital for some time yet but the worst is over and she will recover.'

For a moment Lucy couldn't believe her ears and then she burst into tears.

'Come on, you shouldn't be crying; Anna's going to be all right!' Robert consoled her, hugging her close.

'I know, I'm so relieved, that's why I'm crying,' Lucy breathed thankfully. 'I thought we were going to lose her and life would never be the same without her.'

'Does she really mean that much to you?' Robert asked softly.

'Yes, she does. I love her more than anything in the world,' Lucy told him.

Gently he placed a hand under her chin, tilting her face so that he could look deep into her tear-filled eyes. 'You really do care about Anna, don't you?'

Lucy nodded vehemently. 'Of course I do, Robert. As much as if she was my very own.'

'Even though she's Patsy's child?'

Lucy gave an imperceptible shrug. 'She's your little girl, Robert, and that is all that matters to me.'

Robert sighed as he released her. 'I am so glad about that,' he said softly. 'She means a great deal to me as well. I want her to be happy and as long as you are looking after her I know she will be.'

Sam and Brenda were both elated when Robert and Lucy returned home and told them the good news about Anna.

'Have you any idea how long she will have to stay in hospital?' Sam asked. 'I miss having her around the place.'

'They didn't say,' Lucy murmured. She looked enquiringly at Brenda. 'Do you think it will be very long?'

'I don't know, it depends on her progress,' Brenda said cautiously. 'Rest assured, though, she is in good hands so there is no need to worry about her.'

'No,' Lucy agreed. 'I can get back to worrying about Sam instead. I'm sorry I've had no time for your problems during the last few days,' she told her brother apologetically. 'I am very disappointed that you didn't get the job at Carter's Cars.'

Sam shrugged dismissively, 'What did you say to upset Percy Carter the night you went out with him?' he asked, his voice tinged with bitterness.

'Nothing, nothing at all,' Lucy said quickly but she felt the colour rushing to her face as she remembered the unpleasantness between them when he'd brought her home. She also noticed the frown on Robert's face although he said nothing.

Over the next few days, Lucy felt that Robert seemed to be distracted and it troubled her because she couldn't understand why. She tried to tell herself that he was preoccupied because he was still worried about Anna but she was sure that it went deeper than that.

In the end she could stand the strain no longer and asked him outright if she had upset him in some way. He looked so bemused that she wanted to laugh.

'Of course you haven't,' he exclaimed in astonishment. 'Whatever makes you say that?'

'I don't know; you seem to try and avoid being on your own with me as much as possible.'

'Well, yes, that's true enough,' he said reluctantly, 'and for a very good reason. I keep remembering that I took advantage of you the other evening when you were upset.'

'I don't understand what you mean. As I remember it, you comforted me when I was feeling upset.'

'No,' he said, contritely, his face darkening. 'I took advantage of you when you were most vulnerable.'

The colour ebbed from Lucy's face. 'Is that what really happened?' she said bleakly. 'I thought it was because you had feelings for me; because even after all this time, and despite all that has happened, you still loved me.'

'I do, of course I do. That's another reason why I am trying to keep my distance. Every time I see you I want to take you in my arms and kiss you,' he exploded.

'Then why don't you? It's what I want,' Lucy told him in a strangled whisper.

Robert was silent for a second, looking at her in utter disbelief. 'Do you know what you are saying?' he asked.

'Of course I do,' Lucy said softly, her eyes shining with relief.

'What about Percy Carter?' he demanded.

It was Lucy's turn to look astonished. 'I thought you understood that I want nothing more to do with him. Going out with him at all was a mistake but he said he wanted to talk about Sam's prospects and I was anxious to do anything I could to help Sam.'

Robert nodded but his face still looked glum and Lucy wasn't sure whether she'd explained things well enough or whether he thought she was simply making excuses. She didn't know what else to say so she walked over to him and kissed him lightly on the cheek, hoping he would respond and felt saddened when he didn't.

It was another two weeks before Anna was well enough to come home. Lucy went in to see her every afternoon and sometimes again in the evening with Robert.

Although Anna was still pitifully thin she looked so much better that they both thought she had made a miraculous recovery. On the way home afterwards their conversation usually centred on what Anna's needs would be when she eventually came out of hospital.

Lucy knew that Robert still resented the fact that she'd gone out with Percy Carter even though he knew her reason for doing so and she had told him what a disastrous evening it had been. Neither of them had mentioned it again but they were still not completely at ease with each other and she felt it was important that they should be for Anna's sake.

Anna's coming home from hospital did more than anything else to make this happen. They were both so anxious to look after her and do all they could to restore her to full health that they almost ended up spoiling her.

Lucy was delighted to have Anna back. A lot of her time was taken up trying to keep her amused yet at the same time making sure that she didn't get overexcited or overtired.

She insisted that Anna had a nap after her midday meal if she wanted to stay up so that Robert could play with her when he came home from work. This became the highlight of Anna's day and Lucy liked nothing better than to watch them together.

At night there was a special ritual that included both Lucy and Robert. Anna would happily let Lucy undress her and get her ready for bed as long as Robert would read her a story afterwards.

To fit in with this they began delaying their meal until later in the evening after Anna was tucked up in bed and asleep. Then and only then were they able to relax. Gradually it became a very special time for them as well.

If Sam and Brenda were there, then they would sit talking until it was their own bedtime; if Robert and Lucy were on their own, then they usually discussed any domestic problems and often made plans for the weekend when they both liked to take Anna out.

As summer approached and the nights became lighter, it became ever more difficult to persuade Anna to go to bed so Lucy changed their routine. Instead of delaying their evening meal until after Anna was in bed she served it much earlier so that not only could the child sit there with them but they could also take her out for a walk after-wards.

Some evenings they took her to play in the park on the swings; at other times they merely went for a short stroll and then back home for her bath and a bedtime story.

As July advanced Lucy suggested that she thought it would be a good idea to have a party to celebrate Anna's birthday which was on the last day of the month.

'I think we should make it really special for her with balloons, blancmange and jelly as well as a birthday cake. I'd like to give her a surprise birthday present. I thought perhaps I could give her a doll and you could give her a pram and that would make it really special,' Lucy said with a smile.

'I think she would love that,' Robert agreed, 'but there is one other present that I think she would like even better.'

'Really, what's that?'

'Her very own mother.'

Lucy drew in her breath sharply. What on earth was he trying to tell her? Had he met someone whom he wanted to marry? For a moment all her feeling of security and happiness wilted at the thought of being replaced in both Robert's and Anna's life. She didn't know how she would bear to go on living without them.

She knew she couldn't let that happen. Even if she lost Robert she was determined that she wouldn't lose Anna as well. She loved the child as dearly as if she was her own flesh and blood and she was pretty sure that little Anna loved her. To separate them now, when Anna was still fragile from her long illness, would make the child terribly unhappy.

'I think Anna is quite happy with things as they are,' she told Robert in a stilted voice. 'She has made tremendous progress since she came home from hospital.'

'I know and I want it to stay that way permanently. I think any further upsets would be very bad for her ... and for me,' he added with a huge grin.

'Then I don't understand what you mean about

giving her a mother,' she murmured.

'Don't you?' Smiling broadly he gently pulled her close and his mouth came down to cover hers in a kiss that was as sweet and tender as it was long.

'Lucy, will you marry me?' he whispered softly, lifting his mouth from hers long enough to ask the question.

'Oh Robert,' she whispered, her heart pounding so much that she could hardly speak. 'Of course I will,' she told him, her eyes sparkling and her face wreathed in smiles.

Once more he kissed her, this time jubilantly.

'Come on, let's go and tell Sam and Brenda the good news,' he said eagerly.

'No, wait.' Lucy laid a restraining hand on Robert's arm. 'We can tell them about Anna's party, by all means, but I don't think we should tell them about our plans; not yet.'

'Why not? You aren't going to change your mind, are you?' he asked in a teasing voice.

'No,' she shook her head, 'it's not that. I was thinking about Sam and Brenda. Sam has always said that he intends asking her to marry him once he has a job and, as you know, he has had no luck at all in finding work.'

Robert looked puzzled. 'I don't understand, what have our plans to do with that?'

'Telling them that we intend to get married will only upset Sam and make him even more depressed than he is now. Leave it for a little while and perhaps he will find something.'

'Yes, if that is what you want,' Robert said rather reluctantly. 'I realise that it must be hard for him but I don't see the situation improving. Most firms are putting men off, not taking them on.'

'Yes, I know, but he's trying so hard that his luck must change soon. He scans the paper the minute it comes out and goes after any job he thinks he might stand a chance of getting. I know he's had no success up until now but surely things must change; they can't go on like this for ever, now can they?'

'Let's hope not. I don't think Sam's situation should let it spoil our idea of having a birthday party for Anna, though,' Robert insisted.

'Oh no, neither do I,' Lucy agreed. 'We'll tell Sam and Brenda about Anna's party because we want them to be there, but I don't think we should say anything about our own future plans.'

'Very well, if that's what you want to do, we'll keep them to ourselves for the moment,' Robert agreed as he kissed her again.

Chapter Thirty-One

Anna's birthday party was a tremendous success. She had fully recovered from her illness and was as full of life as she'd ever been.

Brenda bought her a new dress to wear. It was pale blue with a fancy frill down the front and Anna loved it so much when they tried it on her in the shop that she was almost in tears when she had to take it off so that it could be wrapped up.

She was all smiles again, though, when they promised that she could be the one to carry it home and explained that she would be able to wear it at her party.

Lucy attached two big blue balloons to her chair which was placed at the head of the table. There were tiny sandwiches as well as red jelly and pink blancmange. Taking pride of place in the centre of the table was an iced birthday cake with candles on it.

At the end of the tea party Robert lit them and then they all waited for Anna to blow them out. When she'd succeeded in doing so they all clapped and then sang 'Happy Birthday'.

Afterwards they played hide-and-seek and several other simple games. Anna loved it all and the party went on until it was well past her usual time for going to bed. Having a bath was skipped because she was so tired and there was no need for Robert to read her a story; she was asleep almost as soon as her head touched the pillow.

As she came back downstairs Lucy reflected on what a wonderful time they'd had and how good her life had become since she'd moved back to Priory Terrace.

There was still one problem which worried her; Sam had still not found a job. He was becoming increasingly moody and worried because his dole money had run out and it meant the Means Test if he wanted to get any more.

When Lucy had suggested that he ought to start up his shoeshining business again as a temporary measure he had told her that it was out of the question because someone else had commandeered his pitch by the Goree Piazza.

'There's not enough business to make it worth my while to set up in opposition,' he pointed out dejectedly. 'Anyway, after what happened, I'm not too keen on working around that area again. I wouldn't mind betting that those two little sods who caused it would target me again if they got the chance.'

After that, as if he was determined to prove that he really did want to work and was prepared to try his hand at anything, he had gone around calling on all the local newsagents to see if they would let him sell their newspapers on the street corner only to find they had every spot filled by street vendors already.

In desperation he had even resorted to collecting old clothes and selling them on to a rag-and-bone man. He hated doing it and it only brought in coppers.

While she'd been upstairs putting Anna to bed Brenda had restored order to the room and made a pot of tea. The minute they all sat down Robert said that now they were all together there was something he wanted to tell them.

Lucy felt uneasy because she thought that he was going to tell them about their plans to get married even though she'd asked him to delay doing so until Sam had a job. To her surprise Robert had something quite different to announce.

He started off by looking directly at Sam and asking, 'How's the job hunting going? Have you found any work yet?'

'No, you bloody well know I haven't,' Sam said

317

irritably. 'You also know that my dole money is finished and that I can't even pay my fair share towards my keep. What are you going to do, boot me out into the street?'

'No, no, nothing of the sort,' Robert said calmly. 'I wanted to check whether you had anything in mind before I propositioned you. I was wondering if you would be prepared to work for a very low wage for the next few months if you were offered a job that had decent prospects in the future.'

'I don't understand,' Sam frowned, 'it's not some sort of charity set-up, is it? Because if it is, then I don't want to be involved,' he said tersely. 'Do you know what he's talking about, Lucy?'

'No, I'm as much in the dark as you are.'

'Me too,' Brenda echoed looking first at Robert and then at Sam.

'I'm thinking of breaking away from Carter's,' Robert explained, 'and starting up my own business.'

'You're going to do what?'

The outcry came simultaneously from Sam and Lucy who were both staring at him in astonishment. 'You've never said a word about this to me,' Lucy exclaimed.

'I don't really understand what's going on or what you are suggesting,' Sam muttered in a puzzled voice. 'What sort of business are you planning to start?'

'Much the same sort of work as I'm doing now,' Robert explained. 'I'll be repairing cars but doing it as my own boss. I've been thinking about it for a long time.'

'If you're going to start up on your own, then I don't see where I fit into your plans. How on earth can I be of any help?'

'You'd be working as my head mechanic and later on, when things are established and I can afford to take on more men, you'd be in charge of the repairs side of things,' Robert told him.

'Head mechanic! I have no proper qualifications, you know that,' Sam reminded him a trifle bitterly.

'I know you have no actual certificate to prove it, but I do know that you served an apprenticeship at the same time as I did and that it was only a few weeks short of completion and that's good enough for me,' Robert told him.

'You'd take a chance like that in order to help me out?' Sam asked, his voice registering disbelief.

'I'm taking a chance but it's not simply to help you,' Robert assured him. 'I've given it a lot of thought and planned the whole thing very carefully. I even have some premises in view but I would like to have your commitment before I go ahead because I might find it difficult to go it alone. With you there, then I'd know I had someone I could rely on one hundred per cent. Between us we could make a roaring success of the business.'

'It sounds almost too good to be true,' Sam said wryly. 'I'll work every hour there is to prove myself.'

'There won't be any need to do that,' Robert laughed. 'That's part of the problem. At the start we will not have any customers and it may take a good few weeks, months even, to build the business up to where I can pay you a decent wage.'

'I haven't any money at all coming in at the moment,' Sam reminded him. 'As long as I have a roof over my head and enough food to eat then the money side of things doesn't matter to me very much,' Sam assured him.

'Really?' Robert raised his eyebrows. 'I was under the impression that as soon as you had a job then you and Brenda were planning to get married.'

'Yes, that's true and we still are. I meant it, all right, but I am sure Brenda will understand if we have to wait for a year or so. That's right, isn't it?' he asked looking across at her.

'I suppose it is; it rather depends on how long you are talking about before the new business is on a proper footing,' Brenda said, looking questioningly at Robert.

'Well, let's say a year. I hope it won't take any longer than that because I'm planning to get married as soon as I can afford to do so. We don't want to have to wait a moment longer than is necessary, do we, Lucy?'

Sam stared in surprise. 'You've both kept that quiet! Congratulations, anyway – and in that case, then, I'm with you one hundred per cent,' he said enthusiastically.

'Good! I'll start putting things in motion right away. I want to have everything set up and be ready to start work before I hand in my notice at Carter's, so in the meantime, Sam, I shall be calling on you to do some of the leg work.'

'Anything at all,' Sam agreed.

'As I said, I've already found a suitable place just off the Dock Road that I think would be the ideal workshop. It would mean that at first a lot of our work would be commercial vehicles but I'm sure you can cope with those.'

'You bet I can. I can't wait to get back into overalls and get myself greasy and my hands oily again,' Sam said, grinning.

'I will need to fit the place out so over the next couple of weeks that means that I'll be scouting around for the right equipment or rather you will be,' Robert told him.

'That's fine. I'm willing to do anything you ask of me,' Sam told him earnestly.

'Right, well, let's map out a plan,' Robert suggested. He went over to the sideboard and took out a pad of paper and a pencil from one of the drawers and the two of them moved over to the table and began making a list of all the things they considered would be essential.

'I don't think they need any help from us, do you, Brenda?' Lucy said, smiling.

'No, we may as well go and do the washing-up,' Brenda laughed as she helped to collect up the cups and saucers they'd been using and carried them through into the kitchen.

While Robert and Sam planned their future strategy and worked out the cost of the equipment they were going to need, Lucy and Brenda had equally important matters to discuss.

'Have you decided where you are going to live when you and Sam do get married?' Lucy enquired when they'd finished washing up and had put everything away.

'No, there hasn't been any point in doing so because we have no idea when it is going to be possible. I will be able to start thinking about it now, of course,' she added smiling happily. 'It will have to be somewhere fairly cheap.'

'You could live here with us. We've enough room and I'm sure Robert wouldn't mind,' Lucy said. 'There's a scullery off this kitchen that we could turn into a separate kitchen for you to use or you could share this one with me. I don't mind either way. You and Sam could have the middle room downstairs and the middle bedroom. We would have to share the bathroom, of course, but that shouldn't present too many problems.'

'It sounds absolutely ideal; we all get on well,' Brenda enthused. Then her face clouded. 'You don't think, though, that if Sam and Robert are working together as well as living together it might put a strain on their relationship?'

'They may not be seeing all that much of each other at work once the business gets going and they wouldn't see as much of each other in the evenings as they do now. You will be in your own rooms and we'll be in ours,' Lucy pointed out.

'Yes, I suppose you are right,' Brenda agreed.

'The two of them trained side by side years ago when they were both apprentices at Carter's Cars,' Lucy added, 'so they should know how to get on with each other in the work place and they were good friends then, too.'

'That's true and I am sure we could pull to-gether equally well. We can draw up a rota for general cleaning like scrubbing the front step and looking after the stairs and hallway and cleaning the bathroom and keeping everything in good order.'

'I'm sure it would work out fine,' Lucy agreed.

'Let's hope, then, that Robert manages to get the business on a sound footing quite soon so that we don't have to wait too long,' Brenda sighed.

'I agree with you there. We will probably need either to let rooms or take in a lodger to help out until then ourselves. I would sooner have you and Sam here with us than strangers,' Lucy mused. 'Is there any chance of you and Sam marrying right away?'

'I can't see Sam agreeing to that, can you?' Brenda chuckled. 'Mind you, it would have lots of advantages for all of us. For a start, Sam and I would be on hand to look after Anna whenever you and Robert wanted to go out.'

'Yes, that would be useful,' Lucy agreed, 'and I could do any shopping you might need so you wouldn't have to worry about that when you are working shift duty.'

Lucy went across to one of the kitchen cupboards and from the very back of it brought out an almost full bottle of port. 'I think this calls for a toast, don't you?' She smiled. 'I've been saving this ever since Christmas in case there was some special occasion and I don't think anything can get more special than this.'

She put the bottle and four glasses on to a tray and together they went back into the living room where Sam and Robert were still engrossed in their own plans.

'Time to celebrate,' Lucy told them as she poured out the port and Brenda handed it round.

323

'We've nothing very much to celebrate at the moment,' Robert warned. 'We've simply got the prospects of an empty shed on the Dock Road and a head full of ideas.'

'So we'll drink to that shed becoming a thriving business and all those plans you've made working out perfectly,' Lucy told him. 'By this time next year we hope we will both be planning something else; setting the date for our weddings.'

'Surely you don't mean that we should get married on the same day as you and Robert do?' Sam queried looking first at her and then at Brenda.

'Why not?' Lucy enthused. 'What could be nicer than a double wedding?'

'We'll have Anna as our bridesmaid; she'll love being dressed up in a pretty dress and carrying our flowers,' Brenda said smiling.

Lucy looked across at Robert seeking his approval and the deep love in his eyes as he raised his glass towards her meant that words were quite unnecessary.

'Brenda's already agreed that she would like to move in here with Sam and share the house with us when they do get married,' Lucy announced.

'Really?' Robert looked from Lucy to Brenda and back again, bemused.

'You're not the only ones who can make plans for the future,' Lucy told him teasingly. 'We talked it all over; the only thing we can't decide on is the actual date. Would it be too optimistic to say it might be possible in about a year?'

'I'm not too sure about that; what do you think?' Robert asked Sam.

'I can't believe what is happening all of a sudden. First I'm being offered a job, then marriage and now a permanent home as well. It's all too much for me to take in, but of course I'm in favour of what you're all suggesting,' he said with a broad smile.

The four of them sipped their port in mutual harmony. The future looked hopeful but they all knew there was going to be a great deal of hard work ahead of them before their dreams could be fulfilled. So much depended on how successful Robert and Sam were in their new business venture.

'We wouldn't have any objections if you decided to move in here to live with Sam right away, Brenda; without waiting for your wedding day, I mean,' Robert stated.

'Would you consider doing that, Brenda?' Sam asked looking at her hopefully.

'I don't see why not,' she said thoughtfully.

'You don't object to that, do you, Lucy?'

'Are you saying that you would be prepared to live in sin?' Lucy asked in mock horror.

'Yes, I am. That's if you and Robert don't mind doing the same,' Brenda said with a broad smile.

'Brenda! Do you know what you're saying?' Sam exclaimed his face going red.

'I'm afraid they'll have no option, Sam,' she explained. 'If we live here together then it means that they will have to give up one of the bigger bedrooms and unless Robert is prepared to make do with the box room then he will have to share with Lucy because Anna really does need a bedroom of her own.'

'I think it is a splendid idea,' Robert applauded. 'After all, what difference does a scrap of paper make as long as you truly love each other?'

'It does make it official and legal in other people's eyes,' Brenda stated.

'Yes, that's very true,' Robert agreed. 'I think we'd better leave such an important decision to you girls to sort out, don't you, Sam?'

Lucy topped up their glasses with the remainder of the port. 'Right, now I think we should drink to the fact that we know there's a bright new future ahead for all of us,' she said, raising her glass.

Chapter Thirty-Two

Although Lucy knew that setting up their workshop on the Dock Road was of prime importance to Robert and Sam, getting the two rooms in Priory Terrace ready so that Brenda could move in with Sam were equally important to her.

There wasn't a great deal to do but Lucy insisted that the bedroom they were going to use needed a coat of paint to freshen it up.

'I expect you will want to make a few other changes in there and perhaps choose some new curtains and put up some of your own pictures,' she suggested to Brenda. 'The same applies to the room that is to be your living room,' she went on. 'It's supposed to be the dining room but because we usually eat in the living room it is rarely used.'

Decorating the two rooms took them less than a week. Lucy suggested that they should paper the walls and insisted that Sam and Brenda went together on her day off to choose the wallpaper. Sam seemed so pleased by the idea that Lucy left them to do the work involved in putting it up.

Anna was intrigued by all that was going on and it took Lucy all her time to keep her away from all the wet paintwork and to make sure she had something to play with to keep her happily occupied while they worked.

By the time the decorating was finished and Sam and Brenda had bought two armchairs as well as some new curtains their living room was transformed.

'Now you two men can concentrate on the Dock Road shed with a clear conscience,' Lucy told them as they gathered in there to admire the results of all their hard work.

'That will be a lot harder than sticking some paper on the walls,' Robert commented. 'What's more,' he reminded her, 'it means that it will take all of our little nest egg to buy the equipment we are going to need to fit it out properly.'

'I'm sure it will but we've already agreed that it will be a good investment for our future,' Lucy assured him, laying a hand on his arm. 'If there is anything more I can do to help then you have only to ask and I'll be only too pleased to do it. I'm sure I speak for Brenda as well.'

'We'll be on a tight budget both here at home and down there so what about making us up some sandwiches and a couple of flasks of tea each day? If you do that, we won't have to stop whatever we're doing to go scouting around looking for something and it probably won't cost us as much either.'

'Of course I will, gladly. At the moment it will only be Sam working down there, though, won't it?'

'Well, yes, during the daytime. I did think that I would go down there straight from work each evening and put in an hour or two. There are bound to be some jobs that Sam can't manage to do on his own and I don't want to leave all the hard work to him.'

'When are you giving in your notice at Carter's Cars, Robert?' Brenda asked.

'Not until we have the shed fitted out as a workshop and the outside of the place painted and our name up over the door. That's something you two could help us with; we still haven't deci-ded what we should call ourselves.'

'I think we need a cuppa to get our brains working in order to do that.' Brenda smiled. 'I'll go and put the kettle on. Do you want to have it in here?'

'No, we'll all come through into your living room. There's still a smell of fresh paint in here so I'll open the windows and we'll try not to use the room for a couple of days,' Sam told her.

Half an hour later, seated round the table and drinking their tea, the four of them pondered over a name for the new company.

Sam thought it should be Robsam Repairs but Robert said that sounded rather amateurish.

Brenda suggested Robert's Repairs Shop but Robert objected to that because it made no mention of Sam.

'Why don't you call it Merseyside Mechanics?' Lucy suggested. 'That way no one will be too sure who is behind it and also it sounds like a sound company.'

They thought about it for several minutes, saying the words aloud and savouring the sound.

'You don't think a name like that might be a bit too grand for such a small company, do you?' Robert frowned.

'Not a bit of it,' Lucy assured him. 'Anyway, you may be starting small but give it a couple of years and you will have built the business up into quite a big concern and you don't want to have to change the name midstream, now do you?'

'There speaks our business adviser,' Sam said and grinned.

'OK. We'll call it Merseyside Mechanics,' Robert agreed. 'At least there won't be any doubt about what sort of work we do or possibly where to find us.'

Two weeks later and they were ready for action. They'd installed an inspection pit, ramps, a large workbench, and rows of racks to hold all the spare parts as well as various other pieces of equipment.

Lucy thought it all looked very impressive although she wasn't too sure what they were all going to be used for, even though Sam assured her they were necessary.

The following week they painted the outside of the shed in a deep blue colour and the huge double doors in white. The name Merseyside Mechanics was in black on a white fascia and was positioned prominently over the front of the

329

building. When they all went to see it and voiced their approval Robert said that he felt the time was now right for him to give in his notice at Carter's Cars.

'Leave it for another couple of weeks,' Sam suggested. 'That will give me a chance to get some customers lined up. I haven't had a chance to do any canvassing yet.'

'If you are lucky enough to get some jobs right away, then you won't be able to cope with the work single handed,' Robert pointed out.

'We could manage between us. You could help out when you come down in the evening, if necessary.'

'You're probably right,' Robert agreed cautiously. 'I suppose we should be careful about jumping the gun too soon. Once I stop working we won't have any money at all coming in until this place starts to pay. I'll think about it over the weekend.'

'I'm going to move in this weekend now that our rooms are ready,' Brenda reminded them, 'so if we share our meals with you, then my money will pay for our food.'

Lucy offered to help Brenda move her things but Brenda pointed out that there wasn't very much to bring. 'There're only my clothes and a few other bits and pieces and, of course, my cat. I forgot to mention Fluffy.' She smiled. 'I hope you don't mind cats?'

'I've never had one,' Lucy confessed. 'I don't think Robert is too keen on them, though. I remember he used to grumble about Jenny's cats when she looked after Anna.'

'Oh dear, I do hope it's not going to be a problem,' Brenda said anxiously.

'Why don't you bring her along and see what happens,' Lucy suggested.

Anna was enthralled by Fluffy. The black and white cat was quite small and looked like a bundle of fur. Anna squealed with delight as she gently stroked it and Fluffy purred happily in response. From then on they were inseparable.

Anna wanted to be the one to put milk into a saucer for the cat and to put its plate of food down in one corner of the kitchen. She talked to it incessantly and, as Lucy said to Robert, she found it made her own life easier because she no longer had to listen to Anna's constant chatter all the time.

The cat responded well but Lucy warned her that it might scratch her when she announced that she was going to give it a ride in the little pram they'd bought her for her birthday.

Anna promised to be careful. Before Lucy could stop her she'd picked up Fluffy and put the cat in the pram alongside her doll and was covering them both over with the little pink blanket.

For one moment the cat looked as though it was going to object and was about to jump out. Anna stroked it and talked to it, telling it to go to sleep. The next minute, to Lucy's surprise, it had curled up on top of the blanket and was purring contentedly while Anna rocked the pram.

Robert was saved from making a decision about when to leave Carter's Cars. When he went into work the following Monday morning he discovered that someone had already told Percy about Merseyside Mechanics and who was behind it. Percy was far from pleased.

'I'm dismissing you now on the spot. Get your coat and leave the premises right away,' he ranted. 'What's more, I'm having a check done in our workshops to make sure that no tools or spare parts have gone missing. If they find that there is as much as a screw gone adrift, then I'll have the police on to you.'

'You won't find anything missing,' Robert told him coldly. 'What's more, none of the preparation has been done in your time. I've worked my hours here conscientiously.'

'So whom have you hired? Who has been doing the work down there?' Percy challenged.

'Sam Collins. I've gone into partnership with him. You didn't give him a job. He had to do something to earn his living.'

'Sam Collins. He has no qualifications! All he has is a reputation as a reckless driver after crashing one of our most expensive cars and I hardly think that will stand him in very good stead. Who the hell do you think will trust him to drive their car or even want to have it serviced by him? He's not even a fully qualified mechanic.'

'No, and neither are you, yet you manage to run a garage,' Robert told him heatedly.

'You want to remember that I employ mechanics who are fully qualified and I hardly think you'll have the necessary resources to be able to do that.'

'I don't need to; I am a fully qualified mechanic,' Robert reminded him.

'You may know a lot about engines but you

know nothing at all about running a business,' Percy sneered.

'I've managed to run your workshop for the past three years,' Robert pointed out.

'Absolute rubbish! You may have been in charge of the other mechanics but you know nothing at all about how to cost out a job or about the administration side of things. You've no business experience whatsoever. I've been to a top business college in London, remember. In addition I have also learned a great deal of expertise first hand from my father.'

'Yes, and one of the skills he passed on to you was how to treat your workforce with contempt, wasn't it?' Robert said sarcastically.

'That will do! Collect your wages and your personal belongings and leave immediately. Remember, I don't want to see you anywhere near these premises ever again.'

Furious about the way he had been dismissed Robert went straight down to the Dock Road. There would be time enough to tell Lucy about what had happened when he got home that night, he reflected. For the moment it was far better for him to work off his anger doing something useful.

When he reached the Dock Road there was another shock waiting for him. Sam was standing outside the building talking to two policemen and the three of them were staring at what had happened to the doors at the front. Overnight the newly painted white doors had been daubed with huge splashes and streaks of bright blue as if someone had thrown a tin of paint at them.

'What the hell has happened here?' Robert demanded.

'Vandals or drunks having their fun, by the look of it,' Sam said.

'Any idea who it might have been? They've ruined the look of the place,' Robert muttered.

'I was just asking the same question,' one of the policemen commented. 'Can either of you think of anyone you've upset or fallen out with lately? Perhaps someone who might have objected to you opening here?'

Robert was about to say yes, my old boss at Carter's and then he realised how stupid that would be. Whatever else Percy Carter might do he certainly wouldn't throw a can of paint over the front of their freshly painted doors.

'No idea at all,' he said shaking his head. 'Have there been any suspicious-looking characters lurking round here while you've been fitting the place out, Sam?'

Sam hesitated. 'It might sound a bit daft but there have been a couple of young lads annoying me. I've had trouble with them before, a couple of years ago. They were the ones who pushed me in front of the marchers on Orangeman's Day and I ended up in hospital,' he explained to the policemen.

'Right. I remember that incident,' the older of the two policemen observed. 'The two boys who were involved were from around Scotland Road way, weren't they?'

'That's right. Their name's Sparks and they live in Horatio Street,' Sam affirmed. 'I lived there myself in the same house as they did for a short time and they used to follow me around taunting me because I walked with a slight limp in those days.'

'That pair are always in trouble of some kind or other,' the older policeman affirmed. 'They've been up before the magistrates countless times but their mother always manages to come up with some convincing explanation so they are usually let off with a caution.'

'If I had my way, they'd have been put into a home years ago,' the other policeman affirmed. 'You say you think you've seen them hanging around here?'

'Oh I've seen them here, all right,' Sam assured him grimly. 'They've been up to their old tricks of calling me cripple but they always do it from a safe distance because they know I can't run fast enough to catch them.'

'You mightn't be able to do so but I can assure you we will and that we'll charge them with vandalism if we can get a shred of evidence to prove that it was them,' the older policeman told him confidently.

'That won't be easy; they probably waited until everybody had stopped work and gone home.'

'We'll ask around to see if any of the night watchmen on duty at the nearby warehouses witnessed anything. I'm afraid you'll still have to clean off all that mess and repaint the front again yourselves, though,' he said, grimacing.

Robert and Sam spent the rest of the day trying to remove all the blue paint and then applying a fresh undercoat to prepare the surface ready for them to repaint it.

'It might be better if we paint the front blue instead of white so that it is the same as the rest of the building; it mightn't be such a temptation then,' Sam mused.

'That might be a good idea,' Robert agreed. 'Although we've done our best the blue still seems to be showing through the undercoat we've put on.'

'Yes, and that means it may even show through the topcoat if we use white,' Sam pointed out.

Lucy was shocked when they told her their news. 'How on earth did you manage to be down there so early today?' she asked, looking at Robert in surprise.

'Percy Carter has heard about our new business enterprise and he was so annoyed that he sacked me the minute I arrived at work this morning. I was so incensed by the way he spoke to me that I thought it was better not to come straight home but to wait until I'd cooled down a bit. I walked down to the Dock Road only to find that matters down there weren't much better.'

'Still, it will all be sorted out now that we've told the police and they're handling it,' Sam reminded him. 'We shouldn't have any more trouble of that sort.'

'I certainly hope we don't because it has taken us all day to try and clean it off the doors and we'll have to spend most of tomorrow repainting them.'

'If you have a bad start like that then things can only get better,' Brenda told them optimistically. 'What's more, with the two of you working down there then the business should get off the ground all that much sooner.'

'It also means that one of you can stay on the premises while the other goes out scouting for customers,' Lucy added with an encouraging smile.

Chapter Thirty-Three

There were a good many anxious moments over the next few weeks. Robert spent most of his time scouting around the dockside trying to find customers and Sam, left on his own in the new workshop, grew increasingly frustrated by not having anything to do.

'Perhaps I should try canvassing for customers as well as you,' he suggested.

'I'm not sure about that,' Robert told him. 'Don't forget I have distributed well over two hundred leaflets offering our services so if someone comes here looking for us and finds that the place is all locked up, then they'll go elsewhere and we've lost them for good.'

Midway through the following week their patience was rewarded. Quite by chance Robert had met the manager of a small transport company new to the area. It resulted in Merseyside Mechanics being signed up to maintain their lorries.

A few days later Sam had three different dock workers in one day bring their own personal cars in for servicing and attention.

'Sam's customers are very important,' Robert

pointed out when they told Lucy and Brenda what was happening. 'They will be paying us in cash as soon as the work is finished on their cars. In fact, that's the sort of customer we will have to depend on at first. Whatever work we do on the fleet of vehicles, we'll have to wait until the end of the following month before we are paid.'

'The contract you managed to get was more or less due to a stroke of luck because you happened to meet that chap on the quayside,' Lucy said thoughtfully. 'How are other companies supposed to contact you if their car or lorry breaks down?'

'What do you mean?' Robert frowned. 'They'll bring them in to the workshop when they need attention. If the vehicle isn't driveable, then they'll send someone round to tell us.'

'Wouldn't it be better if they could reach you by telephone, though? I know there're not many ordinary people who have a telephone in their own home yet but most businesses do.'

'Of course it would be an asset to have a phone but having that installed is going to cost us more money, isn't it, and we can't afford to do that yet,' Robert pointed out.

'I think you should,' Lucy insisted. 'It might mean us economising a bit more than we're doing now for a few more months but in the long run it will pay off.'

'I have a few pounds saved up towards when Sam and I get married. We don't need it at the moment so you could use that,' Brenda suggested.

'Are you sure? I'll make sure you get every penny of it back when the business starts to pay,' Robert promised.

Over the next couple of months Merseyside Mechanics were so busy that Robert was even talking of taking on an apprentice to help out in the workshop.

'I'm so busy helping Sam that I haven't time to catch up with the paperwork and I'm even getting behind with ordering spare parts and supplies,' he grumbled.

'The answer to that is quite simple,' Lucy told him. 'Let me handle that side of the business for you.'

'How can you do that when you have Anna to look after?' Robert demanded.

'Easily. You keep all the ledgers here at home and then in future bring me the invoices each night and I'll enter them all up and you can stop worrying about them.'

'It all sounds fine but if the accounts are all here, then I will find myself going through them in the evenings when I get home,' Robert protested.

'If I catch you doing that, then I shall hide them away so that you can't find them.'

'No,' Robert shook his head, 'it wouldn't work. I need to keep them where I can refer to them any time I need to do so.'

'All right. In that case, then, I'll come down to the office once or twice a week and collect up the new invoices and the relevant ledgers and bring them back here. After I've entered them up you can bring them all back down here again the next day. When I call in I can also make sure that you have remembered to do all the ordering.'

'I've already said that I think it will be too much

for you to take all that on as well as running the house and looking after Anna,' Robert protested.

'I can make coming down to collect them part of our afternoon walk,' Lucy told him. 'It will make a nice outing for Anna instead of going to the park. Usually we time our walk so that on the way back we are near the school when all the children are coming out, to get her used to the idea of going to school, and we can still do that.'

'School! I know she's growing up, but surely we don't have to think about school, not yet.'

'All the work entailed in starting up this business has occupied your mind for so long that I don't think you've noticed how the time flies by.' Lucy smiled. 'Only a couple of years to go and she will be starting school and then I'll be able to devote a lot more time to helping you. There won't be any need to bring the books back here. I can come and work in the office and answer the phone at the same time which will make things easier for you and Sam.'

'Come here.' Robert pulled her into his arms and kissed her tenderly. 'What on earth would I do without you?' he asked, stroking her hair and looking deep into her eyes. 'Don't you think it's time to set the date for our wedding?' he asked softly.

Lucy raised her face to his. 'Yes, I most certainly do.' She smiled.

'I suppose, if we're sensible, we ought to wait until this miners' strike is over but heaven alone knows how long it is going to last.'

'Perhaps we should live for today,' Lucy murmured as their lips met again in a long sweet kiss that left her slightly breathless and her heart pounding with excitement at the thought of what lay ahead.

'I suppose we ought to ask Sam and Brenda what date they have in mind,' Lucy said as they finally drew apart. 'Not a word in front of Anna, though, at this stage, she is excited enough as it is about Brenda and Fluffy living with us.'

'We'll discuss it later tonight after Anna is tucked up in bed,' Robert suggested.

Brenda and Sam both looked at each other and then burst out laughing when Lucy mentioned the subject after their evening meal that night.

'We were on the point of suggesting the same thing to you,' Brenda told her. 'We'd like it to be as soon as possible because I'm expecting a baby.'

'You're what!' they both stared at her in surprise.

'Oh, Brenda, that is wonderful news!' Lucy exclaimed as she hugged her. 'I know you've put on a bit of weight lately but I thought it was my good cooking,' she teased.

'Well, that hasn't helped me to keep my figure, of course, but I am four months' pregnant,' Brenda said, smiling.

'Now that the business seems to be safely established we were thinking that perhaps some time in late autumn would be possible,' Robert told them.

'I think that Sam and Brenda will want to get married much sooner than that,' Lucy pointed out.

'You're right. It's June now, so by then I'll be on the point of having the baby.'

341

'In that case, then, we ought to fix a date as soon as possible. Are we still going to let Anna be our flower girl?'

'I'm not sure. Do they have a flower girl when the wedding is at a registry office?' Brenda asked.

'I'm not certain either, but if they don't, then they'll have to make an exception for us,' Lucy told her.

'She'd never forgive us if we didn't include her in the celebrations in some way,' Robert agreed.

'Why don't we try and make it some time next month? It will have to be on a Saturday, so what about the twenty-fourth of July? That will be a week before Anna's birthday. Are we all quite happy with that date?' Lucy asked looking at them in turn.

'I will be, if I can persuade my boss to let me have the day off,' Sam joked. 'You do know it will mean closing for the day,' he went on in a more serious voice.

'Don't worry, we'll only be shut for one morning and we'll give all of our customers plenty of notice.' Robert grinned. 'We probably won't be able to stop talking about it.'

Once the date had been confirmed at the registry office their lives became even more hectic as they made their plans. Lucy and Brenda had the responsibility of making sure they all had the right clothes for the occasion even though they were well aware that they had to work to a fairly strict budget.

'I've booked us all into Lewis's restaurant for a celebratory meal afterwards,' Robert told them.

When Lucy protested saying that it wasn't

necessary because she could do them a good spread at home at a quarter of the price he refused to listen.

'That's out of the question. Surely I don't have to remind you that it's a special day for you as well as for the rest of us, do I?'

Anna could hardly contain her excitement. She wanted to be involved in everything that was being planned. Lucy and Brenda promised to take her to Lewis's to choose a new dress.

Anna took this very seriously indeed and even the assistant smiled indulgently as the little girl tried on dress after dress and pirouetted in front of the big mirror in each one of them before agreeing with Lucy on the one most suitable. It was in white georgette trimmed with bands of pale pink, green and turquoise.

Lucy and Brenda also bought new dresses for the occasion but they chose ones which, although they were in crêpe de Chine, they would be able to wear again on Sundays or special occasions.

Lucy's dress was in a very pretty shade of blue that went well with her dark hair and Brenda chose one in the palest of green because of her red hair.

Lucy's had a plain bodice with a scooped neckline and a dropped waistline and the skirt, which had flared panels of slightly darker turquoise inserted into it, ended just below the knee.

Brenda's dress was loose and flowing and had the new handkerchief-style skirt that was rapidly gaining popularity.

Both of them decided to have fairly large hats

343

with dipping brims and for Anna they chose a pretty bonnet-style white straw hat trimmed with artificial flowers.

Lucy was well aware that both men needed new suits for such an occasion. The ones they had were old and shiny but the cost was more than they could afford at the moment. She suggested to Robert that perhaps for once they could use a tallyman but he was very much against such an idea.

'If I left it to you, then you'd probably turn up in your greasy overalls,' she said crossly.

'No, I know it's an important day for you, for all of us, if it comes to that, but no tallyman. Once you get into their clutches you have months of them knocking on your door for their money and when you've finished paying your cheque then they pester you to take out another one. I'd sooner wear the suit I've got than deal with them. Give it a sponging and a good press and it will look like new.'

Lucy didn't argue because she knew he was talking good sense but it worried her so much that in the end she decided they ought to hire suits for the two men. Brenda backed her up wholeheartedly.

'I think that is a very good idea,' she enthused. 'I don't want to spend a lot of money at the moment because I am going to need it for things for the baby,' she confided.

Persuading Robert and Sam to hire suits wasn't easy. In the end it was agreed that instead of doing that the two men would buy new suits from the Fifty Shilling Tailors and pay the money off each week.

'I don't really like having to do that,' Robert grumbled, 'but it's better than going to a tally-man.'

Saturday 24 July was a beautiful sunny day. Anna was awake very early dancing around the house and singing 'Today's our wedding day' at the top of her voice.

The ceremony was due to take place at eleven-thirty. One of their customers had insisted that he would be taking them in his car so Lucy made sure that they were all ready in good time.

All four of them were slightly nervous and Sam even muttered aloud, 'I'll be glad when all this fuss is over,' as Brenda fixed his tie and fastened the cufflinks of his new white shirt.

Anna was too excited to be nervous and both Lucy and Brenda had impressed on her what she had to do when they were in the registry office. Their bouquets of pale pink rosebuds surrounded by greenery and tiny white flowers were small enough for Anna to be able to hold them both without any trouble.

Liverpool was sparkling in the summer sunshine as they drove to the registry office and to their immense surprise there was a small crowd of Merseyside Mechanics' customers standing outside waiting to greet them.

'Good thing there is,' Robert muttered. 'I didn't want to worry any of you but we completely forgot to ask anybody to be witnesses. I'm sure we can find a couple of volunteers from this lot,' he added with a smile of relief.

The civil ceremony went as smoothly as if they'd rehearsed it for weeks. As they emerged into the sunshine they were greeted by a shower of confetti and even one or two people taking their pictures with their Brownie Box cameras.

'It makes me feel like a film star,' Lucy whispered in Robert's ear.

Their meal in the beautiful restaurant over Lewis's department store was equally memorable. They toasted each other in sparkling champagne and enjoyed every morsel of the delicious food that was put in front of them.

It was all so lavish that Lucy was slightly concerned about what the bill was going to be when Robert asked for it. The waiter merely smiled and shook his head.

'That has already been taken care of, sir. Is there anything else that you would like to finish off your meal?'

'What do you mean by taken care of?' Robert asked, frowning.

'The gentleman sitting over there in the corner has already settled your bill,' the waiter explained, nodding with his head to the far side of the room.

As Lucy turned her head to see who it might be her breath caught in her throat. She couldn't believe it; she was sure the waiter had made a mistake because the man in question was Percy Carter.

Before she could warn Robert she saw that Percy had already stood up and was walking across the room towards them and she laid a restraining hand on his arm.

'May I offer you all my congratulations?'

Percy smiled. 'I heard on the grapevine about this momentous occasion. The motor trade has its spies, you know,' he smirked.

'Thank you for your good wishes,' Lucy said quickly as she saw the blood rush to Robert's face and was fearful about what he might say or do. 'I don't think you have met Sam's new wife,' she added. 'Brenda, this is Percy Carter from Carter's Cars.'

Brenda smiled politely at him. Like Lucy she was conscious of how embarrassed Sam and Robert were by Percy's presence.

'And whose little girl is this, then?' he asked, patting Anna on the head.

For a moment there was an uncomfortable silence before Lucy took a deep breath and said in a quiet controlled voice, 'This is Patsy's little girl, Anna, remember?'

It was Percy Carter's turn to look slightly uncomfortable but he swiftly recovered his composure. 'Of course. Now, which one of you entrepreneurs handles the business matters at Merseyside Mechanics?' he asked pompously.

'It depends on what you want to know,' Lucy said blandly.

'I might have known it would be you, Lucy,' he chuckled. 'Well, I wanted to let you know that we had an enquiry a couple of days ago from a Merseyside freight company to service their fleet of lorries. As you know, we prefer to deal with top-of-the-range saloon cars in our workshops. In fact, we don't carry the right sort of tyres or spares nor do we have the necessary equipment to deal with commercial vehicles. I passed your name on to them and I assured them that you would be able to handle their work.'

He paused and signalled to the waiter. 'Can we have another bottle of champagne over here,' he requested.

'They're called Hindley Haulage Company and their transport manager, Austin Maggs, will be contacting you next week,' he went on. 'I understand that they have about twenty lorries in their fleet so they should prove to be good customers. I think we should all drink a toast to that, don't you?' he suggested as he indicated to the waiter to refill their four glasses and also one for him.

'I'm afraid you've been left out of this, little lady, because you are not allowed to drink champagne,' he added smiling down at Anna, 'but I am sure we can find something special for you,' he told her as he called the waiter over again and whispered something in his ear.

A few minutes later the waiter reappeared with a box of chocolates decorated with a large bow in shining gold ribbon.

'Now I must be on my way,' he told them all after he had handed the chocolates to Anna and received a beaming smile in response.

There was complete silence at the table after he'd left. None of them knew quite what to make of the situation but when Lucy summed it up by saying, 'I suppose that was Percy's way of saying sorry', they all started to laugh.

'I was so damned annoyed that he'd picked up our tab that I wanted to tell him to mind his own business,' Robert admitted.

'Well, I'm glad you didn't,' Lucy told him. I know Merseyside Mechanics is up and running but this new client will make a world of difference to us and, who knows what other customers will come our way if they are too commercial for Carter's Cars to deal with in the future?'

'True, and don't forget we are going to have another mouth to feed in the autumn,' Sam joked.

'Why is that, Uncle Sam?' Anna piped up.

'Well, Aunty Brenda is going to have a little baby very soon,' he explained.

Anna stared at them both wide-eyed. 'Will it be a birthday present for me?' she asked.

'No, darling, Brenda's baby won't be born until November,' Lucy explained.

'Will I be able to help you to look after it?'

'I shall be counting on you helping me to take care of it,' Brenda told her gravely.

Anna jumped down off her chair and went over to Lucy who picked her up on to her lap and cuddled her.

'When Daddy tucked me up last night he said that you really are my Mummy now that you and Daddy are married.' She smiled.

'That's quite right,' Lucy assured her.

'Do you think we could have a new baby as well, Daddy?' she asked hopefully, looking across at her father.

Robert tried to keep his face sombre but his eyes were twinkling as he looked across at Lucy before answering. 'Yes, I think that is more than possible,' he told Anna.

The publishers hope that this book has given you enjoyable reading. Large Print Books are especially designed to be as easy to see and hold as possible. If you wish a complete list of our books please ask at your local library or write directly to:

Magna Large Print Books
Magna House, Long Preston,
Skipton, North Yorkshire.
BD23 4ND

This Large Print Book for the partially sighted, who cannot read normal print, is published under the auspices of

THE ULVERSCROFT FOUNDATION